ANYA KELNER

Legacy

Rise of the Red Claws (Book 3)

Copyright © 2024 by Anya Kelner

All rights reserved. No part of this publication may be reproduced, stored or transmitted in any form or by any means, electronic, mechanical, photocopying, recording, scanning, or otherwise without written permission from the publisher. It is illegal to copy this book, post it to a website, or distribute it by any other means without permission.

This novel is entirely a work of fiction. The names, characters and incidents portrayed in it are the work of the author's imagination. Any resemblance to actual persons, living or dead, events or localities is entirely coincidental.

First edition

This book was professionally typeset on Reedsy. Find out more at reedsy.com

Contents

Rise of the Red Claws series	v
Prologue	1
Chapter 1	4
Chapter 2	7
Chapter 3	25
Chapter 4	27
Chapter 5	38
Chapter 6	48
Chapter 7	56
Chapter 8	62
Chapter 9	66
Chapter 10	73
Chapter 11	78
Chapter 12	90
Chapter 13	97
Chapter 14	98
Chapter 15	102
Chapter 16	109
Chapter 17	116
Chapter 18	120
Chapter 19	127
Chapter 20	134
Chapter 21	139
Chapter 22	145

Chapter 23	151
Chapter 24	155
Chapter 25	165
Chapter 26	182
Chapter 27	187
Chapter 28	193
Chapter 29	196
Chapter 30	207
Chapter 31	216
Chapter 32	218
Chapter 33	221
Chapter 34	229
Chapter 35	236
Chapter 36	241
Chapter 37	247
Chapter 38	252
Epilogue	261

Rise of the Red Claws series

Part 1: Awake
Part 2: Hunt
Part 3: Legacy

Prologue

The world was glued to its screens. People stared in disbelief at their phones, tablets, computers and TVs. Live news had overtaken every television channel. No longer could you watch your favorite soap opera or reality show in peace without being interrupted by updates on the 'current situation'.

The world was scared. When newscasters talked of what was happening, their voices trembled. It was entirely out of their control.

The vampires were targeting different cities across the globe, seemingly at random. Nobody knew where they would strike next, although many so-called experts and pundits tried to guess. Their assumptions invariably ended up being wrong, causing mass evacuations and panic for no reason. It simply added to the chaos already engulfing the world.

Self-appointed 'vampirologists' took to social media spouting nonsense about what people could do to protect themselves from the plague sweeping the globe. The list included, but was not limited to, rubbing garlic powder behind your ears, placing thorns around the windows of your home, bathing in holy water, lighting seven bonfires in the shape of a cross, and even ritual shamanic dancing. Of course, none of these worked. They only served to give actual vampires a momentary chuckle.

The American stations always ended their reports the same way, with Nell's alabaster face filling the screen. The spectral image cast living rooms across the country in a milky glow.

Every time Nell saw her own face glaring back at her, looking resolute and menacing, she shuddered. She was being blamed for the massacre in San Luis, where she had been filmed standing atop a mound of corpses. The media had identified her as the ringleader of the vampire swarm that had decimated the quiet border city. She felt overwhelming remorse. While it wasn't her fault, she felt she could have stopped it.

Guilt tore at her insides like a rabid dog. It was her fault that all those innocent people had lost their lives. Nell recalled walking through the carnage. She had seen so many faces twisted in shock and pain. The final expressions they would ever make.

She blamed herself even when Christopher insisted there was no way they could have stopped the vampires from wreaking havoc. It would have been Christopher and her against hundreds of them. The odds were impossible. But that didn't stop the guilt from eating away at Nell, burning her insides.

Hanging her head down, her back pressed against the lumpy couch of the cheap motel room, Nell quietly wept.

Another breaking news headline scrolled across the bottom of the dusty TV screen:

'Russian resort town of Sochi attacked. No reports of survivors.'

PROLOGUE

"What are we going to do?" said Nell, turning to Christopher.

His face was drawn. He seemed paler than ever in the luminescent glow of the screen.

"The only thing we can do," he said. "We fight."

Chapter 1

The ringing jolted Amara from her slumber. The phone display told her it was 2:09am. Ordinarily, it was never good when the phone rang at that kind of hour. In the current circumstances, it was far more troubling.

After fumbling with the device in her half-slumber, Amara pressed it to her ear.

"Hello," she said. Her voice was thick with sleep.

Next to her on the couch, Haiden groaned and mumbled something unintelligible. They had fallen asleep in her apartment watching the news reports. The voice on the other end of the line belonged to the last person Amara had expected to hear from.

"Amara."

One word. But the voice was unmistakable.

Almost instantly the images from the news reports filled Amara's head. This wasn't the Nell she knew. This was a vicious creature who had joined a band of evil murderers. The person on the other end of the line was being blamed for killing more people than Amara could fathom. But could it be true?

The librarian felt torn. She wanted so much to speak to her friend, to ask if she was okay, to find out where she was. But

CHAPTER 1

Nell might not be her friend anymore. She might be the exact opposite. This was dangerous territory. Something terrible must have happened to Nell to turn her into this creature. Amara's disparate thoughts spun and spun.

"Amara...are you there?" Nell said when the librarian remained silent, lost in her own head. "I need to talk to you...Ama..."

"I don't know if I can," Amara said, finally, her voice shaking.

Nell sighed.

"The video. The one they keep showing on TV. I know it looks bad," said Nell. "But you have to believe me, Amara. I haven't killed anyone. Please, let me explain."

The line crackled with static momentarily.

"But the pictures, they..." Amara's voice trailed off as she failed to come up with the words to accurately describe the horror of the images. Nell stood atop a pile of dead bodies.

Amara's thoughts began churning again.

Apart from her brief appearance at Aunt Laura's funeral, Nell had dropped off the face of the Earth. What was she doing? Where was Christopher? He was meant to be teaching her to come to terms with being a vampire. Had he failed? Had Nell lashed out? Had a psychotic episode? Lost her mind? Joined the sworn enemy in a fit of rage? As much as Amara tried to deny that it was possible, that the Nell she knew would never attack innocents, she couldn't be entirely sure. The way Nell was turned, when she was on death's door and without her consent, was surely enough of a shock to...

"Amara...Amara..." Nell called into the silence.

The librarian once again snapped out of her roiling thoughts. Stress and tiredness were clouding her ability to think clearly, to stay in the moment. She took a deep breath and tried her best to focus on the here and now.

"It's not what it looks like," continued Nell, who must have heard Amara's labored inhalation. "You need to believe me. There's been another attack…in Russia. I'm sure you're glued to the news feeds as well. We need to stop them. Stop him. It's Zachariah. He's orchestrating all of this. I believe he's calling his new Family the Crimson Claws. They're the ones behind it, Amara. Not me. I promise you."

'Crimson Claws'. The phrase reverberated in Amara's mind. A dark evolution of the Red Claws, she mused. The name no doubt served as a statement of intent from Zachariah.

Amara could tell from Nell's emphatic tone that she believed what she was saying, but that didn't mean it was true. She knew all too well that Zachariah had plenty of tricks up his sleeve. Nell could easily be a pawn in his game. Amara had been outplayed by him on more than one occasion.

"I want to believe you," said Amara, speaking from the heart, unguarded now. "But how do I know you're telling the truth? Those images, Nell. I can't get them out of my head."

"The video is real," explained Nell. "I'm not for a second denying that. I was there. But it's been taken out of context. Please, let me explain. It'll make sense. I understand why you're skeptical, Amara. Honestly, I can't blame you one bit. But, if you still have any regard for me as your friend, please just let me explain. Please listen."

Amara exhaled fully.

"Okay," she said. "Tell me."

Chapter 2

It had been just over two months since her 'rebirth' and she was slowly starting to wrap her head around living while undead. Christopher, who had been responsible for her strange new existence, was teaching her how to navigate the world as an immortal. It had been quite the learning curve.

While her enhanced physical abilities became an innate part of her very quickly, the more difficult aspect was how to exist alongside mortals. How to feed without taking innocent lives and travel while blending into the shadows. Christopher had been overcompensating with the niceties. He showed her endless patience and brushed off any mistakes she made, even if they could have brought them unwanted attention.

He felt guilty. This wasn't the life she had chosen. He'd changed her for all time when she had no part in the decision-making process. Of course, that logic was muddled. Nell would have died if he had not intervened. This life was better than no life. Surely. She had Christopher. They had each other. It was said that vampires could not love. Nell didn't think it was entirely true.

The physical act of feeding was an instinctive reflex. It came naturally. Scarily naturally, in fact. But Nell had to sustain herself and her body knew just what to do when the time came. Selecting the target was a different matter. It was part effort and part luck. The effort part involved looking up news stories from the local area and then locating the scum who had targeted the vulnerable and innocent for their own gain or twisted pleasure. It also involved frequenting the more unwholesome spots in a given location and keeping your eyes and ears open for who was up to no good. The luck part was that sometimes a meal just fell into your lap.

As a vampire, you saw the craziest things at night, especially with enhanced senses. It had shocked Nell to learn first-hand just how many illegal, seedy and nefarious activities went on all over the country when the sunlight filtered out of the sky. This applied just as much to the quiet suburban neighborhoods that were supposed to be havens of respectability. Sometimes more so. It seemed that when the sun disappeared, so did the morality of a good many humans.

One evening in Westmorland, California, they'd stumbled upon an attempted sexual assault. The assailant had pinned the young woman to the ground behind a crop of bushes and was tearing at her clothes. They'd managed to intervene just in time. The woman ran free without looking back once, leaving Christopher and Nell with their evening meal.

Another time in Tonopah, Nevada, they'd witnessed the attempted murder of a homeless man. The elderly victim was sleeping in a parking lot on a mattress of cardboard, covered with a thin, dirty sheet. The assailant, dressed head to toe in black and wearing a balaclava, approached with a claw hammer raised. Nell's reflexes kicked in, even before Christopher's. She leapt to the vagrant's defense, snapping the neck of the attacker before he even noticed she was upon him. Nell forgot she was a member of the undead when she sprang

CHAPTER 2

into action. She would have done the exact same thing as a human.

This particular evening, Christopher was continuing Nell's education on how to select a suitable target for feeding. They were in Cielo Verde, Arizona. A quiet town close to the Mexican border about thirty miles from San Luis. Christopher was avoiding densely populated areas while Nell was learning the ropes.

They were sitting at a corner booth in Crazy Earl's Cocktails & Pool bar. The sound of country music and pool balls clacking together filled the air, along with the animated conversations and laughter of the patrons. TV screens showed a baseball game while the staff dashed from one end of the long bar to the other serving draft beer and a variety of harder drinks from the dozens of bottles assembled on the shelves behind them. Nell and Christopher were nursing local craft beers while keenly taking in their surroundings. One table in particular.

Christopher felt it was important that Nell was around humans from time to time, as long as it was closely supervised. He didn't want her to feel alienated or detached from the mortal world. It was also important that she learnt the skill of blending in without drawing attention to herself. Since leaving Alaska, they'd been to museums, shopping malls, cinemas, diners and even a crazy golf course on one memorable occasion. Nell suspected that it was also part of Christopher's attempt to show her that being a vampire could be relatively similar to being a human, apart from the whole immortal blood-sucking thing.

It was during these human interactions that Nell discovered that she had a little gift of her own. While Christopher could peer into a person's past, Nell could see their futures. Like Christopher's uncanny ability, it only worked when Nell was in physical contact with the subject. It had started with small flashes. A store assistant who would win $100 on a scratch-card later that day. An elderly lady who would take a fall in her kitchen (luckily her daughter would be visiting at the time). A boy who would come in a disappointing fourth at the inter-school Backgammon tournament. A young woman whose boyfriend would finally go down on one knee, though the ring was a little underwhelming if she was being perfectly honest.

When they walked into the bar that evening, Nell immediately knew that they weren't the only immortals in the joint. This was another sense that Nell was developing, the ability to discern other supernaturals in the vicinity. Whereas the fae could see auras and vapor emanations as non-humans moved about in the world, for vampires it was an instinctive recognition. An internal radar that could recognize on some base level that they were in the presence of other vampires.

The fact that they weren't alone at Crazy Earl's wasn't a complete surprise. Vampires were dotted all over the place and many had the same idea when it came to picking out prey.

The small group of vampires looked up when Christopher and Nell passed them. There were four of them, dressed in biker gear. They wore ripped jeans, clunky military boots and black leather jackets, under which were T-shirts adorned with the logos of classic heavy metal bands.

After Christopher and Nell had taken their seats at the corner booth, there was a small nod of acknowledgment between the two tables. That was all that was needed. *We know, and we know that you know.* Everything was communicated in that subtle gesture of the head.

CHAPTER 2

Nell walked over to the bar and ordered the drinks. The barman almost drooled when he saw her. Vampires had an otherworldly quality that tended to catch the eye. Their skin was usually flawless and their eyes were sharper and brighter than most humans. Nell, like Christopher, was dressed head to toe in black. She wore a velvet dress with a long woolen coat over it and had a lace choker wrapped around her neck. Dressing like a goth, emo or dark wave metal fan was a common tactic of vampires. People assumed their deathly pale complexion was part of the look, so didn't question it. They saw what they wanted to see.

After collecting the beers, Nell made her way back to the table where she and Christopher began making small talk. They were both well aware that, like them, the other vampires had extra-sensitive hearing. They didn't want to delve into sensitive territory when it came to their conversation. After all, they had no idea who the others were.

After about fifteen minutes of furtive looks between the two tables, one of the other vampires stood up and made his way over. Nell held her breath. Christopher looked at her, subtly indicating that he'd take the lead.

"Howdy there, amigos. What brings you to Cielo Verde? The ass-crack of America," said the vampire, laughing at his own attempt at humor. He was well over six-foot tall with long greasy hair, a scraggly black beard and protruding gut, which strained the fabric of his way-too-small T-shirt. "Me and my compadres weren't aware that there were any other...'business associates'...currently residing here," he added, glancing back at his table, where his friends were looking on with interest.

"Not residing, amigo," said Christopher, in a friendly tone. "Just quickly passing through, like eating Mexican food left out in the sun too long."

"I've been there, buddy," said the vampire, laughing heartily and slapping a hand against his chunky thigh. "This town definitely resembles what comes out the other end." He lowered his voice. "Not that we have to worry about that anymore," he added.

Christopher smiled back.

"The name's Jeb…Jeb Crimson," said the biker.

Nell noticed that he arched his eyebrow in a peculiar fashion after mentioning his surname, as if Christopher was meant to know something. A code perhaps.

"I'm Carl and this is Natalie," Christopher replied, looking in Nell's direction.

"Pleased to make your acquaintance," said the biker, before reaching out to shake Christopher's hand.

He then offered his hand to Nell. She stole a quick glance at Christopher before extending her own hand. He gave her a barely perceivable nod.

As soon as her hand was enveloped in Jeb's cold flesh, the pictures came rushing into her mind's eye.

The images were abhorrent. Sickening. Horrific. The visions sent a spasm of shock slicing down her spine. Nell was trapped inside the images. They assaulted her senses. The torture. The pain. The indiscriminate killing. And the bodies. So many bodies strewn across the streets, like trash. The swarm of marauding vampires was like a wave of death. Breaking into homes. Pulling people out of vehicles. Young, old, male, female. It made no difference. Children. Infants. Blood-lust permeated the air. It was a collective frenzy of slaughter.

When Jeb let go of her hand, the awful visions suddenly

CHAPTER 2

ceased. Nell pulled her hand away. But too quickly. There was just a blur of motion. She couldn't help it. She just wanted to be free of those torturous images. But she had made yet another silly mistake. Any humans watching might have noticed that she moved too fast, unnaturally quick. It was a fact that wasn't lost on the big biker.

"Seems I ain't lost my touch with the ladies," he said, in an attempt at humor. "But you might want to be careful there, sister," he added, more soberly. "Don't want to be agitating the locals now. Hick town like this be apt to bring out the pitchforks." He once again chuckled at his own words.

With great effort, Nell contorted her face into what she hoped looked like a smile. She didn't want Jeb to know that she had somehow realized what he was planning to do. That he would be an enthusiastic participant in the slaughter of innocents. A massacre.

"Sorry, it's…it's nothing personal, Jeb," she replied, trying desperately to sound upbeat. "Might just be low blood sugar, if you catch my drift." She gave a half-smirk.

Jeb's eyes seemed to light up at those words and he returned a broad grin.

"I hear ya there, sister," he said. "Me an' the boys stopped in looking for a bite to eat, too. Looks like tonight we're gonna have ourselves a feast."

He cast his eyes around the bar. His gaze fell on a tipsy-looking woman who was trying to line-up a pool shot. She couldn't aim the cue straight in her inebriated state and collapsed onto the table in fits of laughter.

"They have some tasty offerings in here," Jeb added, a keen hunger in his expression.

Nell slowly regained her bearings. She shut the horrific

images out of her mind and recentered herself in the here and now. The visions hadn't provided her with enough information to act on. She needed to do more digging. She hated having to talk to this odious creature, but she had no other options.

"So, Jeb, what brings you and your crew to America's ass-crack?" Nell asked, trying to sound off-hand, as if she was just making small talk.

She noticed Christopher's questioning tilt of the head. She also knew that he could tell that there was something wrong here. Sometimes she felt like he was reading her mind, which he could actually do if he really tried.

"We're here on…official business," Jeb said, straightening up a little and turning his head back to Nell.

"Sounds interesting," said Nell. "Any clues? Seeing as we are 'business associates'."

She smiled broadly.

A sinister grin spread across Jeb's lips.

"Oh, you'll know soon enough," he teased.

That confirmed Nell's suspicions. The killing spree had been planned in advance. It wasn't something that was sparked by a random or unforeseen event. This grim realization made her knowledge of what was to come so much worse.

"Enjoy the rest of your evening," said Jeb, tipping an imaginary hat. He seemed a little more guarded now. There was a sense of wariness about him. He turned towards his table. "We certainly will," he added as a parting remark, before walking off.

After a few more minutes of nursing their hardly-touched craft beers, Christopher said: "I think it's time to call it a night."

Nell nodded and they made their way to the exit, giving a

salute to the other vampires as they passed. The bikers didn't seem so affable now, but still gave weak nods.

Nell's fake smile faded the second she was out of the door and in the huge car park, which the bar shared with an auto parts store and hardware shop. The sounds of the bar faded as the large door swung shut behind them.

"What was it?" asked Christopher, turning to her urgently. "What did you see?"

Nell told him everything. She watched the look of horror slowly creep over his face as she described the details of what she had seen. Christopher was lost for words. He could only stare at her wide-eyed.

"Are you sure?" he said, at last.

"I know what I saw," she said, defensively, crossing her arms. "It was only a few minutes ago."

"Not about that," replied Christopher.

He placed his palms on her shoulders.

"Sorry, I'm not being clear here," he added. "You've got me spooked. Are you sure that these things you see, that they actually happen. That they're not just projections of people's minds or something. Their fears, desires or events that *might* happen, rather than the actual future."

Nell thought for a long moment.

"I can't be sure," she said. "How can I? It's not as if I can hang out with the people I touch and check that what I've seen eventually comes to pass." She stared deep into Christopher's iridescent blue eyes. "But I feel, deep down, in my gut, that I *am* seeing into their future lives. You can see into people's past, Christopher, and we know it's genuine as the events have happened, they can be verified. So I can't see why my ability is any different. Even though it freaks the living Bejesus out of me."

Christopher was silent for a long moment.

"In the name of the Omni-Father," he whispered. "This is majorly messed up."

"We have to do something to stop them," Nell implored as the wind whipped around her, lifting the hem of her coat and ruffling her hair.

"You said there were dozens of vampires?" Christopher asked.

"Maybe hundreds," Nell said, grimly.

"There's only two of us," Christopher sighed.

Nell shook her head in despair.

"Isn't there anything at all we can do?"

"I don't think so," said Christopher. "We need to report this to the Council, but the army dispersed after Zachariah went quiet. I'm not sure how long it will take to form a fighting force again. From what you described, we're going to need serious numbers to stand any chance. Did you get any idea of exactly when the massac…it…was going down, or where for that matter?"

Nell shook her head again. She felt useless. She had seen the horrors of the attack but couldn't provide any of the critical details that would help to stop it.

"Let's head back to the motel," said Christopher. "We need to regroup, think this through."

They set off quickly west, running through the scrub land adjacent to Interstate 8. They had a room at the Meyers Field Inn, close to Yuma International Airport. As they approached the motel they could hear the planes roaring overhead as they descended for landing. The two of them left the interstate and joined South Avenue East, heading for the unremarkable squat building that they were temporarily calling home. That's when the first wave of vampires swept past them.

Nell and Christopher were rooted to the spot as the undead ran past. Some were in groups, others were alone. They had determined looks on their faces and moved with purpose, as if they were taking part in a macabre city marathon. Nell counted dozens of them, both men and women, young and old. Her internal radar pinged relentlessly as more and more vampires streamed by, leaving her and Christopher untouched.

They were heading south along the wide road. Traffic came to a standstill as the vampires weaved in and out between the vehicles. The drivers looked bemused at the sight of streams of people dashing past their stationary cars.

Christopher looked grimly at Nell.

"It's started," he said. It was a statement rather than a question.

"Looks like it," replied Nell. "I thought we'd have more time."

"They can sense us," he said. "They must think we're part of the horde, that's why they haven't attacked us. We can follow them."

Nell nodded. What other option did they have?

They fell in with the vampires, running in amongst the swarm. They moved further down South Avenue East and then across to Cesar Chavez Avenue. More vampires joined the throng. They were crowded thickly on the road, surging ever forward with a primal intensity. Nell could sense the collective blood-lust in the air. It turned her stomach, especially having previewed how this all ended.

She stopped and looked into the distance to read the signpost up ahead. The vampires were converging on the small town of San Luis, streaming in from every direction. Both of Christopher's earlier questions were now answered: when and where. Nell grabbed Christopher's arm and they both sprinted towards San Luis, leaving the vampires around them in their wake. To human eyes they would look like a blur of motion.

As they entered the town they could see the carnage unfolding all around them. Bodies already lay strewn on the street. The vampires hissed as they pulled people out of cars and descended on them, ripping and tearing with their sharp teeth and claws. Groups of vampires were attacking buildings, smashing the glass of storefronts and piling inside. Nell looked down at the sickening sight of bright red blood tricking in the gutters towards the storm drains.

There was nothing she could do here. It was too late. But she might be able to warn people further inside the town where the swarm hadn't reached yet. She put her head down and ran as fast as she could, eating up the ground as houses, shops and offices whipped past her in a blur. She didn't stop to think about Christopher. She only had one thought. Saving as many lives as possible.

After a few minutes she came to a halt. All was quiet around her. Traffic was moving at its usual pace. People milled about on the street. She saw families dining inside a restaurant called Luigi's. All were completely oblivious to the horror unfolding only a few blocks away.

She started screaming in the middle of the road. She stood in front of a white pick-up coming towards her, blocking its progress. She frantically gestured for it to turn around, mouthing the word 'danger' repeatedly.

The driver simply swerved around her, shouting: "Crazy

CHAPTER 2

bitch!" as he passed.

Nell ran across the street into Luigi's, barreling through the front door and bumping into an elderly man waiting for his takeout by the front reception. The lady behind the desk took in her all-black goth garb and frowned.

"Do you have a reserv..." she began.

"You don't understand," screamed Nell. "You have to get everyone out of here. NOW!!"

Diners turned to look at her, many of them with amused expressions. She saw a smartly dressed man at a table-for-two making the drinking gesture and smiling at the woman sitting opposite him. His date, a bottle blonde wearing a low-cut red dress, laughed coyly.

A waiter quickly came over to Nell. He grabbed her by the shoulder and nudged her forcefully towards the door.

"Miss, I think it's best if you leave," he said, sternly.

"You have to get everyone out now, or they're all dead," said Nell.

She knew that she wasn't making any sense to them, but there simply wasn't time. She didn't know what else to do.

"I hope you get the help you need," said the waiter as he continued to push her towards the door. "But you have to leave, now."

Nell could have thrown him across the packed restaurant in a heartbeat. But what was the use? What would it achieve? She looked backed at the diners, many of whom were still eyeing the drunk or stoned goth girl making a spectacle of herself. She spotted the smartly dressed man again. He was giving a sarcastic wave goodbye while his date was now in fits of hysterics. Nell was the highlight of their evening it appeared.

Nell hung her head down and allowed herself to be marched

out of the establishment. She sat on the sidewalk with her head in her hands. She realized there was nothing she could do without coming across as crazy, high or drunk. She even looked the part with her now disheveled hair and all-black goth gear. No one was going to believe her. People generally didn't respond well to a young woman running through the streets screaming at them to leave town. She felt like she was in a bad dream, but there was no chance of waking up.

She heard a scream and looked up at the intersection. A woman had been dragged out of her car and two vampires were feeding on her as she writhed on the ground screaming. A man leapt out of his own car to assist her, but was soon set upon by more vampires who had arrived. Nell cast a despairing look at Luigi's. The diners were still happily enjoying their meals, completely oblivious to the deadly chaos ensuing just outside. How long did they have now? Minutes? Seconds?

The vampires swarmed the area. She spotted Christopher running among the pack, looking around desperately. He finally caught sight of Nell and ran to her side, kneeling down. He grabbed both her shoulders.

"Don't do that again," he said, sternly. "We've got to stick together."

She couldn't meet his eyes.

"Sorry," she said. "I...I just don't know what to do."

He pulled her up for a hug, stroking the back of her neck as she buried her face in his chest.

"There's nothing we can do," he said, bitterly. "This is one fight we can't win."

They stood stock still in each other's arms as the vampires swarmed around them, killing and destroying. Nell heard

CHAPTER 2

panes of glass shatter as they stormed Luigi's. Endless screams echoed out into the night. The undead horde completely ignored Nell and Christopher as they held fast to each other. It was like they weren't there at all, or existed on a completely different plane of existence. The vampires made swift work of whoever was on the street or on the roads, then burst inside homes and buildings, leaving a trail of death.

Trying to fight back would be futile, Nell realized. It would only get her and Christopher swiftly turned to ash and floating away on the wind. Nell felt shame and guilt burning her insides. Innocent people were dying yet she was doing nothing. Why couldn't they have stopped this? Why couldn't she have discovered the vampires' diabolical plan earlier? Wasn't there anything they could have done to save the humans?

It was finally quiet around them. The slaughter was complete. The vampires had moved on to find fresh blood and beating hearts. Bodies lay littered on the ground. Homes and businesses stood smashed and violated, their inhabitants still and lifeless. Nell walked over to a body on the ground. It was the woman who had been dragged out of her car when the first few vampires had arrived in the area. Her glazed eyes looked up at the night sky, deep gouges criss-crossed her neck. Her clothes were ripped and torn from her body.

Nell knelt down and adjusted her blouse so that her exposed breasts were covered up, then carefully placed two fingers on her eyelids and gently pulled them down, so her eyes closed. She looked like she was sleeping. Nell moved to another woman nearby who was lying on the sidewalk. Nell adjusted her skirt down so she wasn't so exposed. She couldn't do anything for these women in life, but could afford them some dignity in death. It felt like a pathetic, inadequate gesture, but it was all she had left to offer.

Nell wandered the streets in a daze, taking in the sheer scale of the carnage. She heard sirens blaring in the distance. Christopher followed behind her, both of them stunned into silence and taking in the surreal scene around them.

Nell caught movement out of the corner of her eye. A shape was moving on the ground. It was small, shuffling at a slow crawl. Nell ran over. A girl. About ten years old. Blood ran thick down her legs. A stream of red against the child's dark skin. Nell could see deep gashes in her flesh.

"It's okay, honey, we're here to help," said Nell. "Are you badly hurt?"

"It's my legs," said the girl, in a weak voice. "They cut me… mommy…they got my mommy."

She began to sob.

"I'll get you help," said Nell. "But you need to be brave. Can you be brave for me? What's your name, honey?"

"Aliyah," said the girl.

"Aliyah, that's a beautiful name," replied Nell. "Mine is Nell, which is so boring, right?"

"It's nice," said the girl, who appeared to be in shock. "But I like Aliyah better," she added.

"Me too," said Nell, placing a hand on the girl's back to comfort her.

"Now Aliyah, I need to lift you up," said Nell. "Is that okay with you?"

"I guess so," said the girl. "I can't walk proper."

"That's okay, honey," said Nell. "I got you."

She scooped the girl in her arms and lifted her up. Nell looked around, not sure of where to head. She turned into a narrow street. Ahead of her was a pile of bodies stacked

CHAPTER 2

up. The gruesome sight stopped her in her tracks. She swung Aliyah's head away from the mound of corpses, so the young girl wouldn't have to witness the horror.

Just then she heard a mechanical chopping sound above her. It grew louder as a helicopter came into view high in the air above. Nell narrowed her eyes, using the limits of her enhanced vision to make out the livery of the aircraft. It was painted red and white with the words 'Arizona MedTech' stenciled on the side. It was an air ambulance. This was her chance.

"Aliyah, sweetie, I need to put you down for a minute," she said to the girl in her arms. "Keep your eyes closed so you don't see anything scary. My friend Christopher here will make sure you're safe and no one hurts you. Can you do that?"

The girl nodded weakly in her arms. She was losing blood and with it her strength. Nell placed her gently on the ground. Christopher stood guard over her, looking around warily in case he had to fight.

Nell needed a high vantage point to attract the attention of the helicopter. Aliyah was weakening rapidly. Nell wasn't sure how much blood she had left to lose. Every second was critical.

Acting on instinct, she leapt high into the air and landed on the pile of bodies. Yes, it might be considered a desecration. But the fact was they were dead, and Nell had the chance to save at least one life in this utter madness. After standing by idly and witnessing so much death, she was prepared to do anything for the chance at any kind of redemption.

She teetered precariously on the bodies before finding her balance. She lifted her head and began waving her arms frantically. The helicopter seemed to fly past before it paused then circled back to where they were. Nell kept waving her arms desperately. Red lights on the underside of the helicopter began flashing. Then it began to descend. Nell pointed in the direction of the injured girl lying under the glare of the street light. A gloved hand appeared from the side of the helicopter and gave a thumbs up, signaling they understood that the person was injured and needed help.

Movement caught Nell's eye on the ground just ahead of her. It was coming from the opposite end of the road from where Christopher and Aliyah were. The sight was surreal. A man was running towards her with his phone held aloft. He'd somehow managed to evade the undead onslaught and was now filming or live-streaming the scene in front of him. Nell looked down at the stack of bodies. This looked bad. Very bad. She stared back at the stranger, looking grim.

"You did it," shouted Christopher, above the din of the ever-louder rotor blades. He couldn't see the man on the other side of the bodies. "The medics will take care of her. We have to leave now, Nell. We can't stay here. It will only complicate matters. They'll blame us."

Nell was torn between staying to help and fleeing into the night. In the end, she knew Christopher was correct. Nothing positive would come from hanging around. With one last look at the lone man, she leapt off her high vantage point and began running with Christopher. They moved as quick as the wind towards the outskirts of town, where a cacophony of sirens from ambulances, police vehicles and fire trucks were blaring.

They silently slipped past the emergency services and merged into the dark night.

Chapter 3

"That's the truth, Amara. I promise. The whole truth."

For the first time since she started recounting her story, Nell's voice quivered.

Amara wanted, more than anything, to wrap her arms around Nell and tell her that everything would be okay. That wasn't possible. So she did the next best thing.

"I believe you, Nell." Amara breathed into the phone. "I believe you."

Haiden was beginning to stir beside her.

"Who is it?" He murmured.

"Nell."

Haiden sat bolt upright.

"The hell! Does she know she's America's most wanted right now?"

"Yes, she's well aware of that," said Amara, dryly. "But it's not true, okay. She told me what really happened. She didn't have anything to do with those deaths."

"And you believe her?" asked the Vampire Hunter, incredulous.

"And I believe her," said Amara, resolutely.

There was an edge to Amara's voice, like she was daring Haiden to challenge her.

"Just like that?" he asked. His tone was blunt.

"Just like that," repeated Amara. "I know Nell. I know my friend. Both what she is, and certainly what she isn't. And cold-blooded killer is very high up on that list."

Amara heard a palpable sigh of relief on the other end of the line.

"The only way we're going to defeat the Red Claws, or Crimson Claws, or whatever they call themselves now, is together," added the librarian. "That means all of us."

Chapter 4

It was the trivial things that always surprised Klaus since becoming human.

It was near excruciating to wake up on a cold morning and clamber out of bed. As a vampire, he never needed to sleep as such, just enter a short restorative trance every now and then and he was good to go.

The huge mansion on the outskirts of Angel Falls was perpetually cold. There was no heating to speak of and the original sash windows let in draughts around the ancient wooden frames.

Peeling the covers away from his soft body and feeling the chill was always enough to convince Klaus to get back under the sheets. He couldn't stand the thought of placing his feet on the stone floor and feeling the icy cold penetrate his flesh.

Klaus found this human side of him disconcerting, weak, but nonetheless always gave in to it. It was one of the very few indulgences he had in his life now. On the many mornings when he would tuck himself back under the thick duvet, he would think of Loris. The sharp lines of his angular face. The trace of stubble that lined his cheeks. They should have been drifting in and out of sleep together in this oversized four-poster bed. Keeping each other warm.

How was it fair that Loris had to die for Klaus to become human? To wake up cold and miserable on days that were equally cold and miserable. Klaus regularly wished that it had been the other way around. That his life had been taken instead. That it was Loris lying here and longing for Klaus with all his heart. The sadness was often too much to bear.

"You pathetic human," Klaus muttered to himself as he rolled over and curled himself into a tight ball.

After about half an hour he was forced to get up thanks to the increasingly unbearable pressure in his bladder. When the discomfort reached critical point he cursed then threw the covers to the floor, before making the bleak march to the bathroom. He winced when his feet touched the frigid floor. This was another aspect of human existence that he found to be utterly inconvenient and tiresome. When vampires imbibed blood, nothing was wasted, none of it ended up being expelled from the body as useless waste.

In all fairness, Klaus wasn't entirely human. He was some strange kind of hybrid. He had largely kept his supernatural powers, the strength and enhanced senses. But he felt human pain and discomfort. He would age. He had to eat and drink and, therefore annoyingly, go to the bathroom. He hadn't considered such mundane bodily functions for decades since becoming a vampire. Now they were always at the forefront of his mind. His stomach rumbled as a timely reminder of what he had become. But sleep, proper deep sleep when he could block out the world for several hours, was the one aspect of human life that he loved.

'Loved'. He could say that word now without ambiguity. Love had never been attainable for Klaus until he'd met Loris and the impossible had happened. The strange thing

CHAPTER 4

was that the love he'd felt for Loris had multiplied since his death. It was like there was always a certain blockage on his emotions while undead. When he became human, the floodgates opened and the love hit him like a tidal wave. It had caught Klaus completely off guard, making the grief that much more unbearable. On many nights Klaus cried himself to sleep at the thought of losing Loris and the gaping hole the older vampire had left in his life.

After stepping out from underneath the sputtering wrought-iron shower, Klaus wiped away the condensation covering the baroque mirror above the enamel basin. All of a sudden, a face that didn't belong to him appeared. It was no longer deathly pale. Color flushed the cheeks. The angles were softer, the lines no longer chiseled. Entirely human. After countless years of looking at his sculpted vampire face, it always took him by surprise when he saw his new reflection. The changes were subtle, but they were undeniable. He wondered what Loris would have made of his new appearance. Klaus would never know what Loris thought of anything ever again.

With a long exhalation, he tramped back to the bedroom and dressed. He then made his way down the grand staircase to the mansion's large atrium. He could hear voices. That was odd. But he wasn't overly concerned. His attitude was surprisingly casual these days. He wasn't too worried about security. He didn't have much of a life to protect, was his general outlook.

He made his way to the long hallway from which most of the ground floor rooms could be accessed. Following the voices, Klaus ended up in the drawing room.

Kavisha sat in her electric wheelchair in the center of the room. She was wearing a purple and gold sari and had an ornate gold chain weaved into her jet-black hair. She was surrounded by the remaining four Magisters.

A wave of revulsion swept through Klaus. It was thanks to the previous leader of these so-called sages, an obnoxious individual who turned out to be Zachariah's own brother no less, that the Red Claws had managed to wreak such havoc. Magisters were supposed to be superior and unimpeachable. Instead, a hidden traitor lay in their midst undetected for years.

Standing beside Kavisha was Amara, the studious librarian, dressed in a beige cardigan and gray slacks. Did librarians swear an oath on graduating to don the drabbest attire imaginable, Klaus mused. It wouldn't have surprised him.

"We let ourselves in," said Kavisha, noticing Klaus. "Hope you don't mind."

"It's your property. I'm just loitering here," said Klaus, indifferently. "Must be important to bring you big-wigs to this hick town," he added.

"Things are moving apace," said the High Chancellor. "I take it you're still oblivious to the outside world. Keeping yourself in the dark, figuratively and literally." She glanced at the closed drapes adorning the tall windows at the back of the room. Small beams of sunlight filtered in through various tears in the delicate cloth.

"The way I like it," said Klaus.

"Then let me fill you…" began Kavisha.

"Toast," interrupted Klaus.

The High Chancellor raised an eyebrow.

"Toast," repeated Klaus. "I need toast. One of the drawbacks of being human. I've got to eat, or I become even more of a curmudgeon."

He turned and walked out of the room, heading in the

direction of the kitchen. He paused in the hallway and popped his head back into the drawing room.

"Sorry, where are my manners?" he said. "Toast anyone?"

The Magisters wrinkled their noses in distaste. Kavisha looked exasperated.

"Do you have any wholemeal bread?" asked Amara, hopefully.

Klaus was just about to reply but the High Chancellor cut him off.

"Klaus, get in here," she said. "This can't wait."

Klaus took in her severe expression then reluctantly shuffled back into the room. Kavisha filled him in on events. His disinterest soon turned to concern as he learnt what was happening in the world outside the stately building in which he had cocooned himself.

"In the name of the Omni-Father," was all he said when Kavisha had finished talking.

"Do you have anything to add, Jiangshina?" asked Kavisha, turning to one of the four robed figures.

The Magister had a delicate, porcelain face with high brows and sleek black hair, which disappeared into her robe.

"We do," she said. Her voice was high-pitched and clear as cut glass. It seemed to reverberate around the room. "The group responsible for the attacks have chosen the moniker Crimson Claws. Like the High Chancellor, we believe they are led by Zachariah Redclaw. It appears that they now have upwards of 100,000 members in their brood."

"Family," Klaus said.

He was met with questioning stares.

"If Zachariah is the head, then they are 'Family', not 'brood'," he informed.

"Very well," the Magister continued, slightly annoyed. "Well, this *Family* is both large and vicious and we don't know the rate at which it is spreading. Vampires have always contained their numbers in order to live covertly amongst the host species. But Zachariah, feeling his life is under threat, has up-ended that balance. The humans now know of our existence. Everything is chaotic and unpredictable. We need to work in tandem with our global bodies if we hope to contain this situation."

"I've made a start on that," said Amara, stepping forward. "I've established contact with the other Councils, but so far we don't have any useful leads."

"Our main task is to track down Zachariah," added Kavisha. "We feel he's key to all of this. The linchpin. Our efforts have to focus on taking him out. But that doesn't fix the immediate problem. We still have to contend with the swarms of Crimson Claws that are causing immeasurable amounts of harm. This has to be stopped."

"The Councils are locked in debate about how to punish the perpetrators," said Amara. "Some have suggested sentencing them to death, others have argued they have to go through the various Councils' judicial systems. But how long will that take? Yet others say they should be placed in a suspended trance for a century, the same punishment that the Red Claws originally received."

"Puhh," Klaus scoffed. "I can assure you from first-hand experience that will do little to calm any blood-lust. It's just deferring the problem to a later date. We'll end up in the same situation that we find ourselves in now." He looked at the tense faces around the room. "At least I won't be around to see it," he added, somewhat bitterly.

Jiangshina turned to him.

CHAPTER 4

"On the subject of your mortality, at this juncture your security is of the utmost concern," she said. "That is why we came so swiftly, and in person. From events that have transpired it seems that you may be the subject of the prophecy contained in the *Adumbrate Invictus*. If that is true, then it follows that you are the key to defeating these Crimson Claws."

"Or it could all be a bunch of horseshit," said Klaus. "And you haven't got the first clue about what is going on with that prophecy, or out in the real world."

"It's an evolving situation," said Kavisha. "These texts are old and not always as straightforward or decipherable as we'd hope. Yet there is wisdom in the words. We would do well to take heed."

"What about the girl?" asked Klaus. "Wasn't she meant to be the chosen one? Our salvation."

"When it comes to Nell, we may have been mistaken," said Jiangshina, looking dolefully at the High Chancellor. "On a number of fronts," she added. "We cannot be sure of where her allegiances lie."

Amara looked indignant.

"Yes we can," the librarian insisted.

Jiangshina looked taken aback.

"She called me last night to explain everything," continued Amara. "I know she called Kavisha, too."

The High Chancellor nodded.

"She wasn't there, in San Luis, to join the attack," said Amara. "She and Christopher were trying to save lives, but there was very little they could do against the Crimson Claw horde. She's not guilty of anything, and she's certainly not one of them."

"What gives *you* the right to decide whether she's innocent or not?" asked Jiangshina, her tone stern. "The evidence to the contrary is plastered on every TV screen across America. And you, a human, are in no position to discern facts that are beyond your realm of understanding."

"You're one to talk," Klaus fired at the Magister, indignation overcoming him. "You had a traitorous scoundrel leading your merry crew for years without any of you knowing what, or who, he truly was." He pointed a finger at Jiangshina. "That's incompetence at best...at worst, it's collusion with..."

"How dare you!" the Magister shot back. "You, of all duplicitous loathsome creatures, think you..."

"Quiet down!" Now it was Kavisha's turn to interrupt. "This isn't getting us anywhere."

She pushed forward the small joystick by her right arm and maneuvered her wheelchair between the former Red Claw and the Magister.

"Klaus, please moderate your tone," she said to him. Then she turned to Jiangshina. "Magister, I'm going to have to ask you to refrain from speaking to Amara in such a manner. The fact she is human is of no consequence. Have we all learnt nothing from the events engulfing our kind? Amara is my most trusted aide. Her insight has proven invaluable to me. And if she believes Nell is innocent, I am inclined to believe her."

"You would take this...mortal's...word?" asked Jiangshina.

"Wholeheartedly," replied the High Chancellor. "Plus, I also know Nell personally, and therefore have a difficult time imagining that she could have become one of these monsters."

The Magister huffed. Amara looked worried. Kavisha cautiously scanned the faces around her. Klaus was rather enjoying himself, if truth be told. This was a refreshing distraction from his usual mundane existence.

CHAPTER 4

The room was momentarily quiet as everyone gathered their thoughts.

"What about the rest of our army?" asked Klaus. "Sounds like we're going to need them."

Kavisha looked more perturbed than ever.

"Unfortunately, after we suffered so many casualties in the previous fighting many of the supernaturals do not wish to come forward this time around," she said, looking down at her delicate hands, which were adorned with a henna pattern. "Thankfully, we still have the wolves on our side, due largely to Devan. They were invaluable last time. Packs all over the world are tracking Zachariah's scent. But there are no leads so far."

The room fell quiet again.

"One more thing," said Jiangshina into the silence. "If it turns out that Klaus is the one referred to in the prophecy, then you should kill Nell at the earliest opportunity."

More than one gasp echoed around the room.

"Her future is clouded," continued the Magister, matter-of-factly. "She is an unnecessary and unpredictable variable right now. It's best to take this particular piece off the chess board."

Klaus noticed Amara balling her hands into fists, before she took a deep breath and probably counted to ten in her head.

"Thank you for your advice, Magister," the librarian said. "But a lot of people love that 'variable', even though that concept probably means nothing to you. We've made our decision. We trust Nell. She is one of us. You will not touch a single hair on her head." Amara's voice was firm, unwavering. Her eyes bored into the Magister.

"That is your prerogative," replied Jiangshina. "And your folly to indulge in. It matters little to us. We are the watchers.

We are the chroniclers. We offer counsel, nothing more."

The Magister looked imperiously around the room.

"If there is nothing more, we shall take our leave," she announced.

"There was one more thing," said Kavisha. All eyes turned to her. "When we lost Loris, we lost not only a powerful ally and wise friend, but also a member of the Council of Elders. So I have a question for you both." She looked from Amara to Klaus. "We don't have time for the proper ceremony and protocol, so forgive me for being so blunt. But I want you both to take up positions on the Council."

Amara and Klaus both looked stunned. Jiangshina's jaw almost hit the floor.

"Given our current situation," continued the High Chancellor. "I think it is important that we show a united front. If we have learnt anything so far, it's that there is strength and wisdom in coming together." She looked at Amara. "In embracing those that are different to us." Then she turned to Klaus. "In showing there is power in compassion and redemption."

"You...you want me on the Council of Elders?" Amara stuttered, as if the words made no sense as they left her mouth.

"I can think of no-one I would want more by my side," said the High Chancellor, smiling up at her.

"But how would that work?" said the librarian. "The other vampires would never accept me."

"It's my decision to make," assured Kavisha. "And I stand by it one hundred percent. Besides, it's time we mix things up a bit on the Council. Have a fresh perspective. Humans know of us now, beyond the fanciful musings of their story books and horror films. There is a new world we need to navigate after the immediate crisis is over."

The High Chancellor turned back to face Klaus.

"And you, Klaus. I know this has been a difficult journey for you, but you're key to this battle. Not least because you have invaluable knowledge about the Crimson Claws. Loris is difficult to replace, but I'm sure he would have been proud to see you pick up his mantle."

Klaus felt emotion welling inside him and had to look away briefly.

"What do you say?" asked Kavisha. "Both of you."

"Yes!" Amara said, not disgusting her eagerness. "I'm in."

"Wonderful," replied the High Chancellor. "Klaus?"

He took a deep breath and stole a glance at Jiangshina. The Magister still looked horrified. She was staring at him, eyebrows raised, eyes wide.

That seemed to tip the scales. With a mischievous little smile, he said: "Okay. Why the hell not."

Chapter 5

Branches flew by as Devan careened through the dense forests just north of Indiana.

He had been tracking her scent for days. It wasn't easy to trail other wolves. Their scents intermingled within packs and weren't as distinctive to the lupine nose as humans, fae or other supernaturals.

Devan had veered off on a few false trails before finally locking on to the scent and heading in the right direction. His heart was heavy with longing for Lupita. In the relatively short time that they'd known each other, she had become everything to him. She was so much more than just the beta wolf in his hastily assembled pack.

It felt like there was a gaping hole in his life that Lupita had once filled. Since she'd left, he hadn't once felt complete. Which was why he was racing through the thick foliage of the Salamonie River State Forest right now. At the very least, he wanted to talk to her. If she didn't want to be with him, then he'd have to find a way to move on. As impossible as he felt that would be, he'd just have to. But he had to know where he stood one way or the other. He couldn't leave things the way they were. Unresolved. Unfinished.

As Devan raced through the forest, Lupita's scent became

stronger and stronger. He breathed in deeply, savoring the aroma. It was a sweet musk tinged with earthy tones. He tasted it in the back of his throat. His longing intensified sharply, as did more primal stirrings. He lowered his sleek head and increased his speed. He was flying through the maze of trees now as his powerful legs worked furiously.

After a few minutes he reached a small clearing in the trees. Young wolves ran freely, exploring their surroundings with enthusiasm. They must be new to the change, having hit puberty recently. A few elderly wolves sat in a semi-circle keeping an eye on the youngsters. Their fur was mostly white, their limbs thin after losing muscle with age.

Heads were swiftly raised from the ground as Devan padded into view. He stopped abruptly in his tracks and tucked his tail between his hind legs and then under his body. The commonly understood gesture of non-aggression and submission.

The elders eyed him coolly. The youngsters were considerably more interested by his arrival and jumped up and down on the spot. They reminded Devan of the wind-up animal toys he used to play with as a child.

"I come alone," projected Devan. "I honor the earth upon which you lay claim. Amity, fraternity, serenity."

"Amity, fraternity, serenity," came the customary reply from the other wolves in unison.

Then came the blunt statement: "She doesn't want to see you," from a female elder. She still had faint traces of russet on her fading fur.

"So she's here?" Devan replied.

The wolves remained silent and impassive.

"Brethren please," implored Devan. "I just want to talk to her." He projected his words far and wide. He knew that if

Lupita was close by, which he was certain she was, she would hear him.

"As I said already, she doesn't want to see you." The same female spoke.

Devan knew he wouldn't get anywhere remonstrating with the elders. He also wasn't prepared to simply turn tail and walk away. Not after his arduous trek. He lifted his muzzle high into the air and projected out with all his mental strength.

"Lupita, please. I just want to talk. If you want me to leave, then I'll leave. But please, just talk to me first. Please, Lupita."

He waited. Silently. Motionlessly.

Just when he thought all hope was lost, Lupita padded out from behind a cluster of trees. His heart skipped a beat when he saw her. The dark eyes, the rust-colored coat, her powerful haunches and distinctive feline walk. Her expression was difficult to read. It seemed like a sad smile.

The elders turned to stare at her. They didn't seem particularly impressed that she'd revealed herself.

"Follow me," Lupita projected, curtly, walking back into the woods. "You're making a nuisance of yourself."

Devan followed behind her. After a minute or so they came to a small brook. Tall pine trees formed a canopy overhead. Water cascaded down moss-covered rocks while broken tree branches and leaves lay scattered on the ground.

Lupita turned to face Devan.

"So you haven't noticed?" she projected.

"Noticed what?" he replied, puzzled.

Lupita began morphing. Fur receded, limbs elongated, sharp animal curves transformed into soft human flesh. Devan looked on, mesmerized. She always had this effect on him. It was like watching a seductive dance.

CHAPTER 5

She stood in front of him, naked. A true woman of nature. He drank her in with his eyes. Light brown skin with a smattering of freckles on her cheeks, clear hazel eyes, a sharp nose and long straight black hair. She had an oval face with full red lips and a high forehead. Lupita was so beautiful to him.

Noticing his intense gaze, she moved her hands slowly down to her midsection, then cupped her swollen stomach.

The breath caught in Devan's lungs. Time seemed to stand still. The trees appeared to sway in his vision. He had to sit down on his haunches.

"You're...you're..." Devan whispered.

"I guess it's not so obvious in wolf form," she mused.

Her bump was large. Too large. Devan tried to do some quick math in his head. It didn't seem to add up. But then he wasn't thinking too clearly. His emotions were all over the place right now.

"You didn't think to tell me?" The hurt was all too evident in Devan's voice. He couldn't help it.

Even if the baby wasn't his, he thought she would at least share something so momentous. They had been so close. She was his beta. That was meant to be a sacred primal bond, built on trust and openness.

Devan shifted into human form, so they were on an equal footing. He just sat there, cross-legged on the grass. Tears stung his eyes, despite his best efforts to remain calm.

"No, I didn't think to tell you," Lupita answered.

Devan felt heat rising to his face. He'd traveled for days, hardly eating on the way. The Crimson Claw threat had engulfed the world. He should be out there right now leading the hunt for Zachariah. Yet he was here. For her. The least she could do was answer his questions properly, instead of putting up a wall. Pack is pack, or so he always thought. He swallowed his anger.

"Is this why you left me?" he asked. "Because of the baby?"

"No," she replied.

Devan didn't respond. He just looked down forlornly at the lush grass. He must have looked like the saddest creature in the world.

"Look, I'm sorry for leaving the way I did," Lupita said, quietly, as the silence dragged on. "But it was for the best. We can't be together. Not after everything that happened." She looked away at the swaying branches of a nearby pine tree.

Devan's exasperation was slowly reaching boiling point.

"After everything?" he said, bitterly. "Everything we've been through. This is what I get? Lupita, please. I need to understand."

Tears were cascading down her face now. She sniffed and met his eyes once again.

"After Lupo died. I just can't get over that," she said. "I know it's not fair to blame you. It was a choice that we made. But I do. I blame you for taking him away from us. If you hadn't come into our lives, he'd still be here. My baby brother would still be alive. Not buried on a desolate beach at the edge of Alaska."

She walked over to a pine tree and gently sat, her back against the wide trunk.

Devan kept his distance, although he longed to take her in his arms.

"I'm sorry, Lupita. I truly am," he said. "I didn't have the first clue of what I was doing. In fighting. In hunting. In leading

CHAPTER 5

a pack. Everything. I made so many mistakes. I did what I thought was my best. But it wasn't good enough. So much was resting on my shoulders. I buckled under the pressure. That's why I relied on you so heavily."

His words hung in the air. Lupita cradled her swollen belly. Birds chirped nearby and water from the brook babbled as it splashed and sloshed over the lime green rocks.

"I felt each death," he went on, reaching down and tearing at blades of grass. "Every one of them broke my heart. Lupo and Flint especially. They were so young. So innocent." He picked up a stone and hurled it at the moving water. "If I could go back in time and convince your family to stay in those woods near Fort Wayne…I wouldn't."

Lupita turned to him, her face hard.

"I wish that Lupo was alive, more than anything I do. The others too," he added, quickly. "But this war isn't over. It's going to claim many more innocent lives. But it needs to be fought, for all our sakes. We can't hide away. It's coming for us one way or another. That doesn't make our losses any easier to bear. It doesn't make the hurt any more tolerable."

Lupita gently stroked her belly as Devan talked. Tears continued to spill from her large hazel eyes. He wanted so badly to touch her. But for the moment he only had his words.

"Also, I would never have met you," he said.

She looked up sharply.

"As utterly selfish and callous as that sounds," he continued. "You have been the greatest blessing that has come into my life."

She had to look away. Her expression seemed pained. Conflicted.

"Given the same choice again, do you think Lupertico and

Lupo would have stayed behind?" he said. "Or you, for that matter? Not the father and son I know. Not the Lupita I know. I don't expect you to forgive me, and I understand if seeing my face brings back painful memories, but I need to know where I stand. Then, if you want, I'll leave you in peace."

Lupita was quiet. She still looked troubled. Torn. But if she did want him out of her life, then there was one thing he simply had to know before the end.

"The baby," he said, tentatively. "It looks like it's nearly due. Ummm, who…I mean is it…"

She gave him a wide-eyed look of consternation that stopped him in his tracks. Then her face softened a little.

"You really don't know much about us," she said. "I keep forgetting that." She began to rub her bump again in a gentle circular motion. "We don't carry babies for nine months if we aren't in human form," she explained. "For wolves, it's more like ten to eleven weeks. That's why I probably look so big to you right now."

Devan quickly tried doing the math again. But a sudden wave of exhilaration gripped his body, making it hard to think. So he just asked outright.

"So you mean, I could be…I mean it could be…" he began.

Her wide-eyed expression returned.

"Of course it's yours, dufus!" she said. "Who else? Do you think I'm some kind of hussy?!"

Devan was way out of his depth when it came to gestational zoology, but only one thing was important right now.

"I'm going to have a baby," he said, with quiet awe. "I'm going to be a dad?"

She looked at him with gentle amusement in her large brown eyes.

CHAPTER 5

"That you are," she said. "For better or for worse, that you are."

For the second time that morning time seemed to stand still and the tall trees appeared to sway in Devan's vision. He looked at Lupita in a state of shock. He'd traveled all this way in the faint hope of winning her back. Now he'd discovered he was going to be a father. A range of feelings churned within him. Elation. Surprise. Trepidation. Memories of his turbulent childhood flashed to the surface. Of his adoptive mother. Of her death.

"I'm going to do this on my own, Devan," stated Lupita. "I have the pack for support."

"Lupita, don't do that, please," replied Devan. He had to think fast. His heart hammered away in his chest. "You ran away because I reminded you of the worst day of your life. But perhaps I can be part of the best day of your life. When this child comes into the world. This baby is mine, too." He said the last statement with more force than he had intended, but he had little control of his emotions. "Let me help you," he pleaded. "If you don't want to be with me then I'll find a way to accept that. But don't shut me out of my own child's life."

He went to her then, kneeling in front of her. He took her delicate hands in his own. She didn't resist.

"Not after my own childhood, Lupita," he implored. "You know I never knew my birth parents. You have to understand what this means to me. Being shut out would tear me apart." Devan suddenly realized that he was crying.

"I don't know how we can make this work," she replied, gently, looking into his distraught face. "You're caught up with this damn war. You don't have time to be part of our life." Lupita's face was a mask of sadness. "And what if…what if…you don't come back. I can't lose someone else." She looked down at her stomach. "We can't lose someone else. It's just too painful, Devan. It would break me, and I need to be strong now."

"If that's what's behind this, then I'll stay," said Devan, resolutely. "I'm not giving up on us, Lupita. On our child. I'll stay here, with you. I'll join the pack, protect you both as best as I can."

Lupita reached up and softly wiped the tears from his wet cheek.

"You'd move here to be with us?" she asked.

"Yes, of course. In a heartbeat," he said. "If that's what it takes. You're my priority now. The only family I have left." Devan sighed, thinking of how Lupita had lost her brother and was now bringing a new life into the world. There was a circularity to it.

"You're a good man, Devan," she said, grabbing his hand and bringing it to her soft lips. "I'm so sorry. For everything. For not telling you. For fleeing. For being a coward."

"No one can ever accuse you of being a coward," he replied. "You're the bravest soul I know. I'm sorry I ever dragged you into this. More than anything I wish we had met under different circumstances, without all this death, destruction and hate in the world."

Lupita leaned forward until their foreheads were touching.

"Go now," she said, looking him in the eyes. "Leave us."

He felt absolutely crushed.

"But come back," she added, with a gentle smile. "Come back to us when it's over. We need you, Devan, alive and healthy. We will be waiting."

"But I can still…" he began.

CHAPTER 5

"Sshhhh," she soothed, placing a hand on his chest. "Don't forget I know you. I know your mind, Devan. You could never be happy here while your friends were risking their lives out there. It would eat you up inside. And that's not the person I want to be with. So go now. I'm setting you free. If you love me, you'll come back."

Relief washed over Devan. He had to admit it.

"We'll get through this," he said, gripping her hands then leaning forward and gently kissing her lips. "I'll be back to take care of you and our baby." He squeezed her hands. "I love you," he added. "More than anything in this world. I just need to help make that world safe for our child to grow up in."

He took a step back then transformed into his wolf form. With one final glance at Lupita he turned and ran like the wind back through the trees, his resolve doubled. He would not let his child grow up in a world where the Crimson Claws were running riot, killing innocents. He knew what he had to do.

Chapter 6

Nell hesitated before reaching out and grabbing the black metal door knocker. It was in the shape of two serpents intertwined and positioned in the center of the huge wooden door that allowed entry into Vhik'h-Tal-Eskemon, an imposing gothic building located deep in the Blue Ridge Mountains. The sprawling complex, complete with turrets and battlements, served as headquarters for the Council of Elders, the governing body for vampires in the United States.

Nell steeled herself then swung the wrought iron knocker hard into the ancient wood. She could hear the echo of the impact inside the grand building.

Her anxiousness swelled as she glanced up and took in the grand façade of the centuries-old structure. She had fled this building the previous year in the dead of night. She had walked willingly into the waiting arms of the Red Claws in a misguided attempt to save those that she loved. From that moment until her eventual rescue she'd been used as a mobile blood bank by Zachariah Redclaw. She had been left an emaciated wreck, barely alive and covered head to toe in savage bruises, gashes and bite marks.

Not that you would know by looking at her now. Her skin was completely flawless and had an ethereal glow. When Nell looked into the mirror, she saw the movie-star version of her old self. Granted, looks weren't at the top of her priorities right now, but it was nice not to have to worry about frown lines, pimples and dark circles. Every girl had a certain self-regard, she reasoned.

The door to the headquarters was flung open. Amara stood on the threshold beaming. She wore an oversized green jumper and a sensible long pleated skirt. Nell looked like the lead singer of a struggling techno-goth band. Amara threw herself into Nell's arms and pulled her in for a tight hug. Nell's slight frame was enveloped in the voluminous soft wool of the librarian's sweater. In that moment, all of the nervousness and worry dissipated from Nell's body. She could have stayed like that forever, in the warm embrace of her dear friend.

Christopher, who had been hanging back a discrete distance, approached the door.

"It's been a while," he said, smiling.

"Too long, stranger," replied Amara, as she detached herself from Nell and embraced Christopher, who patted her back as they held each other. "I hope you've been taking care of my girl," added the librarian.

Once inside the headquarters, Christopher carried their bags up the winding staircase that sat at the heart of the cavernous building. They had two small duffle bags, which contained all their worldly possessions. A few changes of clothes, a burner phone and some toiletries.

Nell briefly turned to look at Christopher. She smiled at him. The brief grin he gave in return showed that he felt the same way. So much could be conveyed with a simple smile, especially when you were as close as they were. It was an empathy that bordered on telepathy. They were back among friends in a familiar place after so long on the road living a vagabond existence. They were also in this together, come what may. All that was conveyed with the simple act of tightening the muscles around the mouth in a certain combination.

Amara led them along the long corridor on the third floor before stopping at a door Nell recognized. It was the room she had previously shared with Christopher in what now felt like the dim and distant past. So much had happened to her since she was last at Vhik'h-Tal-Eskemon. Her mind boggled sometimes when she looked back on her recent life. From unremarkable law student at Vanderbilt University to the (un)living embodiment of a creature that she once thought existed only in the pages of horror novels or mostly lame movies. It made her head spin when she stopped to think about it, which she tried not to do too often.

"We kept it for you," Amara said as she pushed open the door. "We knew you'd be back, eventually," she added with more than a hint of emotion.

Waiting inside the room was an impromptu welcoming committee made up of Haiden, Kavisha and Klaus.

"Welcome back, Crimson queen," Klaus said with a wry smile after the greetings were made. "You've been causing quite the stir out there."

"I was simply in the wrong place at the wrong time," explained Nell as she collapsed into a plush armchair. She'd met Klaus during her time in captivity and then very briefly again in Alaska after her dramatic rescue. His story was almost as unbelievable as hers.

"Nice to see you without a pile of bodies under you," Haiden chimed in. "Christopher was meant to be keeping you safe, not plunging you headfirst into a shitstorm."

"As the lady said, wrong place, wrong time," Christopher said, sitting on the edge of the large bed. "Plus, we were safe, not that it counts for much. The vampires couldn't tell we weren't fellow Crimsons. They sensed we were vampires and just assumed we were also there for the party."

"Hardly a party," Kavisha admonished.

"Yeah, sorry," said Christopher. "Figure of speech." He looked around the room. "So, what have we missed?"

Everybody turned to Kavisha. Her tone was almost apologetic as she filled them in on the global progress. It didn't take long.

"That's it?" Nell asked, failing to mask her surprise. "Everyone is just 'working on it'?" Her tone was a little harsh. Possibly unjustifiably. But she had expected more. Something concrete.

"That's a pretty accurate assessment of where we are right now," said Amara. "Global vampire chapters are trying to locate and hunt down Zachariah. The werwulf packs are trying to do likewise. As far the attacks go, it seems we're powerless to stop them. The only thing we can do right now is let the human authorities deal with the aftermath as best as they can."

"There's no point in us turning up on the scene," added Kavisha. "The humans are angry and scared. They can't differentiate between the Crimson Claws and other vampires or non-humans. To them, we are all the enemy right now. You can hardly blame them."

Nell looked more frustrated than ever. Her face must have betrayed her emotions.

"There are few things we have learnt," said Amara, turning to her. "Mostly from observing the Crimson Claw foot soldiers. They are quicker and stronger than your average vampire."

"Which is going to make our life much harder," said Haiden. He looked disturbed.

Nell wasn't sure if Haiden was referring to the Vampire Hunters in particular or all of them. The Hunters were surely facing an insurmountable task in trying to take out the Crimsons, based on the vampires' strength and sheer numbers. Nell had witnessed first-hand what they were capable of.

"But what is more unique is they seem to operate as a co-ordinated unit," continued Amara. "Kind of like a hive mind or what the werwulfs experience in their packs. They all know what to do at the exact right time. If you watch footage of the attacks, it appears that they are following commands."

"It's difficult to watch and absolutely terrifying for what it could portend," added Kavisha.

If Kavisha was scared, as an ancient, then Nell knew the situation was worse than she had envisioned. And what she had envisioned was pretty dire as it was.

Silence permeated the room as the occupants digested Kavisha's heavy words.

Amara reached out and placed a hand on Nell's shoulder.

"We have one more thing to tell you," she said. "Which might come as a surprise."

Nell noticed that Amara shot a quick glance at Klaus when she spoke. There might even have been a hint of a smile on her face.

Nell had no idea what to expect. In the short time she'd known the people in the room, they'd become like her family. Yet, in reality, she had spent very little time by their sides. The rest of them had bonded tightly while fighting side-by-side.

CHAPTER 6

That much was obvious to Nell. It was easy to feel left out. She had secretly hoped that, as a vampire, she wouldn't experience the more irritating human emotions, such as jealousy. But, the truth was, she was jealous. Jealous that they'd formed such close bonds while she'd been held prisoner and abused.

Managing to keep her face neutral, Nell looked at Amara.

"Well, Kavisha, probably in a moment of madness, has brought us onto the Council of Elders," said the librarian. "Me and Klaus."

Nell couldn't help but notice the tone of satisfaction in Amara's voice. She was proud of herself, and Nell was proud of her. As well as more than a little taken aback by the development, if truth be told. Adversary was certainly making the strangest of bedfellows. But the Council was lucky to have Amara. She had proven herself time and time again.

Klaus's sudden elevation was perhaps a different matter. Nell was unsure of him. He often seemed sullen and cold. The fact that he was a former Red Claw had to have annoyed some of the other Elders. But Nell had to assume that Kavisha knew what she was doing. It wasn't her place to question the High Chancellor's decisions.

"Congrats!" said Christopher, looking from Amara to Klaus. "Proud of you both."

Klaus smiled wanly. Nell had a strong feeling that he was thinking about Loris. She hadn't ever seen them together, but Christopher had filled her in on the burgeoning love affair that was cut short. With everything else going on, Nell had forgotten that Klaus had lost the person he loved. He had suffered the one thing that both Nell and Christopher dreaded. Nell decided that she ought to cut the former Red Claw some slack. She could hardly blame him for bouts of sullenness considering his turbulent life.

"Yes, congratulations," said Nell, graciously. "You'll both make great additions to the Council, I'm sure."

The phone in Amara's pocket began vibrating with a loud buzz. The librarian's face hardened as she hurriedly reached for it and brought it to her ear. She listened intently.

"It's happened again…" Amara said in a faltering voice after the brief call ended. "Another attack."

"Where?" asked Haiden.

"Germany, in Augsburg," said Amara. "It's a university town in Bavaria. Lots of young people, not that it makes a difference. I have to make a call." Amara hurried out of the room.

The rest of the group followed behind her down to the cavernous basement library. Haiden helped Kavisha to use the birdcage elevator. The two of them arrived a minute or so after the rest of the group. Amara was stationed at her large oak desk at the center of the library. Her laptop was perched on one side while various books lay open across the pockmarked wooden surface. There was a large blackboard covered in chalk scribblings close by. The handwriting didn't seem decipherable to anyone but Amara.

Amara consulted a spreadsheet on her computer then took out her phone and dialed a long string of numbers. Nell's sensitive hearing picked up the ringtone. It was an international call. Nell could tell by the elongated rings.

"Hello, Hauptkanzler Wagner," said Amara after the call was answered. "Yes, I've just been made aware. Firstly, I'd like to offer our sincere condolences. Secondly, we need to review the footage. Sorry for being so brusque, but we need to examine any evidence as a matter of urgency." She paused for a moment as she listened. "Thank you for your understanding,

Hauptkanzler. We'll be in touch," she said before ending the call.

"Who was that?" Nell asked.

"Aloysius Wagner," replied Kavisha. "He's the High Chancellor, or Hauptkanzler as he is known, of the Vampire Council in Germany."

"They're sending the footage over," added Amara. "But they are clearly at a loss about what to do."

"As are we all," said Kavisha, bitterly. "As are we all."

Amara thumped a palm onto the desk. She probably didn't mean to do it, thought Nell, but her body was betraying her mind. Nell's heart went out to her friend. Only moments ago Amara had been proudly sharing news of joining the Council of Elders. Now she sat dejected and powerless at her desk. Amara was the team's strategist. The thinker. Yet right now she seemed at a total loss about how to proceed.

"I think it's time we convened another Global Council meeting," said Amara. She began tapping keys on her laptop. "And let's hope it goes more smoothly than the last one."

"I bloody well hope so," Haiden said. "We need to steer the topic away from punishments and retribution and instead focus on how to stop this madness. There will be plenty of time for justice later. Assuming there is a later."

Chapter 7

Haiden had barely seen Amara since they'd moved back into the Council headquarters. She was always so busy. So frantic. But who could blame her? The world was going to Hell and it seemed like there was nothing anyone could do about it. Least of all a mortal librarian.

The irony that a Vampire Hunter was once again currently residing at the nation's vampire headquarters wasn't lost on Haiden. Over the past week or so he'd begun to notice that the ache within him, the one that flared whenever he was in close proximity to a vampire, was dissipating. When he'd first moved to the Council headquarters months ago, that ache had been unyielding. A consistent discomfort in the pit of his stomach that instinctively warned him that the enemy was close at hand. But no longer did the vampires feel like the enemy. Consequently, his internal alarm had switched to a lower setting and then ceased to ping altogether.

Coldly and clinically executing all vampires was no longer a priority for the Hunters. Instead, they had to focus on the extreme end of the spectrum. The Crimson outmoded s. Those who killed without reason, distinction or compunction. The mindless swarms eradicating whole towns and cities as if the human inhabitants were vermin in need of extermination.

CHAPTER 7

While the vampire Councils around the globe had been focusing on ways to combat the Crimson Claws, the Hunters had been doing the same. While they didn't have a global organization as such, the Hunters operated an underground network of chapters in various geographies. They were spread far and wide and hunting was a tradition passed down through the generations. Many of the families that formed the networks had spread out across different territories as new threats arose. Hunters in various locations invariably had familial ties with chapters elsewhere, which served to strengthen the global network.

Haiden had contacts all over the world and was helping to organize the Hunter response to the catastrophic turn of events. Based on the video footage and knowledge accumulated by Amara, it had become abundantly clear that taking on the Crimson Claws head on would not only be futile, but likely a suicide mission. The Vampire Hunters had to take a more strategic, covert approach. It was thanks to Hunter eyes on the ground that the hive behavior of the Crimson Claws was discerned. It wasn't something that was so obvious when you simply looked at video footage alone.

The next task would be to try and take one of them captive. It wouldn't be easy. They needed to proceed with extreme caution. Underestimating the Crimson Claws would mean almost certain death for the Hunters in their path.

After talking to Gunther Müller, his German connection in Hanover, about the Augsburg attack, Haiden made his way swiftly to the grand dining room. It had been set up as the unofficial meeting room. Around three sides of the large wooden table sat the assembled team. A laptop connected to a projector was placed in the middle of the table.

"Ready?" asked Amara as she approached the small computer.

She scanned the pensive faces around the table. Kavisha gave a small nod, seemingly bracing herself. Amara pushed a button on the computer. A screen was projected on the far wall filled with a grid of small boxes. Faces began appearing in the boxes as various Councils answered the group call. One thing Amara had done in her time at headquarters was to update its outmoded technology. Kavisha granted her every request and had eventually just given her a Council credit card, so she didn't have to ask each time.

After twenty or so boxes were filled with faces, Amara addressed the group, welcoming the members and going over what she knew about the Augsburg incident. Haiden was always taken aback by how commanding Amara could be when the need arose. A mortal addressing the world council of vampires, holding their rapt attention, was an incredible sight in his books. God, he loved that girl.

His attention snapped back to the dining room when one of the heads on the screen began addressing the meeting. The man looked to be in his seventies with a shock of white hair and a sallow, thin face. He wore a black formal jacket with white shirt underneath. To Haiden, he looked like a vampire straight out of Central Casting. 'Council Leader Radomir Petrov, Russia' was written in small text at the bottom of his screen.

"We have news," said Petrov in a thick Russian accent. It sounded like 'vee av noos' to Haiden's ear, but luckily automatic captions appeared at the bottom of the screen in case anyone had trouble understanding.

"We captured one of the Crimson Claws," the council leader

CHAPTER 7

continued.

A few gasps were heard. A large number of faces on the grid looked taken aback. Even Haiden wasn't expecting that particular development, he had to admit.

"She was taken to a holding cell in Novinka, near St Petersburg," said Petrov. "It took five of the strongest members of my private guard to seize her. I don't know what in the name of dark creation she was, but she wasn't like us."

Amara was just about to say something, but Petrov continued speaking.

"I say 'was', because the moment we left her unattended she killed herself by ripping her own head from her body. We were left with just ash in a cage."

The other faces on the screen looked perturbed.

"Thankfully, we managed to take some of her blood beforehand," continued Petrov. "This is where more strangeness occurs." The council leader leaned forward in his chair. "It wasn't vampire blood in the traditional sense. What I mean is that it is more liquid, more red. More human."

"Were you able to have it analyzed?" asked Amara, also leaning forward.

"We sent it off to our lab in Moscow," replied Petrov. "They reported that some of the cells were in fact human. This isn't completely abnormal because, as you may know, when we drink human blood, it takes a while to assimilate with our own. But it wasn't like that with her. After her blood assimilated the human cells, fresh human cells appeared, seemingly out of nowhere. It was an endlessly repeating cycle of absorption then rebirth of the mortal cells. The technicians had never seen anything like it."

"What does that mean?" asked a new voice. It belonged to

'Council Leader Axel Lindgren, Sweden', according to the text under his image. He was a rotund man in his fifties with a completely hairless dome of a head and no eyebrows. Or none that Haiden could discern, at any rate.

"It means they create their own food source," replied Kavisha, grimly. "They rejuvenate their own blood."

More startled looks from the grid of faces. It was becoming a recurring theme, thought Haiden.

"It means that these beings, these Crimson Claws, are not like us," said Petrov. "They have evolved, taken the next step. They have the ability to exist without feeding. They kill not for sustenance. Yet they do so on command and with a vicious glee. They are stronger and faster than us and have no regard for prying human eyes." Petrov looked directly into his camera with a piercing look. "Forgive me for saying so, but this is beyond our worst nightmare."

From that moment onward, the meeting descended into chaos. It seemed everyone had something to say and they all wanted to say it at that very moment. A cacophony of voices reverberated around the dining room. Amara had to turn down the volume on the laptop.

Amara and Kavisha looked worried. Christopher and Nell appeared bewildered. Klaus seemed nonplussed.

Haiden was mildly amused. The superior species, he mused. Look at them now. Scared out of their wits. The prospect of 'super-vampires' who never tired, never needed to feed and killed on command was too much for even supernaturals to countenance. What chance did the Hunters have? Not only were the Crimson Claws decimating whole areas, but they were doing so with ruthless efficiency. It was a lot to take in at once. He could sense the fear emanating out of the big screen,

CHAPTER 7

where the assembled council members spoke and gesticulated wildly.

Amara managed to calm the situation somewhat before the meeting concluded.

"Excuse me…excuse me!" she exclaimed, while slapping a palm onto the dining table. "You can't all be heard at once. You need to take turns or we won't get anywhere."

Haiden could imagine the librarian saying the same thing to a group of excited elementary school kids during story hour. A small smirk reached the corners of his mouth.

The chorus of voices slowly abated and all eyes turned to Amara. That librarian voice of hers sure cut through when it needed to, especially when it was asking for every librarian's perennial goal — hush.

"We have better knowledge now," Amara said. "Not all of it is pleasing to hear, I grant you. But we are better for knowing it. Forewarned is forearmed. What we have heard today is a lot to digest. I suggest we reconvene tomorrow to discuss matters further."

She paused and scanned the assembled faces before her. It appeared that no one had any strong objections to her suggestion.

"Tomorrow then," said Amara. "Best of luck to you all. You are in my prayers."

With somewhat bemused looks, the attendees signed off. The various boxes on the wall turned dark gray one by one.

Amara wasn't overly religious. Haiden couldn't remember the last time she had discussed matters of the divine. But he had to admit that if a higher power was willing to lend a helping hand, then he for one certainly had no objections. They needed all the help they could get right now.

Chapter 8

Christopher had sat in stunned silence throughout the meeting. He hung off every utterance. Amara's translation software had enabled him to read the words being spoken by the various council members. His keen eyesight and fast reflexes allowed him to take in most of what was being said simultaneously. Fear and dismay were the overwhelming emotions being articulated. Hardly surprising given events.

Every so often Christopher's gaze drifted over to Haiden, who hadn't taken his eyes off Amara since the start of the proceedings. He seemed transfixed by her. It was clear that he was in love. 'Infatuated' might actually be a more accurate term.

The fact that love could blossom in such trying times warmed him a little. But the subject of the meeting soon put a dampener on his mood. Super vampires. A perpetual mix of human and vampire blood running through their veins. Christopher knew from personal experience that a vampire was at their strongest and sharpest just after feeding. The Crimson Claws were perpetually feeding on their own blood supply. Always on that edge of peak performance as the human blood was assimilated with their own over and over again.

Christopher turned to Nell, who sat quiet and impassive.

CHAPTER 8

Almost as if she knew something important but was afraid to give voice to it. That's when his thoughts began to spiral.

Images of Zachariah drinking a vial of Nell's blood flooded into Christopher's mind. Klaus had described how the Crimson Claw leader had imbibed the fluid in the tunnels under the compound in Alaska. The blood had made Zachariah strong. Almost invisible, in fact, according to Klaus. It was the very reason why Zachariah had kept Nell alive. She'd been his human blood bank. Blood that changed him into a monster, or even more of a monster. Nell's blood wasn't normal, even when she'd been human. That much was apparent. There was something potent about it that could not be explained. Not at the present time, anyway.

What if Zachariah was using Nell's blood to spawn these creatures? Either by feeding it to them directly or by drinking it himself and then turning them. The exact mechanism was beyond Christopher's ability to discern. But he was sure that Nell's blood played a role in the birth of the Crimson Claws. What other explanation could there be? And why else had Zachariah been draining and storing her blood throughout her period of captivity?

As soon as Amara closed the laptop and turned off the projector, Christopher blurted his thoughts out into the room. Nell stared at him with a look of surprise and then horror. He hated having to cause her distress, but this was too important to keep bottled up. He cast her an apologetic look, but continued talking until his jumble of thoughts were out in the open.

After a moment of silence, it was Klaus who spoke.

"I fear you are right," he said, somberly. "What else could it be? I saw Zachariah close up. It was like something from a nightmare after he drank the blood. It wasn't just his strength, but his speed, too. I didn't stand a chance. It was like he could predict my every move, almost as if he saw it before I made it. It terrified me." Klaus paused, considering something for a moment. The rest of the group waited patiently for him to continue. "The only logical explanation is that he is using the stores he took during Nell's captivity. That's why he prized her so greatly and refused to share her once he realized the potency of what was running through her veins."

"In the name of the Omni-Father," said Kavisha, more to herself than for anyone else's benefit.

The whole room turned to look at Nell.

She stared blankly at them, her mouth forming a small oval.

"I don't know what you want me to say," she said finally, sounding strained and defensive. "I don't remember much at all from when they had me. The venom in Zachariah's saliva kept me sedated. He fed on me multiple times a day, dosing me with it each time. Just enough so I remained barely conscious and pliable. As for my blood, I don't have the first clue why it could have been any different from anyone else's. Well, anyone human, that is. I know my blood group was O positive, which I think is the most common type there is. There was really nothing remarkable about me, whatsoever." She scanned each of the faces around the table. Then she looked down, a wet sheen coming to her eyes. "The thought of me being responsible for unleashing the Crimson Claws on to the world. I can't...I just can't..."

"It's just a theory at present, Nell," said Amara, sympathetically. "Nothing more. We don't have any hard facts, so we're just throwing things at the wall to see if they stick."

Christopher knew that Nell was blaming herself. Which

was ridiculous. It was hardly her fault that Zachariah had tricked her into walking into his clutches. That her blood held some seemingly unfathomable secret. If anyone was to blame, it was him for not being able to keep his feelings in check and dragging her into a world where she did not belong. Christopher knew his words would do little to soothe her right now. Instead, he simply held her hand.

Haiden addressed the room.

"If Zachariah drinks Nell's blood before turning a mortal into a Crimson Claw, then we have to assume that the recipient has Nell's blood mixed in with their own. That it keeps being absorbed and regenerating in that endless cycle, giving the Crimsons their heightened abilities. So what happens when a Crimson Claw turns another human into a vampire? Do they also have Nell's blood? Is it just as potent? Is there a diminishing effect the more times it's passed on? Does the blood get diluted somehow?"

The assembled faces were all blank.

"We need to run a more in-depth analysis of the blood drawn from the captured Crimson Claw," said Kavisha, urgently.

"I'll contact Radomir Petrov right now," replied Amara.

Nell looked distraught.

Amara's voice was calm. "Nell, there's still every chance we're wrong," she said. "This is all just a hunch."

Nell gave a weak nod. Amara swiftly left the room.

Christopher appreciated Amara's effort to placate Nell. But deep inside he knew, they all knew he thought, that it wasn't just speculation. They had hit the nail squarely on the head. Nell's blood was fueling this deadly plague sweeping the Earth.

Chapter 9

Amara's phone was chiming with non-stop news alerts. Attack after attack after relentless attack. She flipped the side button to put the device on silent. While it was important to keep abreast of worldwide developments, right now she needed to concentrate.

She had spent a frantic hour researching forensic hematology before calling Petrov and explaining the hypothesis regarding Nell's blood. They had agreed to conduct rapid DNA profiling on the Crimson Claw sample as well as looking at its antigen and protein markers. That would answer definitively the question of whether Nell's blood was present in the Crimson Claw. Luckily, they had a profile of her blood from her first stay at Vhik'h-Tal-Eskemon. Loris had shown the foresight to ask for an analysis when Nell was thought to be the subject of the prophecy contained in the *Adumbrate Invictus*. He reasoned it might offer clues as to why she was so special. In the end there appeared to be nothing unusual about it. At least from a biological standpoint.

It had been three hours since she had spoken to Petrov. She waited nervously at her desk, staring at the display of her phone. As if on cue, the words 'Radomir P, Moscow' suddenly flashed up on the screen. Amara snatched the phone off the

CHAPTER 9

desk and accepted the call before placing it to her ear. In her haste she almost dropped the device.

"Council leader," she said, breathlessly.

"Madam Amara," replied Petrov, his voice sounding grave. "It is as you suspected. The blood is a match."

Amara's breath caught in her throat. Her heart began hammering in her chest.

"Thank you, council leader," she whispered into the phone. "I'll be in touch."

"Do svidaniya," replied Petrov before ending the call.

Amara took a labored breath. Her palms became clammy as she digested the news. Zachariah had turned Nell's blood into a bioweapon. How on Earth did you tell your friend that she was involved in the deaths of millions of people? Not that it was Nell's fault in any way. But she knew her friend. She wouldn't see it that way.

Another grim thought occurred to Amara. Nell had revealed that she had a gift. She discovered that sometimes she could catch a glimpse of a person's future if she touched them. If her blood was present in the Crimson Claws, did that mean that some psychic ability was transferred to them? If so, it would make the Crimsons an even more formidable enemy.

That evening, as she and Haiden lay next to each other, Amara was unable to stop her mind from turning over and over. She had wanted to break the news to Nell right away. But when she saw her and Christopher walking arm in arm across the lush green at the center of the stately building, she just didn't have the heart to shatter her friend's world. One more day, she reasoned. Give Nell one more day of ignorant bliss before informing her and the rest of them. She wasn't sure if she was doing the right thing as far as the grand battle against the Crimson Claws was concerned. But she didn't care. Friendship was going to take priority over battle strategy. Come what may.

Haiden dozed gently beside her. He lay on his back, his hand haphazardly flung across the pillow. Amara turned to look at him, tracing the contours of his aquiline nose, thin lips and defined chin. He was beautiful, Amara thought. She could hardly believe that somebody like him was interested in her. They were opposites in almost every way. Day and night. But it worked. She had never used her analytical mind to examine their mutual attraction too deeply, for fear that the spell might be broken. Some things were better left unexplained, she reasoned.

Amara scooted closer to Haiden and whispered softly in his ear: "Wake up."

She trailed soft kisses down his neck until a soft moan left his mouth. His dark eyes blinked open, perhaps questioning whether or not he was dreaming.

"Hey you," she said as she playfully tapped the tip of his nose.

"Amara," he breathed as he rolled his body to face hers. A smile spread across his lips as he took her in, despite having just been in the grips of slumber. He didn't seem too put out about it.

He reached out and pulled her in for a tight full-body embrace. They fit against each other perfectly.

Haiden ran his warm hands down Amara's spine. He seemed to sense her need. She arched her back then pushed her body closer to his. His kiss was soft, unhurried. She hadn't realized it could be like this. Not before Haiden. That it could be gentle and last for hours as opposed to quick and frantic. They explored each other with the lightest of kisses, the lightest of

CHAPTER 9

touches. Teasing and stroking before finally coming together as one.

After, Amara lay wrapped up Haiden's arms, as well as in the moment. She wished she could freeze the march of time, to keep the Sun hidden beneath the horizon for the next day or two. Then she could just lie here. At rest. At peace. In the warm embrace of the one she loved.

She stirred early the next morning as the unforgiving Sun blazed into the room through partly open curtains. The enormity of the situation dawned on her along with the new day. The sensual moments of last night felt like a distant dream. The harsh reality of life was back with a vengeance.

The first task of the day was to tell Nell about what they'd found in the lab. It couldn't be put off any longer. Amara took a deep breath. Nell seemed so fragile lately. Having her face plastered over every TV screen in the land was bad enough. Amara was worried the new revelation, that her blood was at the root of this vampire plague, might tip her over the edge. She remembered how Nell went running into the clutches of Zachariah the last time she was overcome with guilt.

Amara showered and changed, opting as usual for comfortable unfussy clothing. She then made her way down the stairs. Nell was in the dining room with Klaus. They sat at the large table chatting. Amara had a soft spot for the ex-Red Claw. Even though he had an aloof exterior, she could sense that he had a softer center. He showed empathy for others and had taken Nell under his wing of late. They both had their lives turned upside down by circumstances far beyond their control. It appeared the unpredictable and cruel nature of fate had united them. Yet their growing bond was also completely crazy from another perspective. After all, Klaus had killed

Nell's Aunt Laura. It wasn't something that could be easily overlooked. Amara certainly wasn't going to remind Nell of it. Why rock the boat?

As these thoughts cascaded through Amara's mind, Klaus locked eyes with her. Something in his expression suddenly changed. It became more serious. Harder. For a moment Amara thought he was listening in on her thoughts. Was that even possible? She didn't think so. Yet Klaus had been changed profoundly since taking Loris's life. He was human but not human.

Klaus looked away. She was reading too much into it, reasoned Amara. She was on edge and seeing strange goings on in perfectly ordinary gestures. Also, if he was hiding something, it might be with good reason. Right now Amara had to concentrate on the task at hand.

"Nell, I have something to tell you," she started, tentatively.

Nell's eyes filled with tears. It appeared she already knew what Amara was about to say.

"It's mine, isn't it?" she said, her voice quivering. "Inside of those creatures."

"Yes," replied Amara. "I'm afraid so, Nell."

She held her breath, waiting for Nell to break into tiny little pieces. But she didn't. Instead, she straightened her posture and blinked away the tears.

"So what do we do now?" Nell asked.

Amara would have loved to know what was playing out inside of Nell's mind at that moment. The sudden change in her demeanor was a little disconcerting. Klaus's gaze was fixed on Nell.

"I'm not sure yet," Amara admitted. "We'll figure it out, Nell. Knowledge is power," she added without a great deal of conviction. "But I'll wager that even Zachariah doesn't know your blood continues to live on in his monsters. The way it recycles. He probably just thinks he can use it to create extra-powerful vampires. That extra insight might give us an advantage. I'm just not sure how at the moment."

"Sure," said Nell, surprisingly calmly. "I'll go and tell Christopher the news. He wanted to know right away."

Nell stood up and hurried out of the door, leaving Klaus and Amara just staring at each other.

"Well that was a little weird," Amara mused. "I didn't expect it to go quite like that."

"People cope in different ways," Klaus said. "Give her time."

"When did you become so wise?" Amara replied in a wry tone.

Klaus took a moment before answering.

"When everything I thought I knew turned out to be false," he said, bitingly.

Amara was thrown by the response. She didn't want to upset anyone else today. Nell's reaction was still weighing on her.

"Oh, I didn't mean to..." she began.

"It's okay," said Klaus, raising a placating palm. "You asked and I answered. But about Nell, she's trying to cope with a lot of different feelings right now. I'm sure you're perceptive enough to realize she feels responsible for everything that's happening."

Amara wasn't sure if that was meant as a complement or a dig. It was hard to tell with Klaus.

"If she hadn't willingly run away from here, Zachariah would never have known about her blood," continued Klaus. "Perhaps none of this would have happened. That plays on her mind, greatly. She needs time."

Klaus sounded almost fatherly. It was at times like these that Amara was reminded of just how much older vampires were than mortals, despite their often deceptive looks. Klaus had been born in a very different time and seen so much over his many decades of life. A certain degree of wisdom came with the territory of being undead.

"Thank you, Klaus," she said. "I'll bear that in mind."

As she left the room her thoughts quickly centered back on Nell. In their rush to unravel the secrets of her blood, they had overlooked the much bigger question about her. One that the librarian was determined to answer.

Chapter 10

Klaus exhaled sharply after Amara left the room.

For an unnerving second, he thought the librarian might have figured out just how much he was able to perceive. The way in which he was changing and how his abilities were subtly shifting.

Since he'd taken Loris's life, it seemed that every day brought something new into his experience. His hearing was growing stronger, as was his eyesight. But it was more than that. Over the past couple of days Klaus had noticed that he was able to read people's thoughts and feel their emotional state. The thoughts weren't clear. He'd get a general sense of what they were pondering and a bodily vibration of the accompanying feelings. It felt like a wave when it happened. He was suddenly overcome by an experience of reality that wasn't his own. Very occasionally the thoughts he picked up were surprisingly sharp and clear. Like just a few moments ago, when Amara had thought of Klaus killing Nell's aunt.

Nell might have shut that terrible memory out of her mind, or at least made peace with it, but Klaus never could. It haunted him each time he looked at Nell's face and saw the resemblance between the two women. In fact, every time he saw Nell it reminded him of the person he had been. The one he tried so hard to forget. Also of how much he had to atone for.

As a hybrid 'human', Klaus was finding it hard to run from his emotions. Along with aging and eating, it seemed that feeling was something he could not escape. In his undead life, apart from the ever-present thirst which at times escalated to blood lust, he couldn't remember feeling a particularly wide array of emotions. Plus, could thirst for blood really be classed as an emotion? Yet it was the most common thought that used to occupy his mind.

But now he had to deal with empathy, something he lacked almost completely in his previous incarnation. Empathy for Nell…but not only her. He daren't say anything out loud, but he felt sympathy at the deepest level for Zachariah's army of monsters. That had been him once. Granted, not quite as extreme. But he too had taken the lives of innocents, plenty of them, by mindlessly following orders. Now here he was, with a new life safely ensconced in this grand building alongside people who were actually concerned for his welfare.

It seemed incredibly unfair that he'd been given a second chance, yet hardly any of the Council leaders would grant the same courtesy to the Crimson Claws. They were seen as senseless aberrations that needed to be eradicated. Their underlying humanity or the people they had once been was of no consequence. It hurt Klaus that the Council hadn't recognized the similarities between his life and theirs. If it had, then maybe a thought could be spared to saving them, rather than destroying them.

Yet Klaus wouldn't say anything. As hypocritical as that made him. Even though it tore at him at times. Maybe there would come a time to share his feelings, but right now he didn't want to upset the applecart. It was too risky a trade-in.

CHAPTER 10

Yet more evidence of human emotions coming to the fore – self-interest, pragmatism and expedience. But, ultimately, cowardice.

For the first time since he could remember, Klaus felt like he had a family that actually cared for him. Why put that in jeopardy? His only job was to kill Zachariah and perhaps in the process fulfill that damn prophecy. Without Zachariah, no more Crimson Claws would be made. No more shadows of his former self to haunt his thoughts. Case closed. He had to focus on the prize.

There wasn't much Klaus could do to track down his former master. The wolves were taking care of that. In his previous life, Klaus would have made a crass joke about dogs tracking scents, but he was now free of that ignorance. He had the utmost respect for werwulfs and their unwavering dedication to the cause, despite the painful losses they sustained. It was the wolves who spared his life out in the wilderness when they had every right to tear him limb from limb. Tenacious and noble, Klaus thought the werwulfs had a lot to teach others.

The last phone call from Devan indicated that wolves around Europe were getting fresher, more recent scent trails than their brethren in the Americas. The working theory was that Zachariah was most likely hiding somewhere in the continent, but that wasn't much to go on. Klaus was constantly on standby, his bag packed, ready to go and kill his former leader. To fulfill his destiny. To move on from his whole sordid mess.

Klaus often mulled what his future might look like when all of this was over. His thoughts on the matter changed almost daily, but that was okay. He had plenty of time to figure out what he would do. Before it was easy. Loris was his future. The where, when and how of life were of little consequence.

As long as he was with Loris he would be happy. Fulfilled.

Now he had to confront what it meant to exist without the love of his life. Sometimes, in his imagined future, he lived alone in a forest, nothing but expansive wilderness to keep him company. Other times, he stayed at headquarters trying to be useful in the world after the Crimson Claws. In another variation, he traveled the world, taking in its various wonders. Alone. Always alone. The future was an open book, which was both liberating and daunting. But first, Zachariah. His dreams were mere ash in the wind if they were not victorious in battle.

Making his way to the large grass rectangle at the heart of the grounds, Klaus daydreamed of the day he would be free. When the world would be free. Supernaturals and humans would need to find a way to co-exist once this veil of darkness was lifted from the world. But one battle at a time.

To prepare for Zachariah he needed to test the limits of his new body. The limits of his skills. He worked out for at least three hours a day doing sprints and bodyweight exercises, then tried to stretch his senses as far as he could while sitting still on the grass. He closed his eyes and tried it again now. He could hear birds chirping a few miles away, but that wasn't the sense he was trying to explore. He took a few deep breaths to center himself and then reached out again, imagining a radar at the center of his forehead sending out exploratory waves.

After a few seconds he received a 'ping'. He shut his eyelids tighter and doubled-down with his mental energy on the signal. It slowly came into better focus. Amara. In her study. He was sure of it, having just been in her head. The texture was the same. So many thoughts whirling around. She had the capacity to juggle disparate pieces of data simultaneously to try to discern patterns. That wasn't how Klaus's mind worked, and he found the experience jarring. If he moved closer to her he could probably decipher the jumble of thoughts occupying her mind. But that felt like an invasion of privacy. He was only practicing now. She was owed the sanctuary of her own head.

Klaus opened his eyes and exhaled, bringing the gray stonework of the old house into focus in front of him. He was changing. Evolving and devolving at the same time. There had to be a purpose behind the way he was being shaped. A higher plan, if he could put it in such lofty terms. He could spend time pondering it. But no answers would be forthcoming. So instead he lowered his head and began running sprints through the lush grass. The physical exertion would offer a brief respite from his unsettled mind. For that he was grateful.

Chapter 11

Nell heard her name being called out repeatedly on the edge of her consciousness just before she was thrust out of her sleep state. It was like being propelled rapidly up from the ocean floor and breaking through the waves into the light of day. She actually gasped as she opened her eyes.

It had been a few days since the revelation that her blood was running through the veins of the Crimson Claws. She had hidden herself away in her room to catch up on rest and avoid the whispers and pointed fingers. Of course, no one was whispering or pointing figures, but that didn't stop her imagination from getting the better of her.

"Nell! Nell!"

Amara bounded into the room, past a startled Christopher, who was holding the door open for her.

Nell sat bolt upright, slowly regaining full control of her faculties as she shed the final remnants of her restorative trance.

Amara was out of breath. It looked like she had run all the way up from the basement library.

"I figured it out!" exclaimed the librarian. "I know why your blood is special. Hang on a minute though, I need to get my breath back."

CHAPTER 11

Amara sat heavily on the bed and took a series of gasping breaths.

"Take it easy, Amara," Nell said, crossing her legs and leaning forward.

She felt surprisingly calm considering she was about to find out why her blood appeared to be the deadliest weapon in the world. Christopher took the armchair on the far side of the room.

"Okay, so first things first," said Amara, regaining some of her composure. "This doesn't change anything...about the person you are, and how we all feel about you."

"Now you're really starting to scare me," said Nell.

"Right, sorry, that wasn't my intention," said Amara. "Anyway, I did some digging...on your parents."

Nell's eyes widened, her mouth opened.

"My parents?"

"Yes," said Amara. "The first breakthrough was an absolute fluke, actually. I was telling Haiden I was looking into your family history and happened to show him a picture of your parents. He recognized your dad!"

Nell's eyes grew even wider.

"Patrick Cartwright," continued Amara, "was...and I'm sorry you have to learn it like this...a Vampire Hunter."

Nell stared at Amara, stunned. Then burst out laughing.

"This is a joke, right?" she said.

Amara wasn't laughing.

"He wasn't a Vampire Hunter?" said Nell, incredulously. "He was an insurance salesman...and then a work-from-home realtor. Amara, he was normal. Boring. There's no way on Earth my dad was a Hunter. That's ridiculous."

Nell scoffed at the idea. Haiden must have been confused,

mixed up her dad with somebody who looked similar. Besides, Vampire Hunters inherited their traits from their ancestors. It was passed down in the family. If her father had been a Hunter, then she...

"Haiden was positive, Nell," continued Amara, before Nell could finish her train of thought. "He actually worked with your dad when they were stalking a nest in upstate New York. Didn't your father travel a lot when he was in the insurance business?"

"Yes," admitted Nell, casting her mind back. "But that was for risk assessments. He needed to do site visits. It's not something you can do sitting at a desk."

Amara looked sympathetically between Nell and Christopher.

"And did you ever have concrete proof he was actually out on these 'insurance calls'?" asked Amara.

"Obviously not," said Nell. "Why would we need to? Why would he lie to us?"

"I can think of one reason," interjected Christopher, glancing at Amara.

Amara bit her lip.

Nell placed her head in her hands.

"It can't be true," she said, without full conviction. "Dad. A Hunter?"

She felt like she'd been hit by a freight train. She was physically winded by the news.

"There's more, Nell..." Amara said, almost cringing with apprehension. "...it's about your mom."

"Her too!" exclaimed Nell. She felt like the bottom was falling out of her world. She had to place her palms on the mattress to steady herself.

CHAPTER 11

"It's not quite the same," explained Amara, shooting a worried glance at Nell.

"Go on," instructed Nell. "Just tell me." What was the point in backing out now?

"I ran an ancestry check on your blood sample then traced your family tree. Those genealogy websites are amazing, by the way. I was able to track your family all the way back to the fourteen-hundreds. The amount of information they hold is incredible."

Nell was nonplussed.

"Anyway," continued Amara. "It turns out your mother's side originally hails from Europe."

"What's surprising about that?" asked Nell, slightly miffed. "We're hardly Native Americans."

"But do you know where in Europe?" asked Amara.

"England…Ireland?" suggested Nell. "Peters is about as plain a surname as you can get."

"Your mom was named Florence Peters," explained Amara. "But Peters wasn't the original family name."

Nell raised her eyebrows. Christopher leaned forward in his chair.

"It was anglicized from 'Petre', which is a fairly common surname in Romania."

"Romania?" repeated Nell.

Amara nodded.

"Turns out your mother is a direct descendant of Zaleska Tepes, who was the daughter of Vlad Tepes."

Nell was hit by a sudden recognition. She knew that name. Memories came back of poring over books of ancient folklore at Henry Freeman Memorial Library in Angel Falls. It seemed like a lifetime ago. It certainly felt like a different life to the one she had now.

"Vlad Tepes had a more famous name, didn't he?" ventured Nell. "Vlad the Impaler."

"That's right," said Amara, with undisguised delight. "Well done, Nell!"

Nell internally rolled her eyes. She wasn't in a library reading class now.

"He was the inspiration for Dracula," explained Amara. "Also arguably one of the most evil and sadistic people to have ever walked the Earth."

"Hey, you're talking about my family there!" said Nell, with what she thought was undisguised irony.

"Um, yeah, I'm sorry about that," said Amara, completely missing the humor. "Zaleska Tepes is your great, great, great, great, great, great…well you get the idea. The key point is you share your bloodline with Vlad the Impaler, the Voivode of medieval Wallachia himself, son of Vlad Dracul, the Blood Brute of Romania, the scourge of the Ottoman Empire and…"

"Yeah, we get the idea," said Nell, rather dryly. "He was a big bad dude back in the day."

"Sorry," said the librarian, reining in her enthusiasm. "It's just that history fascinates me."

"So I'm a direct descendant of the guy who created vampires in the first place," said Nell. "And that makes me special? Well my blood anyway."

"I think that's part of it," said Amara. "But my sense is that it's because you're the child of a Hunter and a descendant from the original vampire family. When the bloodlines joined it created an incendiary mix. Sort of like Yin and Yang. Light and dark. I can't put it in scientific terms and we know that the biological markers show that your blood is normal. But there's something extra there, woven into its fabric, undetectable to laboratory testing because medical science can't test for the presence of anything…arcane or esoteric. Those are the best words I can come up with to describe it."

"So my blood is magic?" asked Nell.

"Not magic as in child's magic," said Amara. "But definitely out of the ordinary. Powerful. Does any of this make sense to you?"

Nell was silent for a few moments.

"It makes as much sense as anything else you've said," said Nell. "It's a lot to take in, Amara."

"I know," said the librarian. "You're in the right room, at least. I know I'd need to lie down after hearing this."

Nell cast her mind back to her childhood. She remembered her dad teaching her how to hunt and shoot during camping trips. But why wasn't the Hunter tradition passed down to her? Did she not show enough aptitude? Was it because she was a girl? Perhaps her dad was jaded with the life of a Hunter and didn't want to place the same burden on his only child. She'd like to think it was the latter reason. That he did it out of love. But the truth of the matter had followed Patrick Theodore Cartwright to the grave. Nell would never know.

The three of them sat in silence for a while. Nell could tell that Amara was itching to say something else, but was keeping it bottled inside, allowing Nell some breathing space. Rather than allowing her friend to stew, Nell asked her what was on her mind.

"I just think you were destined to be here, whatever choices you made in life," said Amara. She reached out and squeezed Nell's knee. "It would also explain why Christopher was so drawn to you in the first place. I think something inside of you was calling to him."

"I knew it had to be something more than her personality," said Christopher.

His attempt at humor fell completely flat. Amara gave him a withering look.

"I just want to say again that none of this is your fault, Nell," assured the librarian.

"I know. Thanks, Amara," Nell lied, hoping Amara fell for it. It wasn't a discussion she wanted to have right now. She knew that nobody else blamed her for the mess they all found themselves in. But she couldn't honestly say the same of herself.

Just then Haiden popped his head around the door.

"Devan's on the phone," he informed, animatedly. "There's been a development."

The announcement served to break the mood of the room.

Nell, Amara and Christopher quickly set off after him. A few moments later they were in the dining room. In the far corner stood the Magisters, almost melding into the shadows, trying to be inconspicuous. Nell didn't know what to make of them on the whole. They seemed to come and go as they pleased, working to a strategy that wasn't immediately apparent. But the fact that they were in this room meant Kavisha had deemed it necessary. That was good enough for Nell.

"Devan, I'm putting you on speaker," Klaus said into the mobile handset before tapping a button and placing the device on the table.

"Hey everyone," came Devan's voice.

Nell's heart swelled. It was the first time she had heard Devan's voice in a long while. He had been her first friend when she'd moved in with her aunt back at Angel Falls. He

CHAPTER 11

had also looked out for her, in a somewhat harebrained way. But his heart was in the right place. He wore his feelings on his sleeve, which Nell thought was an admirable quality in a world where 'friends' were often virtual or fair-weather.

"I'll get right down to it," continued Devan. "Our brethren in Europe have tracked the scent trail. They believe they're closing in on Zachariah."

"Where?" asked Amara, shooting a glance at Kavisha.

"Italy," replied Devan. "Venice to be precise. The wolves have his scent entering the region but there's no exit trail as yet. They believe he's still there. The pack is trying to narrow down his location. This might be our chance, Amara."

Amara gave another glance to Kavisha, who nodded resolutely.

"I'll make the arrangements," Amara said.

"Good," said Devan. "Time is pressing. We have a window of opportunity that we need to use before it closes. How are our numbers?"

Everyone in the dining room turned to Kavisha.

"Not as we hoped," the High Chancellor conceded, lowering her head slightly. "I heard from Sanya only this morning. You all remember her? The spell-caster who fought alongside us with her twin sister, Yansa."

The team responded with somber nods. Yansa had been killed by the Red Claws during the battle in Alaska. It had virtually broken her sister.

"She told me that the spell-casters are reluctant to participate further in this war," continued Kavisha. "The general feeling is that they sacrificed themselves once, and now the odds are heavily stacked against us due to the emergence of the Crimson Claws. The fae feel the same way. Everyone is scared and trying to protect their own. It's hard to blame them."

"Shit," said Devan. "That doesn't sound promising."

"Sanya will fight with us, though," added Kavisha, by way of conciliation. "She said she has nothing left to lose after her sister was taken from her."

The room was silent for a long moment.

"The wolves?" said Amara, finally.

"We'll be there, rest assured," said Devan. "This is personal now." There was a steeliness in his voice.

Nell surmised that he was thinking about the fallen members of his pack, particularly Flint and Lupo, who were hardly more than just pups.

"Will Lupita be there?" asked Amara. "I haven't heard from her in a while."

"No," replied Devan. "She won't."

It was a curt response. Nell could tell that there was more to it.

"She's staying with her pack in the north," added Devan, who must have realized he was being unduly brusque. "She's not in a position to fight."

Nell had an inkling, but she kept her thoughts to herself.

"Thanks, Devan," said Amara. "We know we can count on you. I'll get back to you very soon with the travel details."

Devan hung up the phone. Nell surveyed the room. The faces looked serious. Focused.

"I've always wanted to see Venice," ventured Klaus. "But perhaps not like this."

***

Once back in their room, Christopher shut the door firmly

CHAPTER 11

behind him.

"I need to know that you're okay, Nell," he said. "I want you to be honest with me. Completely honest."

"What do you mean?" said Nell, defensively. "I don't keep anything from you. You should know that by now."

Internally, it felt like her world was turning upside down. Everybody around her seemed to be coping with the situation. Like it was their calling in life or something. But this wasn't her calling. She didn't want her existence to be like this. Not one bit. But how do you tell the person who risked their life for you, who valued you above the rest of humanity it seemed, how you truly felt?

"You're not fine, Nell," said Christopher, approaching her and placing his hands on her shoulders. "Come on. It's me. In the name of the Omni-Father, Nell, I can tell when something's wrong."

Christopher's voice was loud. Not shouting, but frustrated. She couldn't blame him for being annoyed. He could read her like a book and knew she was swallowing her feelings. Plus, she'd been a pain to be around ever since they'd witnessed the massacre in San Luis. She'd only gotten worse since coming to headquarters and finding out about her blood connection to the Crimson Claws.

"You know something, Christopher?" she snapped. She could feel the floodgates slowly opening. "I can't even explain what it feels like. Can you imagine hating the very thing that gives you life? Your own blood. Because it's been used to spawn a legion of monsters. Then you find out that your father lied to you your whole life. All this after you fall in love with a vampire, only to be told that he has to kill you to save the world. Then, you run away to save the ones you love and end up making everything one hundred times worse. Only then to be told that the vampire was only attracted to you because something in your damned blood 'called to him'? So, yeah, Christopher, I'm not okay. Far from it."

Christopher wrapped his arms around her shoulders and held her tightly. Nell knew that part of her torment stemmed from not having come to terms with her time as a hostage. She most likely had post-traumatic stress due to that tortuous experience. But she wasn't ready to face it head on yet. And wasn't it her fault in the first place for stupidly walking into the hands of the Red Claws? What right did she have to feel sorry for herself? Her reckless actions resulted in the world being plunged into darkness.

"I love you for you," soothed Christopher. "Not your damned blood. I couldn't care less where it came from or what manner of voodoo it contains. Yes, your blood is part of you, but you are so much more than that."

"Everything that's happened is because of me," said Nell. "When I look back on the events of my life. My parents' accident. Having to move to Angel Falls. Meeting you. None of this would have happened if things had been different."

Christopher pulled back from her and placed his hands on her shoulders again.

"You're wrong," he said, staring at her with those intense blue eyes. "The Council were always going to wake up the Red Claws. That darkness was always going to revisit the world, with or without your involvement. That prophecy would have still played out, through Loris and Klaus. They appear to be at the root of it, rather than us."

"But my blood…" she began.

"Zachariah was always going to wreak havoc on the world,

CHAPTER 11

one way or the other," said Christopher. "Without you, I'm not sure we would have had Devan and the wolves on our side. Also Amara, who's proven to be invaluable in our fightback. Not least because she built a truce with the Hunters. You think we vampires could have done that?" He began to rub her shoulders. "Nell, you keep dwelling on how things have gone wrong, without taking account of all the positives that have come from you being here. Not least in my life, as selfish as that sounds."

"You can't mean that," said Nell. "Not after everything that's happened."

"I mean it from the bottom of my heart," replied Christopher. "My life was hardly worth living before I met you. I was just a hollow shell. Now I have everything to live for."

Resting her head against Christopher's chest, Nell felt safe. Not absolved of her actions, but calmer. She trusted Christopher with her life and knew he meant what he said. She just wished that the circumstances were different.

She tilted her head up and kissed him gently. It had been so long since they'd been intimate. Neither of them had been in the right headspace. But in that moment, all she wanted was to be with Christopher and block out the entire world. She pushed her body against his and deepened her kiss. She slid her hand down his body, finding its final resting point. Their clothes quickly formed a messy pile on the floor.

Nell finally felt the guilt, anger and frustration ebb away. If only for an all-too-brief moment.

Chapter 12

Amara used the credit card Kavisha had given her to book the private jets. The fact that the Council appeared to have unlimited funds made her life so much easier. After Devan's phone call, they had all swiftly packed what they needed. Amara had triple the baggage of everybody else. Not only did she have her personal belongings, but she took her work things, too. Books, laptops, external hard drives, a whiteboard, markers, folders of notes, the lot. Haiden helped her heave the cases onto the plane.

The ragtag group boarded the aircraft on the private strip at Chattanooga airport mere hours after their call with Devan. It helped when you could pay the carrier triple its standard fee to rearrange flight schedules. Amara managed to grab Nell for a private word just before they climbed the mobile stairs into the belly of the executive aircraft.

"You look like you're feeling better," Amara said, scanning Nell's face.

She could have sworn she saw Nell blush, despite her deathly pale exterior, but decided not to pry.

"I am," said Nell. "I got a few things off my chest, which helped. You don't have to worry about me, Amara. I won't be a liability."

CHAPTER 12

"I would never think of you as a liability, Nell," replied Amara. "I just didn't want you to carry your burden alone. These are crazy times."

Amara leaned forward and hugged her friend before the pair boarded the plane.

After take-off, Amara called an impromptu meeting.

"So, this is where we stand," she said to the assembled group. "We know Zachariah is believed to be in Venice. The wolves are headed there by plane, or their own four legs if they are already on the continent. Oh Kavisha, I forgot to mention, I wired them the money for their flights. I hope that's okay."

"Sure," Kavisha said, nonchalantly.

Amara had known it would be fine but sometimes she felt like a child using daddy's credit card. She thought it polite to double-check that the expenditure was approved. Being frugal all her life, especially on the salary of a librarian, she was not used to throwing money around.

"The wolves are meeting us there," continued Amara. "As are a contingent of Hunters, right Haiden?" She turned to him.

"Yeah," he replied. "Hunters from the region are converging on Italy. However, we decided to leave a significant number back in their home geographies, in case they're needed. We just don't know how this is going to play out and where new threats will materialize. We can't discount the possibility that Zachariah is trying to distract us, divert our resources. Better safe than sorry. Oh and Kavisha, I paid for our transport using Council funds."

Kavisha simply waved a hand, as if it wasn't even worth mentioning.

Amara turned to Klaus, who was staring out of the window, seemingly minding his own business.

"Klaus, if the prophecy is correct, you might have an important role to play," said Amara. "May I ask where you're at with your, erm, changes? Do you feel able to fight Zachariah if the time comes?"

Klaus looked taken aback.

"I've seen you training at Vhik'h-Tal-Eskemon," explained Amara. "I know your progress has been quite…quick."

Klaus smiled. He should have known that the ever-vigilant librarian would not have missed a beat.

"I'm getting stronger," he said. "My senses are sharp. Which is all to the good. But the changes also mean that if I sustain a severe blow I don't have the capacity to heal. So the strengths are balanced with weaknesses. I have no idea whether it will be sufficient to defeat Zachariah, particularly if he has enhanced himself with…"

He glanced at Nell, who looked uncomfortable with the topic of discussion.

"…his elixir," Klaus said, diplomatically.

"Okay then," Amara said. "That will have to do. On the subject of exceptional abilities, Nell, what about you?" She looked at her friend. "Are you still able to catch glimpses of people's futures? We need to marshal every resource we have at our disposal. It all might come into play in ways we can't foresee as yet."

"It's hit and miss," replied Nell. "I could do with a little more practice. I haven't really been around that many people lately." She looked around at the assembled faces. "So if there are any volunteers," she added brightly, more as a joke than a serious request.

"Everybody will take a turn," said Amara. "Won't we guys?"

Amara turned to the group, most of which nodded their

assent, perhaps a little reluctantly. It seemed no-one was overly keen for their future to be divined.

"Thanks," said Nell, somewhat surprised. She hadn't expected her request to be taken at face value.

"When we get to Italy we'll be staying just outside of central Venice, on the island of Murano," informed Amara. "That way we won't draw attention to ourselves. The wolves, Hunters and other vampires will be staying in small groups at venues nearby. Lucia Verga, leader of the Venetian Council, is aware of our arrival and she has extended the offer of any help we may require. But we need to assess the situation on the ground before making any decisions."

Amara studied the notepad in her hand. Despite the modern technology that she'd asked Kavisha to invest in, the librarian believed that pen and paper was the way to go for the most important things.

"I think that's everything," she said. "Now let's get some rest."

Instead of sleeping or entering the trance state, as she'd encouraged the rest of them to do, Amara continued her research using the surprisingly quick onboard Wi-Fi. She was digging into Christopher's past, using the same set of tools that she'd used to uncover Nell's history. Amara had a number of questions bouncing around her head and she needed to satisfy her curiosity. Sleep could wait. It was like an itch that needed to be scratched. Why were Nell and Christopher so different from other vampires? Why were they bestowed with gifts of seeing and was it something beyond attraction that had drawn them together?

Haiden was gently snoring in the plush leather seat next to hers, an eye-mask covering his face. She envied his ability to fall asleep at the drop of a hat.

Amara turned her attention back to her laptop. The family tree in front of her was growing, sprouting branches spreading far back into the past. Names were falling into place. It was exhilarating. Information on Christopher's maternal side was very limited and she quickly hit a dead end. But his father's side blossomed out, covering centuries past. A name appeared on the screen and Amara had to do a double take. She blinked but the name at the top of the tree was still the same. Four simple letters. Radu. But it was the surname that gave it the extra weight of history, and infamy — Tepes.

Amara's fingers flew across the keyboard as she began researching furiously. Radu was the brother of Vlad the Impaler, Nell's distant relative. It seemed that Radu was the opposite of Vlad in every way possible. While Vlad was known to be ruthless and cruel, Radu was merciful and just. He was even affectionately known by many as 'Radu the handsome'. He'd had one child. A daughter named Maria, who was born in 1457. Christopher descended from Maria, who would eventually become the Princess consort of Moldavia.

Amara stared at the screen open-mouthed. Did this explain Christopher and Nell's connection? Why they had the same gift, but in reverse. Christopher could see into the past while Nell was able to glimpse the future. Opposites. Much like Radu and Vlad. Nell was descended from darkness. Christopher from light. Did the Tepes family blood recognize itself and draw both of them together. If so, to what end?

She couldn't keep this to herself. Her heart was actually drumming in her chest. She released the metal clasp of her seatbelt and wandered to the back of the aircraft, laptop precariously balanced in one hand. Nell and Christopher sat next to each other, her head resting on his shoulder as he took in the view out of the window.

"Nell, Christopher, can I tell you something?" Amara said, taking a deep breath and steadying her jangling nerves.

She pulled down the tray in front of Christopher and placed the laptop in front of him, angling it so Nell could also see the screen. Then she told them what she had discovered, pointing out the names on the digital family tree. She used the touchpad to zoom in and out of the sprawling diagram, highlighting dates, locations and titles.

Both Christopher and Nell were lost for words when Amara concluded her impromptu presentation.

"I know," said Amara, more than a little proud of herself if she was being honest. "It's nuts, right?"

"It could explain a lot," said Christopher, who seemed to recover from the revelations quicker than Nell. But then, his family's history was decidedly less blood-soaked and murderous than hers.

"You're both anomalies, it would seem," said Amara. "Your lineage likely plays a part in what makes you different, but also perhaps in what draws you together. Maybe there's something greater at play here. Nell sees the future, you see the past. It's kind of like you complete each other."

Christopher addressed the subject that seemed to be the most concerning to him.

"That's great and all," he said. "But she's not like my cousin or something, is she? Now that would be weird."

"You're okay on that score," assured Amara. "The only relations between you go back six hundred years. There's been an awful lot of dilution since that time."

"Yet blood still outs," said Nell, finally finding her voice. "We can't seem to escape the past."

"Hey, keep it down back there!" shouted an annoyed Haiden, his eye-mask askew. "Some of us are trying to sleep."

With a wry smile, Amara closed the lid of the laptop.

Chapter 13

Nell needed to clear her mind. Amara's discovery had added to the jumble of disparate thoughts whirling around in her head. She knew that her friend hadn't meant to cause her any more anxiety. The studious librarian was just excited to share news of her research. Nevertheless, the continued revelations were doing little to calm Nell's agitated spirits.

In order to get out of her own head, she decided to see if she could enter someone else's. She was testing her gift of foresight by working her way around the cabin, touching hands and then screwing her face up in the most unflattering manner as she tried to see into the future. So far nothing. Just a few bemused looks.

Perhaps she needed to be in better spirits for the power to work. Perhaps she knew these people too well for the ability to take hold. Perhaps the skill had deserted her altogether. Nothing would surprise her at this point.

She approached the only person that she hadn't tried yet.

Chapter 14

Klaus was sitting on his own on the row of seats furthest back in the cabin. He sat by the window, mesmerized by the view of thick white clouds drifting by. He'd never seen anything like it in his long life. It seemed like magic. While mortals no doubt thought of vampires as extraordinary, they took for granted sitting in long metal tubes that flew amid the clouds. The miraculous was only a matter of perspective, he mused.

He looked up as Nell slowly approached along the narrow aisle. She looked apprehensive. It saddened him a little to know he was thought of as aloof and grouchy. But he was who he was. It seemed that prophecies and fate could change nearly everything about him, but not fundamentally who he was at his core. Yet he tried. He strived to be better with people.

He smiled warmly as Nell came to a stop and stood over him.

"My turn?" he asked.

"If you don't mind," said Nell, sheepishly.

"Ready when you are, fortune teller," Klaus replied, sounding, if not feeling, enthusiastic.

He stretched out his hands towards her. Nell looked momentarily surprised. She no doubt wasn't expecting him to be so accommodating. She then gently placed her palms on

CHAPTER 14

the backs of his hands and closed her eyes.

Klaus observed her face closely. Nell's eyelids began fluttering wildly. She suddenly let go of his hands as if she had been struck by a tidal wave of electricity. Her eyes flew wide open and she inhaled sharply. Klaus knew she didn't need to breathe. It was an instinctive reaction carried over from her mortal life. None of this seemed particularly promising to Klaus.

"Thanks, Klaus, all done," Nell said, turning away from him to make off.

"What did you see?" he asked, hurriedly.

"Nothing," replied Nell, not turning back to face him. "It doesn't seem to be working today," she added as she swiftly walked away.

This wasn't good. Wasn't good at all. It took every ounce of restraint for Klaus to stop himself from attempting to delve into her mind. One part of him wanted to probe her thoughts and feelings. But from her reaction, perhaps it was best not to know. Nell was no fool. If it was something that was crucial to the mission, she surely would have told him. She had decided not to. He had to trust her. As hard as he found it to trust anyone.

He looked out of the window but the clouds no longer held the same fascination as they did before. To distract himself, he decided to test his own abilities. He needed to be sharp for what lay ahead. He cast his mind out to the pilot and attempted to listen in on his thoughts. It was rude, but he would never know, Klaus reasoned.

Mundane. Very mundane. His wife, children. What he'd eat for dinner that evening at the layover. Klaus had never felt quite as jealous of a human before. He would give anything for a boring existence at this point. A life of routine and certainty. A dependable partner, perhaps not the children, but a life of habit and stable structure.

Klaus tried for the remainder of the flight to subdue his brain so he could find sleep. Sleep was one of his favorite things about being human(ish). Long periods of nothingness where sometimes he joined Loris again in the dream realm. Yet right now it was evading him. It was far simpler as a vampire, almost like an on/off switch. You relaxed the body and mind then sank into the restorative trance. There was no trying. It just happened. Without fail. But now, as he sat reclined in the darkened plane cabin, hearing the steady hum of the twin engines, sleep just would not visit him. His mind drifted. To Loris. To Zachariah. To love. To loss. To betrayal. To Nell's vision. To what lay in store in Venice.

Eventually, he gave up on his quest for sleep altogether. Once again he needed a distraction from his spinning thoughts. Klaus began to stretch his mind out a little. He looked along the length of the cabin. Just up ahead he spotted Kavisha. Her distinctive jet-black hair gave her away. She was sitting on an aisle seat with her wheelchair placed next to her. Her head was perfectly still. Klaus assumed she was deep in the sleep trance.

He had a mischievous thought. Could he peek into the mind of the High Chancellor herself? It would be a big test of his growing ability. He was feeling agitated and antsy being cooped up in the cabin with its recycled air and constant mechanical thrum. He decided to throw caution to the wind and stretched out with his mind, keeping his gaze fixed on the back of Kavisha's head. It was like focusing an old-fashioned camera. He had to twist and adjust his internal focus until the signals became stronger. Then he saw something. A memory. He was sure of it. Kavisha was shaking hands with…Zachariah. Huts rather than houses lined the primitive streets. Just before the scene faded in his mind, she spoke. Five simple words. "You have yourself a deal."

Chapter 15

They'd barely been at the hotel on Murano island for a few hours when the massacre started. The first thing Klaus noticed were the helicopters, just on the edge of his hearing. He heard them flying miles overhead before any of the others in the room could detect the sound. The churn of the rotor blades was soon accompanied by the distant sirens of emergency service vehicles.

Hurrying to the window, Klaus strained to focus his vision into the far distance. Across the wide expanse of water he could make out frantic activity on the mainland. His enhanced senses were both a blessing and a curse. He was witnessing carnage as the Crimson Claws rampaged across the area of Campalato, which was about three miles from their current location on Murano.

Bodies already lined the streets, ripped and torn as if they were dolls discarded by an angry child.

The others quickly joined Klaus at the window facing the mainland, straining to take in the scene. Evidently their vision wasn't as sharp as his. One of the perks of being 'chosen by fate', he thought, sourly.

"What do you see?" said Amara.

"I can't see much of anything," said Nell. "Just the coast and

CHAPTER 15

the outlines of buildings."

"It's another massacre," Klaus informed, grimly, without peeling his eyes away from the unfolding horror.

He watched as paramedics knelt by victims, looking for signs of life. They wouldn't find any, Klaus lamented. The Crimson Claws were as efficient as they were savage. He wondered how many of his former brothers and sisters were among the deadly swarm only miles away from where he stood now.

Klaus finally averted his gaze from the window and turned to look at his companions. A rag-tag bunch he now thought of as his family. Each of them looked like the blood had drained from their face. The humans looked like vampires while the undead were even more ashen-faced than normal. In other circumstances, it might even have been funny.

His eyes lingered on Nell. Klaus was struck by how young she looked at that moment. Fragile and lost. He didn't need to probe her mind to know she felt responsible for what was happening out there. She took each death personally. Klaus was worried that she would drive herself over the edge if she carried on like this. She could do something reckless again. He made a mental note to pull her to one side later and try to talk her down from the ledge he was sure she had climbed.

"So what do we do?" asked Christopher. "We need to go out there, right? We have to help?" His voice wavered, as if he didn't have the full conviction of his own words.

He was glancing at Nell nervously. Klaus could gauge from his look that Christopher had the same misgivings as him. Then he caught a thought. It was fleeting but strong and clear. Christopher was thinking back to the time when Nell had run into the arms of the Red Claws after being tricked by Zachariah. He was terrified she would do something similarly foolhardy. Especially with Crimsons in such close proximity.

"No, we can't," said Amara, firmly.

Klaus snapped back to the here and now.

"We can't afford to draw attention to ourselves," continued Amara. "Zachariah doesn't know we're here. It's the only advantage we have right now. Plus, we don't want to come to the attention of the human authorities. That would just add another layer of complication to an already chaotic situation."

"Also, what can we hope to achieve out there?" added Kavisha, forlornly. "The numbers and strength of the Crimson Claws would overwhelm us almost instantly."

"We can't just stay here and do nothing," Nell pleaded, looking from face to face, imploring anyone to support her.

"We're not doing nothing," said Klaus, feeling the need to speak up. "We are here to track down Zachariah and take him out, so we can end this cycle of death. To prevent more situations like this from occurring. That's not nothing, Nell."

"It feels like nothing," Nell said, bitterly. "I've seen this before, close up. I know how it ends for all those people out there. Innocent people."

The room fell silent. It seemed there was no adequate response to that statement.

Klaus turned to Amara, who was furiously tapping away on the keys of her laptop, no doubt trying to find live news about the unfolding attack.

"What the hell…" Amara muttered to the computer screen. Her eyes were wide, as if she'd just seen a ghost. She turned the screen towards the rest of them. Klaus could now see what had caused such a visceral reaction in the librarian. His own blood ran cold at the sight.

Zachariah's face filled the screen. Dark eyes and hair, sharp features and a fire in his eyes. It appeared to be a video message playing on one of the news channels. Amara clicked on the triangle at the center of the image and turned up the computer's volume to maximum.

"Hello humans," said Zachariah, addressing the camera. "You might be wondering who I am, but that's not really important right now. You are by now familiar with my work. That's the salient point here." Zachariah sneered into the lens. "For the past few months, my Family and I have been striving to achieve one goal. To subdue human life and allow vampires to reign free over the Earth. Humans are fit for only one purpose. To feed us. Every vampire feels this way, yet I am the only one bold enough to come out of the shadows and let you know precisely where you stand in the pecking order. There is no way out for you. We will take over the world. Our destiny is assured. What you have seen so far is only the beginning. Any attempts to stop us will be futile. We *will* reign supreme."

Klaus glanced at the High Chancellor, who looked open-mouthed at the screen. While Zachariah was expressing sentiments Klaus knew that many vampires shared, he was saying the quiet bits out loud.

"Attempts to thwart us will end in more death," continued Zachariah, any hint of humor vanquished from his expression. "Agonizing, prolonged death," he added. "As opposed to the swift, merciful release from your dreary lives that I am offering you. I am now your leader. You will bow to me or you will suffer torment the likes of which you have not even imagined. My name, for the record, is Zachariah Redclaw. I am the leader of the Crimson Claws. Remember my name. Remember my Family. Keep us foremost in your thoughts." Zachariah made to turn away from the camera, but he suddenly swiveled around to face it once again. "Oh, and Klaus, I'll see you again soon, my brother," he added. The video stopped.

Klaus stood frozen. All heads turned to face him, but he had nothing to offer. He was completely blindsided.

"You don't think I...that I..." he began.

"No," said Amara, firmly. "We don't, Klaus."

Haiden raised his eyebrows.

The video played over and over again across every news channel. Journalists were scrambling to figure out who Zachariah Redclaw was, also the mysterious 'Klaus' he had referred to in the broadcast. Speculation ran wild, but only Amara had figured out the truth. So far.

The librarian began fielding a barrage of phone calls and firing off hurried emails. She was attempting to placate the various Vampire Councils around the globe. Many now suspected Klaus of being a Judas in their midst. All on the strength of Zachariah's words, his reference to the former Red Claw as 'brother'. Amara explained over and over again that it was just a tactic to sow discord, and also a veiled threat aimed at Klaus. She had her work cut out trying to allay their misgivings.

Zachariah's speech had also ensured that any hope of trying to work with the humans was now out of the question. He had implicated every vampire in his maniacal scheme to soak the planet in blood. The humans wouldn't trust any of them. At this point, with so many murdered, who could blame them?

While the rest of the group had been hanging on Zachariah's words during the broadcast, Klaus had noticed other things. He took in Zachariah's posture, coloring and the sharpened iridescence of his eyes. It was almost as if the Crimson Claw leader thrummed with energy and vigor. So much so that

CHAPTER 15

Klaus could almost feel his aura radiating out of the computer screen. Klaus recognized this version of his former master, and the sight brought back horrific memories of pain and loss.

"He's high on Nell's blood," Klaus announced to the room.

That word 'high' felt like exactly the right term. The blood was like a drug. It intoxicated Zachariah as well as endowing him with heightened powers. There was no doubt in Klaus's mind about the timing of the video, too. Zachariah knew they were there, in Italy and on his trail. It sent a shiver up Klaus's spine to think that soon he might be face to face again with his creator. The one he used to love like a brother. More than that. Their last battle had left him wounded and broken, with hidden scars that would never heal. He thought again of the look on Nell's face when she had touched his hands on the plane. She claimed that she hadn't seen anything. He knew it wasn't true.

"Are you sure?" Amara mumbled as she continued to type furiously on her keyboard.

"Yes, positive," answered Klaus. Then he shared a thought that had come to him just after using the drug analogy. "I think he needs more of it, in his system, to have the same effect, so he's taking larger quantities now."

"Yeah," said Christopher. "That's the way it works. The body builds up resistance. You need to keep upping the dose." He spoke from personal experience, Klaus surmised.

"I dread to think how much of Nell's blood he extracted when he was holding her captive," added Haiden, without thinking much before speaking.

Klaus looked to Nell, who seemed to physically shudder.

"It would explain why I was woozy the whole time, and why I can't remember much," Nell said as she shook her head.

"But he has to run out eventually," replied Haiden. "He hasn't got an indefinite supply. So what happens then? That's what worries me. Does he do something really destructive with his final batch?"

"Desperate people are dangerous people," Kavisha suggested.

Klaus cast his mind back to the plane journey. To the interaction he'd seen between Kavisha and Zachariah. He wondered whether, at one point, Kavisha had been desperate, too.

"We need to adjust our strategy," Amara said, closing her laptop with a loud snap. "We need to think carefully about what we do now."

"We visit an old friend of mine," said Kavisha. "That's what we do now."

Chapter 16

The Venetian chapter of the Italian Council was housed in a magnificent building. Despite the dire situation facing humanity and the relentless demands being placed on her, Amara paused for a long moment to take in the sheer splendor of the structure. It was made of bright white stone with four marble pillars flanking the tall black front entrance. To the general public, it looked like a disused historic building. Amara knew that somewhere in the walls of the structure was buried a talisman that ensured prying eyes and feet were kept at a distance. It was the same Old Magick used to protect vampire properties around the world.

Amara and her entourage walked with purpose through the ornate door, which was embedded with carved serpents along its length. It never failed to amaze Amara that vampires, supposed blood-thirsty undead fiends, had a governance structure. A Council with all the requisite bureaucracy, administration and organization. A body to ensure that vampires didn't do too much harm, and thus were able to exist in the shadows. Until now.

Council Leader Lucia Verga greeted them in the vast marble hallway before escorting them upstairs to the meeting room, an equally enormous space. It seemed everything was done on a grand scale in Italy. Kavisha, rather awkwardly, had to be carried in her chair by Haiden and Christopher as there was no lift. Christopher had his enhanced strength, but Haiden was red in the face by the time they reached the top of the stairs.

"I have to say, Kavisha, you have a very unique team," said Verga once they were all seated. She was a tall, slender woman with a prominent nose and jet back hair that was tied back in a severe-looking knot. She wore a figure-hugging black dress with stiletto heels and had a gold choker around her neck. To Amara she looked like a pantomime witch who had undergone a glam up. "One might even begin to question your judgment," Verga added, looking rather disdainfully around the circular table. Like everything else, it was made of expensive white marble.

Kavisha smiled. Amara bit her lip. The sheer audacity of the woman. She didn't even try to be subtle. After they had come all this way to help her. Amara had to take a deep breath to swallow her anger. Even though it was vampires of the world against the Crimson Claws, it didn't mean those on their side were progressive, or even nice for that matter. Amara had to remind herself of that. Once the battle was over, old enmities would resurface. Amara had a feeling that Council Leader Verga would turn particularly cold towards Kavisha and the American Council.

"On the contrary, dear Lucia," said Kavisha, warmly. "I am very proud of my team. We have been able to glean unique insights that otherwise would have eluded us. Perhaps other councils should take a less...myopic...view of how they should function."

Verga wrinkled her nose and looked like she was sucking

on a bitter lemon.

Amara decided to interject, for the sake of the all-too-pressing common cause.

"We are very sorry to be here under these circumstances," she said in as pleasant a tone as she could muster. "However, it is a pleasure to meet you in person."

"I'm sure it is," replied Verga, offering a strained hint of a smile. "So, to business," she added, placing a palm firmly down on the gleaming table. It was clear she had no more time for pleasantries, even if they hadn't been particularly pleasant. "We're here to talk about the human culling that just occurred on my doorstep. Also of the wave of darkness that has crossed the ocean from your mighty America."

The irony was palpable. Verga looked around the room with an accusatory gaze. It was clear that she blamed the Americans for engulfing the world in chaos and blood. On that point, Amara had a degree of sympathy for the vampire. But now wasn't an ideal time for pointing fingers.

"As you know, our intelligence suggests Zachariah Redclaw is here, hiding somewhere in your country," said Amara. "At the moment we have scouts attempting to locate him, notably the werwulfs."

Verga's nose wrinkled even more at the mention of the lycans.

"So far we've had no luck," continued Amara. "The pack are keeping their noses close to the ground, so to speak. We're hoping to have him on our radar soon."

"And the impure...one?" asked Verga, giving a pointed look to Klaus. "He will be ready to fulfill his part of this prophecy?"

Klaus seemed unbothered. He'd heard much worse over the years, Amara assumed.

"My colleague, friend and fellow Council member Klaus knows what is asked of him," said Kavisha, her tone hardening. "He, I might remind you, is no longer a Red Claw and has made a number of painful sacrifices for our cause. His loyalty is beyond question. Please watch your tongue when speaking about somebody that I hold in the highest regard."

Verga looked like she had just been slapped.

"I hope your faith turns out to be well placed, for all our sakes," she said, pointedly. "This calamity you have unleashed threatens…"

She was interrupted by a commotion coming from downstairs. There were strained shouts accompanied by the sound of angry growls. Christopher bolted from his seat and ran for the stairs.

Amara stood and turned towards the door. An arm reached across her chest and blocked her from moving any further.

"No," said Haiden. "Not until we know it's safe."

In her eagerness to investigate, Amara had forgotten how breakable she was. Haiden was right, however frustrating that fact was. Amara was left sitting in the meeting room with Kavisha as the screams continued to echo in the cavernous hallway.

All Amara could do was wait. She could hear fierce shrieks, roars of frustration, but she couldn't tell from whom they were emanating. After what felt like forever, a limp body was dragged into the room. It was carried by three vampires wearing sharp black suits. Two propped up each arm while the third held his lolling head. The captive was beaten and bloody with large chunks of hair ripped from his scalp and congealed black blood covering his body from multiple wounds. He wore a tattered black T-shirt with loose-fitting military pants.

CHAPTER 16

A captured Crimson Claw.

The vampire was deposited unceremoniously on a chair at the other side of the table. As soon as he was forced to sit, he suddenly came alive, struggling to break free, shaking wildly. But the three captors holding him down, combined with the Crimson Claw's weakened state, meant he was unable to escape.

Lucia Verga re-entered the room followed by Haiden, Nell and Christopher. The three of them stood between Amara and Kavisha, forming a sort of protective guard, in case the Crimson had any ideas, and the strength to back them up. Verga was carrying a glass vial filled half-way up with dark blood, no doubt extracted from the captive. She screwed on the plastic stopper and deposited the vial in a drawer pulled out of the meeting table.

The Crimson Claw stopped struggling and raised his head, looking around the room. He stopped when he caught sight of Klaus.

"Zachariah sends his regards, brother," he said to the former Red Claw. He smiled, showing teeth covered with thick dark blood.

Klaus looked disturbed, which was no easy feat.

"Family takes care of family," added the captive, never taking his eyes off Klaus. His smirk widened, making him look like a demon.

"Enough," said Verga. "Tell us what you know and we can help you," she said to the Crimson Claw. "There is a way out of this for you."

"There is only one way out of this for me," said the captive, his grin even more demented.

Amara recalled Radomir Petrov explaining how the Crimson captured in Novinka had ripped off her own head. She looked across the table. The vampires from the Italian council were holding the Crimson's arms down firmly. They had been versed on this possibility and were taking no chances.

"How does Zachariah plan his attacks?" demanded Verga. "How does he get all of you to follow his orders?"

"I'm not telling you anything, betrayer," the vampire hissed, before spitting thick black blood onto the pristine white table.

Verga looked outraged.

"The mass killing of humans is one thing," she said as she cautiously approached the restrained Crimson. "But defiling my beautiful furniture is another magnitude of transgression."

In a seeming blur, Verga bent down and bit one of the captive's fingers clean off at the first knuckle. She spat it out across the room as if she was taking a chomp out of a cigar end. The vampire screamed with pain and fury. He tried to shake his bonds, but the three council vampires held him in place.

Amara had to look away. She detested torture. But as much as loathed the practice, she knew the vampire would not sustain permanent damage from the interrogation. He had the capacity to heal and regrow lost body parts.

"You will receive nothing from me, deceiver," snarled the Crimson.

"Then you will just have to keep learning hard lessons," said Verga, coldly. "How does Zachariah plan his attacks?" she asked again. "How does he get the horde to act as one?"

The Crimson Claw remained silent, showing his uneven teeth in that familiar rictus grin.

Verga approached again.

"Hand," she said to one of the captors.

CHAPTER 16

The suited vampire stretched out the Crimson's hand and placed it flat on the table. The bloody stump of the missing finger oozed thick black blood. Verga reached for it and began peeling the skin back from the stump. The captive roared in pain.

Amara had to close her eyes. It was too much for her. Then she heard Christopher's voice.

"Stop," he said.

Amara opened her eyes and saw that he had made his way over to the captive.

"This won't get us anywhere," he said. "He won't talk. We know this already. It's futile."

For the countless time that day, Verga looked offended.

"And you have a better idea?" she exclaimed.

"I think so," Christopher replied before reaching down and clamping his fingers around the Crimson Claw's wrist.

Chapter 17

Christopher concentrated hard, trying to force his way into the vampire's mind. He was worried that Nell's constantly recycling blood within the Crimson Claw might provide some level of defense against his gift. Thankfully, this didn't seem to be the case, as the memories slowly came to the surface.

***

Zachariah stood before Sebastian, who felt like he was receiving the highest possible honor. A personal audience with the Omni-Father-Reborn, Zachariah Redclaw.

Sebastian understood the importance of his mission. It was an act that would save vampires from a subservient, barren future. A life of hunting for scraps and existing in the dark crevices of the world. Zachariah explained that because vampires had lived lives of meekness and docility, humans had contrived a mythology of the undead existing only in the shadows of night. It was in their books and lore. This fact alone was an unbearable humiliation for the dominant species.

These cullings were the symbol of a new dawn. A future that would see the undead crawl out of the gloom to walk where they pleased, when they pleased. To take what they pleased, when they pleased. The humans needed to be subdued. Overwhelmed into submission. They needed to offer themselves up for feeding without resistance or defiance. Only then could a calm be restored to the world. A new natural order.

Humans needed to be farmed, like cattle, for their liquid life force. They provided nothing else of value to the world. They had their chance to dominate. What did they have to show for it? A wounded planet, useless wars, famine, disease, suffering, while a chosen few enjoyed obscene wealth and privilege. They were vermin, a plague on creation itself. They needed to be taken in hand. For their own sake.

Not all vampires felt the same way. Some believed in the sanctity of human life. Those that would have us hide away from the light. They were the traitors and needed eradicating.

Zachariah knew what was best. He was Lord and Master, and he so loved his Crimson Claws. He so loved his only Family. Since Zachariah had bestowed the gift of eternal life on Sebastian, his mortal past had faded into irrelevance. His life started with Zachariah and ended with Zachariah. Sebastian was one of the lucky ones. The chosen ones. He was at the vanguard of a revolution. His name would be spoken of in revered tones down the ages.

The task ahead was simple. Eradicate as many humans as possible. But also turn some. Only the strong. Only the young. Only those worthy to join the ranks of the ruling class. No one old. No one weak. No one deformed, disabled or unwhole. Purity mattered. Choose wisely.

The future was bathed in glory. The future was bathed in blood.

***

Christopher pulled his hand away. He had seen enough. It sickened him.

"His name is Sebastian," Christopher announced, once his head was clear. "And he is a true believer. When he says you will get nothing, I'd be inclined to believe him."

Christopher looked down on the captive. He was battered and bruised. A pulpy mess. Pathetic in many ways. After being in his head, he knew Sebastian felt a burning humiliation for allowing himself to be captured. His physical wounds were nothing compared to the mental injury he was suffering.

Christopher knew full well how this was going to end. Sebastian felt he had failed his master by being captured. He knew that returning to Zachariah was not an option.

Sebastian began to writhe around in the chair, attempting to escape again. Christopher knew he had been given time to heal, even though outwardly the Crimson Claw looked just as damaged. But under the skin, bones had knitted together, muscle had regrown and blood had started to cascade more forcefully around the body. Christopher could have joined the effort to hold him down, but he didn't. He simply let the scene play out.

Sebastian's movements became more frantic. He gave the impression of a condemned man in an electric chair. He managed to lift an arm up, despite a captor pushing down on it with both hands. A moment later he had both arms up. Then he quickly stood and pushed the chair backwards with the back of his legs. It hit the back wall and toppled over. The Crimson Claw pushed all three of his captors away in quick succession. It was just for a moment. But a moment was all

CHAPTER 17

he needed.

With lighting speed Sebastian reached up and grabbed his own head. Christopher looked away. There was nothing to be gained from witnessing the end, apart from nightmares. But the visceral ripping and pulling sound would live long in his memory. Christopher hadn't thought to cover his ears. He heard screams reverberate around the room, echoing off the marble walls. He gave it a few more seconds before opening his eyes. In front of him, dark ash slowly cascaded to the ground, covering the dirt-stained clothes Sebastian had been wearing.

Just another life extinguished in a sea of slaughter.

Chapter 18

Devan felt a twinge of nerves as he walked into the foyer of Hotel San Pietro on Murano island. It had been a long time since he'd seen his friends face to face. A lot of things had changed since then. He felt as if life had chewed him up and spat him out. He was halfway across the world, while Lupita and his growing baby were alone. Admittedly, not totally alone. She had the rest of the pack. But a big part of him felt he should be there with her, giving them both the support they needed. He couldn't win either way.

He walked past the reception desk and up the plush carpeted stairs to the first floor, following Amara's directions. Then along a long corridor until he came to room 134. He rapped on the door with his knuckles and stood back, taking a deep breath. The door opened and Nell flew into his arms in a blur of motion. He certainly wasn't expecting that. She wrapped her slender limbs around him in a tight bear hug.

"I've missed you," she said.

"Hey," said Devan, trying to catch his breath. "Super-human vamp strength meets mortal dude. You might want to loosen your grip, blood-sucker…or this might be a very short reunion."

"Oh, sorry," said Nell, relaxing her hold. "Sometimes I

CHAPTER 18

forget." She smiled at him sheepishly.

God, she looked beautiful, thought Devan, while taking a much-needed deep breath. The last time they'd seen each other was when Nell had been freshly turned by Christopher. She was still weak, anemic and traumatized after her ordeal. Devan couldn't believe the difference a few months made. It was true what they said about vampires. When they were turned they became far more attractive than the mortals they once were. Flawless even. Attractive wasn't the correct description, actually. It was more ethereal. Enthralling. Also kind of spooky. This was the first time Devan had known somebody both before and after they had been turned. The difference was stark yet subtle. Weird. Perhaps that was the right word.

After steadying his breathing, Devan walked into the room, where he met the rest of the group. Amara and Christopher both hugged him. Haiden gave him a manly fist-bump, while Kavisha took both of his hands in hers and squeezed them tightly. Klaus, true to form, was cooler. He offered a simple handshake accompanied by his best attempt at a smile. Devan remembered sparing the vampire's life when his pack stumbled across him in the wilderness. Perhaps some appreciation was due. But memories were short and a lot had happened in between. And Klaus, well he was Klaus.

It took a while for Devan to find his bearings. Having lived solely amongst wolves for so long, he found he had to re-acclimatize to speaking out loud rather than projecting. He also had to re-acquaint himself with the other subtle cues of in-person interaction, such as reading body language and facial expressions.

Amara had booked four rooms at the hotel, but they were currently congregated in the suite that the librarian shared with Haiden, which was the largest of the four. This was principally to house all of Amara's materials, as opposed to her trying to nab the nicest room. At least that was what she told the others. Devan was inclined to believe her.

"So, we're still no wiser than we were yesterday," said Devan. It was both a statement and a question.

"At the moment, yes," replied Amara. "We need to focus on Zachariah. We can't let the Crimson attacks, as sickening as they are, distract us from our primary purpose."

"But the attacks are spreading," said Nell. "We can't just continue to ignore them."

"Our latest intelligence suggests there's close to a million Crimson Claws out there," said Amara, grimly. "There's no way on Earth we can fight them all."

Kavisha addressed the room.

"The global Council feels if anything is to be done about them, then we need a strategy that allows us to attack them from a distance."

"Do we have any ideas?" asked Haiden. "Seeing as hand-to-hand combat is out of the question." He sounded annoyed at his own words.

"There are some suggestions floating around among the Councils but nothing solid we can implement right now."

"What kind of ideas?" asked Devan.

Amara looked to Kavisha, who gave what looked like a reluctant nod.

"We were thinking along the lines of chemical warfare," said the librarian, pausing to let the statement sink in around the room. "As absolutely horrid as those two words sound. Various labs are working on it based on the Crimson blood analysis. But there's no way to ensure any novel compound

CHAPTER 18

would be safe for humans. They would be collateral damage in any attack."

"Jesus," Devan exclaimed. His mind conjured up images of Hiroshima and Syria, where chemical agents were used to devastating effect on the local population.

Amara rubbed her hand across her forehead, as if trying to wipe similar scenes from her mind.

"The other strategy mooted was an air-born vaccine," she continued. "To reverse-engineer the Crimson infection. That would be a more elegant solution, but it's proving even more difficult to formulate."

"It's wishful thinking," added Kavisha, bitterly. "A non-starter in practical terms."

"Poor Nell has been poked and prodded within an inch of her life for tissue and blood samples," said Amara, looking apologetically at her friend. "The Councils believe her blood might hold the key to creating a line of attack, seeing as it's constantly being recycled within the Crimson Claws. But so far nothing."

Nell looked stoic.

Devan knew that the tests wouldn't bother her. If they offered the prospect of eradicating the Crimson Claws, she would be only too happy to become a pin cushion for the cause.

"Any news on the ground, from the wolves?" Haiden asked.

"We're closing in," said Devan. "We think Zachariah is definitely in Venice, but we can't quite pinpoint him. His scent trails lead off in various directions and then abruptly stop. I've never experienced anything quite like it."

"Can we use Lupita?" asked Amara. "I recall she was the best tracker in your pack."

"No, we can't," said Devan, flatly. "She won't be joining us." He felt a well of sadness stirring within him.

Amara looked surprised, as did a few other faces, but she didn't press the matter.

"We don't talk much, with me being away," added Devan, somewhat cryptically. "But she's safe, and that's all that matters." Devan tried to smile, but his facial muscles didn't seem to want to cooperate.

Nell gave him what he thought was a knowing look, but she also remained silent on the matter.

Devan brooded for a moment, not knowing what to say. Thoughts buzzed around his brain and emotions tugged at the pit of his stomach. Lupita. His child. The wolves. His pack. Crimson Claws. Humans. Vampires. Chemical warfare. Combat. Images of the previous battle in Alaska flashed into his mind…followed by a thought.

"The spell-casters," he said.

Amara raised an eyebrow.

"They're sitting this one out," she said, forlornly. "Along with the witches, warlocks and fae. They don't want to lose any more lives in what they view as a vampire civil war. With the horrific Crimson attacks, we can hardly blame them."

"But Sanya," said Devan. "She's still in this fight, right?"

"The offer is there," confirmed Amara. "But it's just her."

"Maybe she's all we need," said Devan.

He looked around the room. All faces were turned to him. Devan wasn't one for tactics and war games, but he had a feeling he was on to something.

"You said yourself, Amara," he continued. "The Councils are trying to formulate a weapon in their labs. They're approaching it from a scientific point of view. But what about the things science can't explain? Like alchemy. Potions. Enchantments. Sorcery. Things the spell-casters are experts in."

He shrugged his shoulders, not feeling too sure he was on solid ground.

"Maybe Sanya could create a…weapon or something," he said. "She's one of the most prominent spell-casters out there. It's something to think about, at least."

Devan glanced at Amara, who appeared to be deep in thought. She hadn't dismissed the idea, which meant she probably considered it had at least some merit.

"The spell-casters and witches could disperse this agent, seeing as they can fly," said Haiden. "But they're not with us, which adds another layer of complication."

"One thing at a time," countered Devan. "If Sanya is able to come up with a solution in the first place, then maybe she can get some of the others on our side. She'd have something to show. Something tangible that could be used to attack the Crimson Claws. It could instill confidence in the others."

"What have we got to lose?" said Amara.

"Exactly nothing," Kavisha added. "Anything is worth a shot at this stage."

She smiled at Devan, who felt a tinge of self-satisfaction.

"No time like the present," said Amara, grabbing her phone from the desk in the corner of the room.

She scrolled through her contacts before finding the one she needed and tapping the dial icon. She put the call on speaker and placed the handset back down on the desk. The call was picked up after the first ring.

"Hello dear," the soothing voice at the end of the line said. "I knew it was only a matter of time before I heard from you."

"How are you doing?" Amara asked, beginning a string of pleasantries.

"I know you didn't call just to enquire about my health," Sanya said, at last. "As touching as that is." As always, her voice was soft and kind.

"As you probably guessed right away, we need your help," confessed Amara.

"And who is 'we'?" Sanya asked, her voice steady.

Devan couldn't blame her for the question. It seemed that everyone was scared of what would happen if the Crimson Claws were allowed to continue their deadly rampage, but equally worried about the consequences of fighting back. It was a finely balanced equation.

"The vampire Council, not just back home but around the world," said Amara. "The wolves and the Hunters. Plus Kavisha, Christopher, Nell and Devan…and me."

Clever, thought Devan. Make it personal.

"We need you to make good on your promise of help, Sanya," added Amara. "We wouldn't ask if we weren't so desperate. But you might just be our only hope."

Chapter 19

Kavisha could hear Sanya's gentle voice on the other end of the line as Amara explained their thoughts to her. Devan's out-of-the-box suggestion was encouraging. It opened up a new avenue to explore. Kavisha made a mental note to involve him more in strategy in the coming days or weeks. At least Kavisha hoped it would only be days or weeks before there was a resolution. The prospect of this turmoil dragging on far into the future was enough to make her break out in a cold sweat. If she was able to sweat, that was.

Amara was still chatting to Sanya while at the same time tapping away on her laptop trying to book a flight. While spell-casters could fly, traversing an ocean was asking too much of them, Kavisha learnt. She was a little ashamed to be gleaning these facts now. For too long vampires had only consorted only among their own kind, choosing to shun other supernaturals. Due to their lofty sense of superiority, they failed to build bridges or even comprehend that there could be any kind of common ground.

Kavisha turned in her chair to look at Devan, who was catching up with Nell and Christopher. She recalled her surprise just now when he came up with his suggestion. It was a source of embarrassment, even shame, for her. Like the rest of her kind, Kavisha had viewed the lycans as unsophisticated animals who were good for hunting, tracking and fighting, but not necessarily thinking.

Vampires had a lot to learn about others. Especially humans, who were generally thought of as little more than cattle. Kavisha hated to use a word that was used by Zachariah in his unhinged rant to the world. However, she could not deny that his sentiments were widely shared among her brethren.

Kavisha turned once again in her chair, this time to glance at Amara, whose hands flew across the keys as she took notes while listening to Sanya. In the name of the Omni-Father, if it wasn't for that ingenious mortal woman she didn't know where she would be right now. Even as High-Chancellor of the Council of Elders she wasn't equipped to make the alliances and perform the diplomacy that came so naturally to the gifted librarian.

Kavisha looked down at her impotent legs. Cripple, she thought. Not just physically but in her ability to lead in a time of crisis. Just like the Crimson Claws, there would be reckoning for her, she predicted.

Her morose thoughts were interrupted when Amara put down the phone and announced that Sanya would be with them in the flesh by tomorrow. The spell-caster had requested a few things in advance, so she could get started on her experiments as soon as she arrived.

1. A vial of Nell's blood. The poor girl needed to be poked once again. Yet it was Nell's blood that helped birth these abominations and her blood that was cycling within their veins. Kavisha surmised that any potion or substance would need to target the blood.

CHAPTER 19

2. A vial of blood from a Crimson Claw. This should be straightforward as Lucia Verga from the Venetian Council had the foresight to take a sample from the now-deceased captive. While Kavisha wasn't overly fond of the stern vampire, she had to give credit where it was due. They would need to arrange for the sample to be transported to the hotel.

3. Bessington's Speciality Blend Earl Grey tea, loose leaf, not in bags. This was a necessity, apparently, and probably the toughest challenge. But Sanya insisted she couldn't concoct her formulations or 'get into the zone' without her favorite herbal libation. So all stops had to be pulled out to secure a ready supply. Klaus, of all people, was on the case.

Watching from the sidelines, as she so often did lately, Kavisha was impressed with the operation taking shape around her. Her mood had been in a state of flux since Loris's death. Even though he was a new Council member, Kavisha had come to rely on his wisdom and counsel. She missed him greatly, which was one thing she shared with the aloof Klaus.

Kavisha wasn't one to outwardly show her feelings, preferring to view herself as a stoic matriarchal figure. Recent events, however, were making her *'kamzor'* as her mother used to say, which translated to 'fragile' or 'weak' in Hindi. The word triggered a memory. Her mother, Advika, cradling a cripple-born girl centuries ago. Advika was a servant in the court of Akbar the Great, a noble ruler who took pity on the unfortunate and gave her mother lodgings in the servant quarters along with a job. However, Akbar died fairly young and his son, Jahangir, who succeeded his father as Mughal Emperor of India, wasn't as charitable. Kavisha and Advika soon found themselves out on the dirt streets, having to rely on strangers to throw coins of pity on a homeless woman wearing a tattered sari and her disabled daughter.

"Life was hard, you can't be *kamzor*," her mother used to tell her.

Kavisha needed to be '*mazaboot*' — strong and steadfast, or else the world was going to chew her up. It was a message that Kavisha had taken to heart. However *mazaboot* Kavisha had been up to now, she felt deep down that she wouldn't survive the coming battle. *'Takadeer'* was another word her mother used to use frequently. It meant 'destiny'.

Kavisha's history with Zachariah meant there was a personal vendetta to settle. A side story to the bigger picture playing out. The deal she had made so long ago would come back to haunt her. Yet that deal had saved so many, kept so many safe for so long. Before it all unraveled in death and betrayal. She'd had no choice back then, when the Red Claws had begun their rise. Kavisha did what she had to do to protect those around her. If that meant others would suffer, it was unavoidable. Life was hard, you couldn't be *kamzor*, after all.

Kavisha remained in her head into the next day, brooding over past choices and the unpredictable nature of the future. She sat back, quite literally, and allowed those around her to make the necessary preparations. Amara pretty much had it under control, and it usually wasn't wise to get in her way when she was in the flow of her work. Did Kavisha rely on the librarian too much? Had she abdicated her own responsibility? The answer seemed to be self-evident. Yet she would still be

CHAPTER 19

there to offer guidance and support. She knew her team, ragtag as it was, was up to the task, and that made her feel better. Hopeful, in fact.

Vampires had tried for decades upon decades to stop Zachariah Redclaw and his Family from wreaking havoc. They'd failed. As evidenced by the growing number of massacres currently spreading around the globe. Maybe it was time to give humans a turn. Or, more specifically, one particular incredibly smart human, who saw everything with fresh eyes and new ideas. Collaborating with mortals, wolves and Hunters was new territory. But perhaps swallowing your pride and admitting defeat was the key to redemption, for her and her species.

Kavisha passed the hours in quiet contemplation. Her reverie was finally broken when Sanya came bounding into the room. She wore a trademark flowing floral dress and her arms were adorned with dozens upon dozens of bracelets, each one colorful and unique. Kavisha noticed a few more streaks of gray in her blonde hair, which fell to her waist in curling tendrils. But her wide smile and bright hazel eyes were just as vibrant as she remembered.

"My dearest, Sanya," said Kavisha, genuinely delighted to see her old ally. She stretched out her arms.

"It's so lovely to see you again, Kavisha," replied the spellcaster as she leaned down and hugged the High-Chancellor. "I trust you've been well despite...everything."

Christopher bustled into the room after her, carrying a stack of boxes up to his nose. Devan followed hot on his heels, holding several heavy bags. He looked like he was struggling. Werwulfs in human form were not physically stronger than other humans, yet their senses remained sharp.

"That's quite a lot of stuff," Kavisha laughed.

"That's not the half of it," replied Sanya. "There's more sitting in the lobby."

Devan didn't look pleased. He deposited the bags on a couch before Christopher slapped him on the back and they both shuffled out of the room. Devan looked markedly less enthusiastic.

"I need my bits and bobs," said Sanya, in her soothing, mellow voice.

She turned to Klaus, who was minding his own business in a corner of the room.

"I'll have a cup of tea now, young man, if you're making one," she instructed. "I'm ever so parched after the journey."

To Kavisha's surprise, and relief, Klaus simply smiled.

"It just so happens I was about to put the kettle on," he replied, diplomatically.

"Excellent," said Sanya, giving him a wide grin. "Give it plenty of time to steep and don't sully it with milk and sugar."

"I wouldn't dare," replied Klaus, looking mock offended, as he headed to the kitchen.

"Marvelous," replied Sanya. "Making tea is a delicate operation, much like formulating a potion."

Devan and Christopher were soon back, brimming with more boxes and bags.

Sanya started extracting various tools and paraphernalia from her luggage.

"You can set up in this room," informed Kavisha. "It's the biggest one we have."

"You have the blood samples ready for me?" asked Sanya. She glanced at Nell, who was sitting quietly on one of the armchairs.

CHAPTER 19

"Yes," replied Kavisha. "They're in the mini-fridge."

"Okay," said Sanya, exhaling and looking around the room. "Now leave me in peace. No interruptions. Apart from tea-related matters."

Even though the spell-caster was feigning sternness, her soft melodic voice took any sting out the words. They ended up sounding almost comical.

As the group exited the room, accepting the orders with grace, Kavisha watched as Sanya pulled a wand from the folds of her dress. It looked like a simple tree branch, but Kavisha's keen eyesight saw that it was made of some kind of charred bone. Sanya flicked her wrist as Christopher walked by her.

Kavisha watched in astonishment as fine droplets of dark blood exited his skin. It hung in the air like mist before Sanya flicked her wand once more. The cloud of blood vapor flew into a glass vial she was holding in her other hand, settling back into a thick liquid form. Christopher hadn't noticed, or felt, a thing.

Sanya winked at Kavisha.

"Call it a hunch," she mouthed to the High-Chancellor. "Our little secret."

Kavisha nodded.

"I'll leave you to your work," she said, before pushing the small joystick next to her right hand and maneuvering the wheelchair out of the room. Spells, hexes and potions were way beyond her understanding. Best leave it to the expert.

Chapter 20

"Ladies and gentlemen, vampires and lycanthropes…" Sanya glanced sideways at Klaus. "…and those of an indeterminate nature, who make remarkably good tea, I must concede…" (Klaus couldn't help but smile). "…I give you probably the greatest weapon of mass murder ever created."

Words as brutal as those should never come out of the mouth of a woman who looked so folksy and grandma-like, Nell thought to herself. The juxtaposition between the homely, earthy woman in front of them and her damning speech was stark. It made Nell like her even more.

The spell-caster held up a tiny glass vial containing an innocuous-looking light blue powder. It looked like kids play sand, as opposed to anything sinister.

It had been two days since Sanya had locked herself away in the room, seemingly never sleeping and only surviving on her beloved Bessington's Speciality Blend Earl Grey tea. Hissing and bubbling sounds emanated from the room, along with a variety of pungent odors. The sound of exploding glass vials accompanied by a string of colorful curse words also peppered the air. Amara had to use all of her diplomacy skills to convince the hotel staff that they were not in fact attempting to manufacture a bomb. Of course, an unlimited credit line thanks to the Council's buoyant finances helped to soothe the jitters of any concerned hotel managers.

Now, finally, the spell-caster was able to reveal the fruits of her labors.

Nell noticed that Sanya looked tired. No, it was more than that. She looked physically and spiritually drained. Her soft hair was now coarse and strands of it were sticking up at odd angles. There seemed to be significantly more white hairs streaking her head. She had dark circles around her eyes and what looked to be smudges of ash down her face. The effort had taken a lot out of her. Literally, thought Nell. She didn't know the ways of spell-casters, but she was willing to bet that Sanya had to pay with part of her body and soul to achieve the result so quickly.

"Is that it?" Devan asked. He sounded a little disappointed.

Nell could understand the sentiment, even though it sounded monumentally ungrateful. Typical Devan. The fine baby blue powder swishing around in the vial looked so tame. In her mind, Nell had been expecting a bubbling black liquid giving off a foul stench of death and decay. But then perhaps she watched too many cartoons as a little girl.

"Well observed, young man," said Sanya, a little stiffly. "This is indeed it. It needs testing in the field to demonstrate its efficacy, but I am certain it will prove quite…life-limiting…for vampires of the Crimson Claw persuasion. I'm also quite sure it will not affect humans or vampires that do not have Nell's blood running through their veins."

Sanya turned to face Nell.

"That is why, my dear, you need to stay well away when this is dispersed," she warned. "It will have precisely the same effect on you as on the Crimson Claws, namely corrupting the blood and causing it to effectively boil the host from within."

Nell's eyes widened and her mouth hung open. Christopher reached out and held her hand.

Nell's mind raced. But not with thoughts of her own mortality. That factored very little in her thinking. She was solely focused on ending the global killing spree. Taking out the Crimson Claw hordes once and for all. Stopping the wave of death that was born of her blood and finally putting an end to the rabid guilt that consumed her every time an innocent life was taken. This soft blue powder offered redemption for the unforgivable mistake of willingly walking into the hands of Zachariah Redclaw and allowing him to uncover the potency of her blood. Then turning it into a weapon of mass destruction.

Nell looked at Sanya. She could have kissed the spell-caster at that moment. Picked her up and spun her around in jubilation for creating the chance for Nell's atonement. But Sanya looked so fragile. Also, Nell thought it wasn't the polite thing to just grab someone and start squeezing them. But this moment felt almost too good to be true. Nell reminded herself not to jump too far ahead. There was still a chance that the agent wouldn't work as anticipated. Also, it was never wise to underestimate Zachariah. He had continued to pull surprise after surprise out of his sleeve. Yet, the hope was palpable. She could see it in the expressions around her. Eager eyes fixed on the blue powder held in Sanya's slender hand.

"When do we test it?" Nell asked, breathlessly.

Klaus shot her a disdainful look, which took her by surprise. What was his problem? She stared back at him, not willing to be cowed.

"Killing begets killing," he said, facing her down. "But it's okay if it's the 'right' kind of murder."

Nell could feel her blood boil, without the help of Sanya's concoction.

"It's justified if it's mindless zombies killing innocent people," she said.

"Innocence is to be found on both sides," Klaus replied.

Nell was about to fire back, but Devan interrupted. No doubt in an effort to stop the tension from escalating.

"The central square in Venice," he said. All eyes turned to him. "Piazza San Marco," he added. "That's where we should do the test. My pack is sure Zachariah is in the vicinity of Venice. His minions have blended back into the shadows of the general population, waiting for further instructions. The wolves picked up their scent. They know Crimsons are lurking around the piazza."

"Sanya," said Amara, turning to the spell-caster. "You said you were 'quite sure' the agent will not affect humans or other vampires. Umm...not to appear unappreciative, but that doesn't sound like you are one hundred percent sure."

"I'm sure as I can be without having done the field test," Sanya replied. "Everything done in the lab is theoretical until proof is provided in the wild. Spell-casting is no different than your human science in that regard."

Sanya looked very tired now, Nell observed. Physically and mentally spent. She needed to recuperate.

"The tourist numbers have thinned," said Haiden. "After the attack, people are staying inside. Now might be our best chance."

"I've been doing this a long time," said Sanya, who seemed to be wilting before their eyes. "Do what needs to be done. Do it now. Get those bastards."

Nell was once again taken aback by the normally genteel spell-caster's words. The hardening steel in her eyes, despite her fatigue. It wasn't too much of a stretch to figure out what was driving her. What was propelling her through the fog of weariness. White-hot anger. Anger at the death of her beloved twin sister Yansa at the hands of the enemy. No amount of revenge would fill that void in her life, Nell knew. Yet the fact that she was taking action at least served to distract her from her grief. There was some solace to be found in that.

Preparations were made. Nell was to remain in her room with the doors and windows tightly sealed. She needed to be strictly quarantined. Sanya, who was finally getting some much-needed sleep, had estimated that the half-life of the agent was two hours. This meant that the concentration of particles in the air would halve every two hours. It would take the best part of a day for the air to be safe again for Nell. Not that she needed to breathe. She just needed to avoid sudden and agonizing death through contact with the substance.

Nell had to smirk at what she found herself doing. Despite the array of magic, spells and supernatural beings at their disposal, she was tearing off strips of electrical tape bought from the local hardware store and covering the gaps in the window frames. Her dad would be proud of her, she thought. Using thick layers of electrical tape was his solution for nearly every break, tear and repair around the house. Nell felt the stinging pang of loss when she pictured his face.

Once the room was as air-tight as it could be, Nell sat heavily on the bed. Then she waited...for what felt like an eternity.

Chapter 21

Klaus held in his hand probably the most powerful bio-weapon ever created. He looked down at the marble-sized ball of pressed powder which, purportedly, had the ability to cook Crimson Claws from the inside out by corrupting their blood. All he had to do was crush the tiny sphere in his palm and then blow. As if blowing a kiss. But this would be the kiss of death. The extremely fine powder would be carried on the natural air currents and dispersed around a wide radius. With his team stationed at various points around the piazza, each armed with their own innocent-looking tiny blue ball, the agent would be spread across a wide area.

Klaus looked up and took in Piazza San Marco, an expansive square lined with historic buildings and ornate arches. It was dominated at its eastern end by St Mark's Basilica, which looked like a grand gothic temple with its domes, spires and ornate carved statues. Despite him being centuries old and not given much to exuberance, the sheer splendor of Piazza San Marco took Klaus's breath away. Now that he could breathe. He turned around in a full circle to take in the square's sheer magnificence. A brief moment of calm and contemplation before the inevitable chaos ensued. At least that was the plan.

The square was filled with a surprising number of tourists.

Those who had chosen to brave the streets following the Crimson attack. Plus a fair smattering of vampires. It was easy to tell who amongst the crowd was undead. Vampires shared a sixth sense, one that had not abandoned Klaus. But differentiating which ones were Crimson Claws was beyond his capability. That's where the wolves had the sensory advantage. Their noses had evolved over millennia to pick up the most subtle of differences.

Klaus looked at his watch. 2.57pm. Three minutes before the designated time. He glanced again at the inoffensive-looking sphere in his hand, then once more at all those milling about around him. Just going about their business. His heart sank in his chest. The familiar guilt accosted him. Once upon a time, he'd been a Red Claw. If things were different, he'd be the one carrying out Zachariah's orders right now. He too had been brainwashed into thinking that Zachariah was some kind of deity. To be obeyed at all costs.

But there was nothing for it now. Killing the Crimson Claws would prevent further loss of human life. He could not argue with that logic. He needed to step out of the gray zone and start viewing things as black and white. For the moment, at least. For his own sanity. There simply was no good choice available.

He glanced at his watch again. 2.59pm. Klaus watched the seconds tick down. It seemed like the longest minute of his life. Finally, the allotted hour came. With a heavy heart he crushed the soft ball, which dissolved into sand-like fine powder in his hand. He pursed his lips, closed his eyes, hesitated a moment, then blew. He exhaled until all the air from his lungs was expelled, all the while keeping his eye-lids tightly shut.

He held his breath for a long moment. Half a minute at least.

CHAPTER 21

Then he slowly opened his eyes to witness…precisely nothing. The world continued to turn. People still milled about. The lavish surroundings remained magnificent. The stone statues atop St Mark's Basilica continued to peer down imperiously.

Klaus scanned his surroundings for any hint of change. There was nothing he could detect.

Then the first body fell.

Followed by another. Then another.

They were like heavy sacks falling to the earth with dull thuds.

They lay motionless for a few seconds then started to shake as if possessed. Screams of abject terror and searing agony came from the maniacally writhing bodies. More and more bodies began to fall. More and more shrieks began to echo around the piazza.

The humans and other vampires looked on with a mix of confusion, fear and bewilderment. Many fled the square, no doubt fearing a repeat of the devastating Crimson assault.

A cacophony of hellish screams now echoed across the square.

Klaus caught sight of Christopher and Devan in the distance. Like him, both stood frozen, captivated by the scene unfolding around them.

Klaus looked at the first body that had fallen. A heavy-set male who looked to be in his early twenties wearing black jeans and a blue and white checkered shirt. His scream morphed into a gurgle as thick black blood poured from his mouth. His face had turned a dark shade of purple and he continued to spasm on the ground as if he had a thousand vaults searing through him. Klaus noticed that steam was coming off the blood that was spilling out of his mouth. It fell onto the paved ground, where it bubbled and hissed.

Klaus looked on in horror and fascination. Sanya had been true to her word. The compound they had released in the air was boiling the Crimson Claws' blood. It was frying them from the inside. The vampire held out a hand towards Klaus, for what reason he would never know. Klaus watched as the tip of the Crimson Claw's index fingers slowly turned to ash, followed by the top of the finger, then down to the knuckle, and on and on. Soon the whole hand had cascaded away. Then the arm, followed, eventually, by the whole body. A large mound of dark ash was the only evidence that a vampire had once walked the earth.

Klaus noticed the screams starting to fade as more and more bodies disintegrated. He stood there open-mouthed. Soon Piazza San Marco was completely silent, littered with piles of dust.

This was the beginning, thought Klaus. The beginning of the end.

***

The mood in the hotel that evening was jubilant. Sanya was looking remarkably better after a little rest. Color had returned to her face and the dark circles had faded, although not entirely. She held a steaming cup of tea, which she had to keep putting down as various people felt the overwhelming need to hug her. She was the hero of the hour.

Klaus feigned a few smiles but mostly kept to himself. The others no doubt assumed he was just being his introverted self, so he was able to conceal the misgivings that he felt deep in his bones. He badly wished Loris was still with him. He always

CHAPTER 21

knew how to assuage Klaus when his soul was troubled.

After tipping her cup upside down above her mouth to extract every last drop of her precious Earl Grey, Sanya announced that she must leave. Her work was not over. She had to share her knowledge among the spell-casters, witches and warlocks. They had agreed to rejoin the war after Sanya had shared news of her breakthrough. The growing army was another source of giddy excitement in the room. Sanya needed to show them how to produce the compound. Its complicated and delicate formulation meant that she had to demonstrate in person the various intricate steps. Her first point of call would be a coven in Zagreb, Croatia.

The spell-caster collected the vial containing the remaining Crimson Claw blood. She also had to extract more blood from Nell, which she did by simply waving her wand. The others watched in awe as a mist of dark liquid exited Nell's body and hung in the air. Sanya deftly twirled her wand and the cloud snaked its way into a glass tube. Then she did the same with Christopher. Kavisha looked on knowingly.

"Hey," said Christopher, as the mist of blood left his body and was suspended in the air. "I didn't know I was part of the magic!"

"The one who birthed the one who birthed the many," said Sanya, cryptically. "Your essence is the seed."

No one questioned her. This was firmly her realm. They were just glad she was so adept at her arcane craft.

After another round of tight hugs, Sanya finally walked out of the door. But not before Klaus presented her with a parting gift. A jumbo two-for-one pack of Bessington's Speciality Blend Earl Grey. Her face lit up.

"You should consider potion preparation, young man," she

said to him, warmly. "You have the finesse required."

With that she hurried out, accompanied by her two packhorses, namely Devan and Christopher, who were loaded with bags and boxes. This time Devan didn't seem put out at all. He was only too glad to help. It seemed that nothing was able to dampen spirits after their 'success' with the Crimson Claws. Klaus almost envied their optimism.

However, something nagged at him. In life he knew that if things appeared too good to be true, they usually were.

Chapter 22

Amara's phone chimed just after 2am. Another news alert that contained one of her selected search terms — 'vampire', 'Crimson', 'Zachariah', plus a few others. Amara sat on the plush couch while Haiden was fast asleep on the expansive emperor-size bed. She could see his chest rising and falling rhythmically. Amara was too buzzed from the day's dramatic events to find sleep. Haiden, true to form, was out like a light as soon as his head had hit the pillow.

She unlocked her phone then tapped the alert to bring up the full news story. The picture at the top of the page was fuzzy, a screengrab from a video. But she could make out just enough for the breath to catch in her chest. Then her blood ran cold. She was frozen, fixated by the image. It couldn't be. Surely not.

Forcing her eyes away from the screen and kick-starting her body to start moving, she sprang onto the bed. She began to shake Haiden wildly.

"Wake up! Wake up!" she cried, frantically. She was loud enough to be heard in the adjacent rooms, especially as the occupants of those rooms had abnormally sensitive hearing. Within a few minutes the whole team was assembled in her room.

The librarian grabbed the remote control and switched on the TV. Every channel was showing the same thing. The room fell silent and still. The only light came from the blue glow of the television set. Amara turned up the volume as a newscaster addressed the camera.

"This is the second video we, and many other news outlets, have been sent by the self-proclaimed leader of the Crimson Claws. As you are likely aware, they are considered to be the number one terrorist threat in the world right now. The video we are about to play depicts scenes of a distressing nature. Viewer discretion is strongly advised."

The screen cut to a grainy image of an empty room with bare white walls. A small round window high up cast a diffused hazy light into the space. The video remained on this stationary image for a while before two men dragged a woman into view. She was tied to a wooden chair with thick white rope. Her body was bound at the legs, arms and waist while her head lolled down onto her chest. Amara could make out that she had red hair. The legs of the chair made harsh screeching sounds as they were dragged across the hard floor.

The woman was deposited in the center of the room, head still bowed. The two men left. Another figure came into view. He needed no introduction. Amara's heart began hammering in her chest.

"This video is a warning for those who would attempt to hurt my Family," said Zachariah, peering straight into the lens. "Your actions serve only to make matters much worse for yourselves. Kill one of us, and we will kill hundreds of you."

Zachariah approached the captive and grabbed her hair in his fist. He yanked her head backward with violent force, so that her face was visible to the camera.

CHAPTER 22

Nell screamed. Haiden gasped.

"No, no, no, no..." Christopher repeated, staring at the screen, as if reciting the word would somehow make what they were seeing go away.

Sanya stared back at them. Sweet, motherly, kind Sanya. Her face was bloated and bruised. Her bottom lip was bloody. Angry purple welts framed her swollen, tear-stained eyes. Amara realized with horror that her hair looked red because it was caked in blood.

"This is what happens when you test me," snarled Zachariah. He opened his mouth wide, showing a mouth full of razor-sharp teeth.

Sanya suddenly raised her head.

"You can still do this," she yelled, blood spilling from her ruined mouth. "Don't let him win...for Yansa...for..."

Zachariah swiftly clamped down on her neck with his teeth and tore away a chunk of flesh. The spell-caster screamed in pain. Zachariah pulled his mouth away and then spat at the camera. Flecks of bright red blood stained the lens, partially obscuring the view.

Amara was shaking now. She couldn't help it.

Still Sanya tried to speak, looking back up, but her voice was wet and muffled. Amara couldn't make out the words. Yet the spell-caster's eyes still contained their fire. That unbowed iron resolve. They communicated everything Sanya wanted to get across. Words were not needed.

Zachariah quickly moved behind her and placed his hands on her neck. He looked into the camera with a demonic grin, his mouth covered with Sanya's blood.

"Let this serve as a warning," he said.

Amara had to look away. Piercing shouts and screams

echoed around her in the room.

When Amara finally looked back, Sanya sat still. Her head rested once more on her chest. Zachariah was nowhere to be seen. Yet the camera lingered intrusively on Sanya's lifeless body. The image faded to black.

Not a word was uttered for a long while. The occupants of the room were left with their thoughts. Of Sanya, of Zachariah, of the battle, of the world, of life and of death.

Amara was the first to speak. She didn't want to. It felt like sacrilege. An intrusion on a solemn silence. But what choice did she have? She was placed in charge of strategy. And what was it that Sanya had said…"You can still do this".

"The video has gone global," said the librarian in a soft tone, after looking at her phone. "The international councils will know by now."

"How on Earth are they allowed to show this on TV?" said Nell, finding her voice. The anger was palpable in her voice. One of the stages of grief.

"Because they need to warn people," said Haiden. "The old rules are out of the window with the Crimson Claw threat. If the newscasters had simply described the video, it wouldn't have had nearly the same impact. People wouldn't have understood what's really at stake here. This is an international emergency. A new set of rules apply."

Amara wanted to bring up the elephant in the room, but thought better of it. They all understood the consequences of what they had just witnessed. They weren't stupid and didn't need to be spoon-fed. The knowledge of how to defeat the Crimson Claw army had died with Sanya. She hadn't had the chance to share her knowledge. All that hard work, the testing, the promise that the compound held. It had all been

CHAPTER 22

for nothing. They were back to square one.

It was actually worse than that, Amara realized. Sanya's tragic death revealed that Zachariah was keeping tabs on them. Somehow. He knew the spell-caster had rejoined the battle. He knew she had created the weapon that could devastate his plans. He was aware of her movements so that he could abduct her. In this game of chess, Zachariah was always one step ahead.

Amara was just about to voice her thoughts when her phone began ringing. She recognized the number so put the call on speaker.

"Hey," said Devan, on the other end of the line. He was staying with his pack in the Dorsoduro area in Venice's art district.

"We know," said Amara. "We saw it."

"It's not that," replied Devan, his voice heavy. "There's more bad news, I'm afraid."

Amara looked to Kavisha, who had sat in stunned silence. Her eyes were wet with tears. She had known Sanya longer than any of them.

"I just received a call from somebody called Margot Malfeena, not sure why she decided to use my number," continued Devan.

Amara recognized the name. She knew where this was going.

"Anyway," continued Devan. "She just told me that the spell-casters have revoked their offer of help. She added that we should expect the same from the witches and warlocks. They feel it's too dangerous an undertaking, given what…just transpired."

Kavisha thumped the armrest of her wheelchair in frustration.

"Margot said the chances of them being able to replicate the compound were next to none," added Devan. "Sanya was the best they had when it came to potion work. They wish us well but want nothing more to do with the war."

"Fuck," Amara breathed. There were no other words in her extensive vocabulary that seemed to fit the bill. She exhaled sharply. "How are we doing on the hunt for Zachariah?" she added as an afterthought. She had little hope of a positive response. If the wolves had made a breakthrough they would have told her by now.

"No new progress," confirmed Devan, almost apologetically. "We lock on to the scent, then it goes cold abruptly. He's laid false trails around the islands so we end up going round in circles."

"Thanks, Devan," said Amara with another long sigh. "I'll be in touch."

She ended the call and sat heavily on the couch next to Haiden.

The thought of starting from scratch again, after coming so far, was absolutely heart-wrenching. Amara looked at the dejected and despairing faces around the room and the flicker of hope she carried inside of her dimmed even further.

For the first time, Amara questioned whether they would be able to defeat Zachariah Redclaw. For the first time, she questioned whether humanity stood a chance.

Chapter 23

The idea came to Devan in the dead of night. He tossed and turned after viewing the video of Sanya's cold-blooded murder. He didn't want to sleep but, after spending long hours racing through the streets trying to locate Zachariah, his body had other ideas. Now he was in a fitful half-way state between slumber and wakefulness. His disturbed dream state was conjuring a host of dark images.

He was with his pack. Lupita was by his side. That reassured him a little. Darkness fell and they needed to find shelter. Somewhere safe and secluded to camp for the night. The darkness was thick. Impenetrable. Not a single star shone in the sky. It was a blanket of inky blackness.

A scream pierced the night. He recognized the voice instantly. His mother. That familiar cry had forced him awake on countless nights. Shaking and sweating with his heart racing like a freight train in his chest. But not tonight. He was still there, on his haunches in the dark wilderness dreamscape. Coiled like a spring, ready to take flight. The scream echoed out again. Devan registered its direction and ran like the wind, leaving the safety of the pack behind.

Branches and foliage whipped at his face as he ran. He couldn't make out his surroundings clearly due to the oppressive darkness, yet he didn't slow down. He thundered towards the screams, which continued to ring out, ragged and breathless.

Devan plowed on blindly through the darkness. He was desperate to reach her. Desperate to save her. He knew how this story played out. He'd lived this heartache hundreds of times before in the small hours. Yet this time it would be different. It had to be.

He came to a grassy clearing. It morphed before his eyes into the ramshackle garden of his childhood home. He looked down and saw his human body. He was twenty years old. Fit and strong. He ran to the back door and barreled into the house. Devan knew he was too late. The creature holding his mother by the neck was already squeezing. He always thought of him as a creature. But in reality he was all-too human. His mother's face was a deep shade of red, eyes bulging from the sockets.

"NO!" Devan screamed as ran towards her.

Devan's stepfather turned towards him. A perpetual drunkard, Merle somehow managed to remain sober long enough to make his mother fall head over heels in love with him. It was a state of affairs that Devan tried to reverse every day of his life. But she wouldn't listen. He had her tightly wound around his finger. Despite the beatings. Despite the bruises. Despite the furniture and appliances going missing to feed his addiction. She could not see a life beyond this pathetic man.

Leona Copeland was Devan's adoptive mother, but that didn't make the slightest difference to him. Blood didn't make you family. Love and commitment did. This woman had raised him from practically a newborn. He loved her with all his heart.

CHAPTER 23

"LET GO OF HER!" Devan screamed, the anger surging in him until he felt he might explode.

Her neck was bruised. He'd seen plenty of bruises before. On her lower arms mostly but he was sure there were many others. She tried her best to hide them with oversized clothing and Merle was always careful not to strike the face. It was like some twisted pact they had to cover up his brutality. The very definition of co-dependent but with a sick twist. His mother swiftly changed the subject every time Devan brought it up. It was insane. She felt that if she didn't talk about it then it wasn't real. Devan knew Merle was a violent abuser, but he didn't think of him as a potential murderer. Until now.

A guttural noise escaped Devan's mouth. Then his body began to change. It hurt. Badly. His bones seemed to shift under his skin. Needle-like pain began to sting his flesh, but from the inside. Merle seemed to shrink. Either that or Devan was growing taller. Sights and sounds suddenly became more intense. His vision was too sharp. The vivid colors hurt his eyes. Sounds flooded his ears. His mother's gasps. Merle's grunts. Crickets in the garden chirping. A dog barking far away. A car trundling down the road out by the nearby creek. His senses were assaulting him, scrambling his brain. He lost his balance and fell forwards. He stretched out his arms to break his fall. Not arms. Something else. Long, muscled, powerful. Covered in thick, coarse hair. Sharp claws on the end of huge hands. Not hands. Paws. He couldn't make any sense of it. He felt like he was going to vomit. Yet he had to keep it together. His mother's life was at stake.

Devan looked up. Merle appeared horrified. His face was a mask of terror. He let go of Devan's mother, who crashed to the floor. Devan knew it was too late before she even hit the ground. Discarded like trash. Life had left her eyes. She stared vacantly up at nothing. Her soul didn't reside in that body any longer. It was just a broken shell.

Devan fixed his gaze on Merle, his rage burning incandescent. He felt so strong, so savage, so wild. It was as if his mind had turned his body into exactly what he needed to be in that very moment. A beast that would leave not a single trace of the evil man that cowered before him. With a thunderous growl he pounced with a fury, grace and power he'd never known before in his life.

The scene changed. Devan was back with his pack in the inky black night. The wolves surrounded him. Lupita's warm body was nestled next to his. Her pregnant belly protruded from her midsection. She looked up into his eyes as if she could read his soul.

"What am I supposed to do now?" Devan projected.

Lupita spoke softly using her mouth. It was his mother's voice that Devan heard.

"My precious boy, you can do this," she said. "Remember what I told you. There's nothing that you can't do, or be. The world is yours. Show them who you are, Devan. Trust the wolves. Trust your family. I love you, my boy. Stay safe. Always. Find her. She can help you, even in death."

Devan awoke with a jolt. The idea was clear. He took a moment to quietly thank his mother, or at least her memory. Then he jumped out of bed and threw on his clothes.

Chapter 24

Amara awoke abruptly on hearing the banging on her door. She cursed under her breath. This was becoming an annoyingly common occurrence. Didn't they know that she was human? She needed to sleep or very soon she wasn't going to be much use for anything. Let alone a global war between good and evil. Working with supernaturals was an enriching learning experience, but it had its downsides.

Throwing on a white oversized dressing gown provided by the hotel, she opened the door. She fully expected to see Christopher or Nell, no doubt having had another late-night epiphany that needed to be shared right away. Perhaps even Kavisha for an impromptu strategy meeting.

But it wasn't any of them. Instead, Devan stood in the doorway, much to Amara's surprise. He'd obviously dressed in a hurry. His shirt buttons were inserted in the wrong holes, making the shirt lopsided and his collars uneven. His jacket was inside out. Sleep lines still wrinkled his face.

"I've had an epiphany," said Devan, breathlessly.

Urghhh…same crap, different face, thought Amara, grumpily. She performed an internal roll of the eyes. Here we go.

"It came to me in a dream," said Devan, as he virtually barged into the room.

"Always nice to see you, dude," said Haiden, groggily. "Do make yourself at home." The sarcasm dripped like thick honey. He buried his face into his pillow before grabbing Amara's from her side and placing it over his head.

Amara huffed. She felt more put out than ever. She turned to face Devan, hands on hips. Her face was like thunder.

"We might not be able to track Zachariah," said Devan, oblivious to her irritation. "But we can track Sanya. We just need to identify her scent here at the hotel, from where she's been and anything she interacted with. Tracing her would lead us to where Zachariah took her. It doesn't guarantee that he'll still be there, of course, but at least it tells us where he's been recently. It's better than anything we've managed to ascertain so far."

Amara's hands slipped from her hips and her face softened.

"Devan, that's pretty damn good," she said, even managing a small smile.

Internally she was kicking herself for not coming up with the idea. Strategy was meant to be her strong point. Perhaps sleep deprivation was already impairing her ability to think clearly.

Amara stepped forward and wrapped her arms around Devan. Irrespective of whose idea it was, it was promising. She felt an overwhelming sense of relief after being stuck in neutral for so long.

"Get a room," Haiden muttered as he sat up, unable to find sleep for once. "They have plenty here I'm told."

Amara picked up a wet towel and threw it at him. He caught it deftly.

After the dark shadow cast by Sanya's death, this was a small chink of light. Also, it seemed fated that it was the beloved spell-caster who offered them salvation. Again. Amara recalled her last words once more…"You can still do this… Don't let him win."

***

Amara actually managed to get a few hours of sleep before her phone alarm started emitting digital birdsong. Haiden slept like a log next to her. She stared up at the ornate ceiling rose and gathered her thoughts.

She needed to hold her morning meetings with various Councils around the world. The attacks were spreading. Nowhere was safe now. She had to assure them that progress was being made on the hunt for Zachariah. They were looking to her for salvation. She needed to balance being realistic with offering some hope. It was a tricky tightrope to traverse. Yet she had to walk it.

***

By the afternoon she was drained mentally. The Councils were more frantic than ever and Amara could offer very little to placate them. She thought about taking a nap. But instead she fired up her laptop and started working on an idea that had taken up residence in the back of her brain since yesterday.

She downloaded the video of Sanya's final moments from an online news forum and then opened the file in a video editing program. The video began to play. She saw the empty white room. Amara hit the pause button and then saved a high-resolution still of the image onto her desktop. She exited the video program and then hurriedly deleted the video file. A sense of relief washed over her once the gruesome film was expunged from her computer. Next she opened the still image in the laptop's default photo viewer. It had basic functions like crop, zoom and rotate. She zoomed in on the image and then began to move it around.

She was looking for clues. Anything. Perhaps something in the architecture of the building. The materials the walls were made of. Markings. Indentations. Something. She spent twenty minutes forensically scanning the image, working from the bottom of the white room upwards. She had just reached the small circular window when Haiden interrupted her.

"I'm afraid it isn't good news from us, Amara," he said.

Haiden seemed to have aged. Even though he was generally a positive person, the war was having an impact on him. He was used to hiding his fears. But his face was beginning to betray his innermost thoughts.

"I've just been speaking to Sofia and Ciro, the Hunter liaisons for Italy," he continued. "We're also having no luck with Zachariah. Unlike the wolves, we can't distinguish between the Crimson Claws and ordinary vampires, so to speak. So, until the fighting starts, I'm not sure we can offer much assistance."

He looked thoroughly dejected. Amara patted the space next to her on the bed. He sat down heavily. She roped an arm around his neck and pulled him in for a kiss on the cheek.

"I know you're trying," she said. "We all are. We can only do what we can."

Haiden glanced at her computer screen in an attempt to deflect the attention. The Hunter didn't seem too comfortable being consoled. He studied the image.

CHAPTER 24

"Wait," he said. "Just there. Zoom in."

He pointed to the view outside the small window high in the wall.

"It's just trees," Amara said. "It could be anywhere."

"No, please Amara, humor me," he insisted.

Amara zoomed in as far as she could without the image turning into just a bunch of shaded pixels.

"They're cypress trees," said Haiden. "I can tell by the shape. They're not that common, as they need certain conditions to thrive."

Amara raised her eyebrows.

"Geography major," he said. "I did do *some* schooling," he added, a little indignantly. "Botanical topography was one of the modules."

Amara opened a browser window and her fingers flew across the keyboard.

"There's a few locations in Italy where cypress trees are native," she said, studying her screen. "Including the alps. The locations are fairly spread out so it doesn't narrow down the geography."

She switched back to the image of the room.

"What about there?" asked Haiden. He pointed at a cluster of gray pixels that stood out among the green of the trees. "It's a structure of some kind."

Amara squinted her eyes in an attempt to improve her focus.

"It could be," she conceded. "But it's too unclear. It's just a gray smudge."

"Can't you enhance it?" asked Haiden.

"I can try," she replied.

Amara exited the photo viewer and then launched an image editing program. She opened the picture then cropped it to just the window. She zoomed in and used the sharpen filter. The pixels fused together. The blurry outline of the mass of gray resolved itself into something more coherent. Amara then started playing with the contrast and color levels of the image to make the shape better stand out among the green of the trees. She was working at speed now, a new enthusiasm in her movements.

When she was done she looked at the image, then at Haiden. He smiled back at her.

"It's something," he said.

"It's more than something," she replied. "I can work with this."

She opened the maps site on her browser and hovered over Italy. She then selected the satellite view. Nearly the entire country turned green. She switched back to her first browser window, which listed the locations of indigenous cypress trees in the country. She copied the first location, 'Val d'Orcia in southern Tuscany', pasted it into the search bar and hit enter. The view shifted to the region. Amara zoomed in and then started panning around. She was looking for a structure that could possibly match the shape from the enhanced video still. She began with hope in her heart and a spring in her fingers as she flew enthusiastically over the landscape.

By hour six she was decidedly less enthusiastic. In her initial excitement she had failed to take account of just how big Italy, or how small a laptop screen, actually was.

"Just give it a break," said Haiden, bringing her the fifth black coffee. "It can't be good for your eyes."

He sat next to her and began rubbing her shoulders. She melted into his touch. After sitting on the bed without back support for so long, her muscles were tense from the effort of

CHAPTER 24

holding her upright. In her quest to make a breakthrough in her search, she hadn't even thought to move over to the chair and desk.

Haiden left and she brought her eyes back to the screen. She started moving around the lush green terrain of Turin once more. She suddenly saw a patch of gray among the green of the cypress trees. She hovered her cursor over the structure. The text 'Torre della bell'Alda' came up. There was an English translation under it — 'Tower of the Beautiful Alda'. It was part of the Sacra di San Michele monastery on Mount Pirchiriano, located in Sant'Ambrogio di Torino. It was built between the twelfth and fourteenth century but fell into disrepair due to wars, earthquakes and plain old neglect.

Amara held down the CTRL key and moved the cursor with the trackpad. Suddenly the terrain shifted into 3D mode. She was able to fly around the landscape, getting a side-on view of the various buildings that formed the monastery. She spun round the Tower of the Beautiful Alda, trying to view it from all angles. She again brought up the still image in the photo software and studied it intensely. She then went back to the map and slightly adjusted her view of the tower. Once more she brought up the still image. Then flipped back to the map, where Torre della bell'Alda was silhouetted against the lush green cypress trees. Her pulse started racing.

"Haiden," she shouted. "HAIDEN!"

He was there in a flash, a panicked look on his face.

She beamed back at him, which put him at ease.

"I think I've got a hit," she said. "Take a look."

He sat beside her and studied the map view of the tower, then the still image, and back again to the map. He raised his eyebrows and looked at her with his mouth open.

"In the name of the Omni-Father, as those blood-suckers always say!" he exclaimed. "I think you might just be right, Amara. I thought you were wasting your time with this."

She looked outraged then punched him on the shoulder. Hard.

"All these hours you thought I was just wasting my time?!"

"No…I…" scrambled the Hunter. "I just thought that it couldn't be done. It was like looking for a needle in a proverbial haystack. I should have had more faith in you."

"That you should have," replied the librarian, indignantly, and perhaps a little playfully. She began rubbing his shoulder. Guilt. She had given him a good old whack.

She began reading a brief history of the tower, which probably wasn't the best use of her time at that moment. But she simply had to know. It seemed you could take the woman out of the library, but you couldn't take the library out of the woman.

Alda, a peasant girl, went to the monastery centuries ago to pray for an end to the civil war that was engulfing the nation. Unfortunately, she was ambushed by enemy soldiers. She attempted to escape but there was no way out. She found herself trapped at the top of the tower. As the soldiers approached, she threw herself off while praying for the help of Saint Michael and the Virgin. Moments later she found herself standing at the bottom of the tower. Completely unharmed.

Wow, thought Amara. Quite a tale. Did the tower also hold a miracle for them, too? She was going to find out. She asked Haiden to gather everyone before calling Devan.

"Hey Devan, you're on speaker," Amara said, excitedly. "We have news."

"That's great," he said. "I have news too."

CHAPTER 24

"Okay, let me go first," said Amara. She felt giddy with excitement. "We've got a strong lead on Zachariah. We might know where he is hiding. At the very least we're confident we know where he took Sanya."

"What? How?" various voices chorused in the room. Devan remained silent on the other end of the line.

"It was Haiden, actually," Amara said, smiling at him. He looked taken aback by the praise. But it was his idea to enhance the blurry image of the structure in the first place. Also, she still felt guilty for hitting him so hard. "He spotted a landmark…." she continued, before going on to explain how they honed in on the Tower of the Beautiful Alda. She passed the laptop around the room so the images could be viewed.

Devan was silent the entire time.

"So that's where we need to head," said Amara, resolutely.

"But that can't be," Devan said, breaking his silence.

All faces turned to the phone.

"What do you mean?" asked Amara.

"Well, that was my news," explained Devan. "We tracked Sanya's scent. But it was to somewhere completely different… Parco Nazionale del Vesuvio."

Amara translated the same in her head.

"But that's…"

"The national park of Mount Vesuvius," Devan finished for her. "It's actually a huge region. Sanya's scent stops by a cluster of disused huts on a low-lying plane. It's off the tourist trails. The wolves found some of her clothing close by. I told them not to go further until we formulated a plan."

Amara was lost for words. She reclaimed the laptop and began searching the maps site again. Mount Vesuvius was just over four hundred miles south from Venice, close to Naples.

The Sacra di San Michele monastery was nearly three hundred miles to the west, in Turin. Completely different directions.

"Perhaps you were mistaken," suggested Devan. "The monastery could be similar in shape to…"

"Not possible," interjected Amara. "The Tower of the Beautiful Alda has a very unique shape, plus…" She looked at another of her browser windows to confirm something before continuing. "…plus cypress trees aren't native to the region around Mount Vesuvius. We're not mistaken, Devan. It's a match."

"Zachariah," said Nell, looking from face to face. "His games again."

"I think it's safe to say that a trap has been laid," suggested Klaus. "The only question is in which location."

Amara looked at Kavisha, who had little to offer. She seemed to shrink in her chair.

Klaus was right. It was highly likely that one of the destinations was a trap. But there was only one way to know for certain.

Chapter 25

The plan was made. They would split up. Cover both locations, but with minimal numbers. It was purely a scouting assignment. At least to begin with. Simply locating Zachariah was the principle aim of the missions. Once they'd done that, they would cross the bridge of actually trying to defeat him. One thing at a time.

Nell had misgivings about splitting up. It never seemed to go well in the movies. During the previous battles, she'd been pretty useless. So this was all new to her. She was placing her trust in Amara's hands. They all were. Last time Nell was a mere mortal when all Hell broke loose. Not this time. She was strong, quick and eager to get into the thick of it. She owed that much to the world.

Losing Sanya was tragic. Yet the compound that she created had died with her. That compound had excluded Nell from being anywhere near the heat of battle. But now she was thrust back into the fray. For that she was grateful, yet the price of that freedom had been far too high.

Amara outlined her thinking. Half of them would go west to Sacra di San Michele and the rest would head south to Mount Vesuvius. Haiden, adamant that he and Amara were right in their research, would head the group going to the monastery.

Joining him would be Klaus and Ezra, the older Hunter who was built like a brick outhouse. Devan, accompanied by Nell and Christopher, would head south to Mount Vesuvius national park. Neither Haiden nor Devan wanted to concede that they could be wrong. The mission had turned into something of a contest between the werwulf and the Vampire Hunter. Testosterone was flying. If the situation wasn't deadly serious, Nell might have even found it amusing.

Amara swiftly arranged for internal flights and car hire. Having never left the US before, Nell was enjoying seeing another country. It was an odd admission to make in the middle of such chaos. Yet these might be her final glimpses of the world, so she vowed to take in the wonder of her surroundings without guilt. It was a thin silver lining to an otherwise bleak situation. Plus she was traveling with Christopher and Devan. The two guys she first met when she came to Angel Falls in what seemed a lifetime ago. There was something circular about where she found herself. Destiny wasn't repeating, but rhyming.

***

The charter plane landed at the small domestic runway of Capodichino airport in Naples. Only twenty minutes later Devan took the wheel of the hire car and they headed south-east towards Mount Vesuvius National Park. The satnav showed a journey time of only thirty-seven minutes. Nell braced herself. She looked in the interior rear-view mirror and caught Devan's expression. He looked pensive. Nell didn't need to touch his flesh to know he was thinking of the new life he had brought forth into the world with Lupita. Sometimes a woman knew things without the help of esoteric powers. Female intuition was a mystic force in its own right. She made a vow to do everything within her power to protect him, for the sake of the child.

She turned to look at Christopher. His face was grim, too. He was usually calm and collected, but when something pushed him over the edge, boy did you know about it. Amara had told Nell that while she'd been held captive, Christopher had exploded at pretty much everybody. He had also regularly taken his frustration out on innocent plaster and brickwork around Vhik'h-Tal-Eskemon with his fists. It broke her heart to think of him in that state.

The car journey was quiet. The three of them were lost in their own heads. Nell's thoughts spiraled to Zachariah. Even though he had tortured her for so long, she had no real clear memories of him. She was weak and delirious for most of the time she was held captive, with only flashes of lucidity. Yet it sent a shudder down her spine to think that soon she might be face to face with her captor. But face him she must. Even though the prophecy might not be about her, she felt she was an integral part of this war. Why else would she and Christopher, two vampires with the same bloodlines yet opposing gifts of hindsight and foresight, have come together. It had to be fate. There was a larger plan at play. Wheels within wheels, as she once heard the Magister Jiangshina say.

Her thoughts were interrupted as Devan abruptly swung the car into a gravel parking lot. The sign read 'Valle dell'Inferno'. That sounded about right for what they might be entering, Nell thought, darkly.

"We walk from here," Devan said, grabbing his backpack from the passenger seat and stepping out of the car.

Nell and Christopher followed suit. Once outside, they looked up to take in the majestic grandeur of Mount Vesuvius in the distance. It dominated the landscape with its sloping angles and rich reds and browns near the wide summit. Around them was lush greenery and various hiking trails that snaked across the expansive park. A constant throng of tourists wound their way along the various pathways headed for the imposing dormant volcano. Zachariah would have chosen this location because it was densely packed with humans, Nell thought. They would become bargaining chips if his back was against the wall.

Devan paused for a moment and breathed in deeply, filling his lungs.

"Wow," he said. "That's some of the freshest air I've ever breathed."

He looked back at the two vampires.

"Not that you blood-suckers would appreciate it," he added, before trudging off.

Christopher gave him the finger behind his back. Nell smirked. Then they set off along the nearest trail, mingling with the tourists so as not to look conspicuous. Devan was following his nose. Even in human form, his senses were razor sharp. They walked on an upward elevation along the wooden boards of the trail. Nell's unease grew the further she walked. Alarm bells started ringing. She had a feeling that something was waiting for them. The fear kept growing as the seconds passed, until she couldn't take it any longer. She had to know, or at least try to know.

"Christopher," she breathed, before reaching out and grabbing his hand.

She cast her thoughts into Christopher's mind, trying to see

CHAPTER 25

what the future held for him. She saw swirls of merging colors in her mind's eye, but they wouldn't coalesce into anything discernible. They kept shifting and merging like a living tapestry. Suddenly she felt a sharp pain in her neck as if she had been…bitten. The pain was so intense that she had to let go of Christopher's hand. The colors suddenly vanished and the pain faded as quickly as it arrived. She was left disorientated and shaken.

Christopher was taking in the sights, thinking Nell was just being romantic in reaching for his hand. But Devan had noticed something was wrong. He stopped walking and double-backed, coming to a stop in front of Nell.

"Hey, is everything okay?" he asked.

Nell saw an opportunity. She reached out and grabbed his forearm, as if to steady herself. Then her mind went searching.

Devan, still in human form, walking back down the hiking trail. But his clothes were different. It didn't make much sense. But he was alive. That was the only important point. He was alive.

"Yes, fine now," said Nell, letting go of his arm. "I just had a brief spell of vertigo. Thanks for the arm. I'm good now."

Christopher looked at her quizzically. She just shrugged. Devan looked around at his surroundings and breathed deeply.

"That way," he said, pointing away from the trail to an area of woodland.

"You sure?" Christopher asked.

There weren't any trails or signs of disturbed ground in that direction. Just unspoilt wilderness. Devan raised his eyebrows.

"Yes Christopher, I'm sure," he replied, softly, as if talking to a child. "You'll be able to smell it soon enough, if you try."

The dig wasn't subtle. 'Don't question a werwulf when it comes to tracking, you ingrate blood-sucker,' Devan was saying, without saying it.

"We'll just have to make a jump for it and hope nobody notices," said Devan, looking at the barrier.

Nell looked back along the path.

"Let's wait for this cluster of people to pass, then we go for it," she said.

"Agreed," said Devan.

They pretended to have stopped to take in the view of the mountain. When the crowd of people passed by, Devan jumped over the wooden barrier in a swift motion, falling to the rocky earth on the other side. His boots crunched on the gravel. Nell and Christopher followed with the grace and speed of the undead. Werwulfs may have the edge when it comes to tracking, but vampires could move like the wind.

"Stay low and quiet," Devan said, rather pointlessly. When it came to stealth, vampires also had the edge, by a wide margin.

Devan lifted his head and sampled the air again, then led the way into the dense growth of the forest. Nell and Christopher trailed behind, deftly avoiding jutting branches and the denser areas of undergrowth. They progressed as quickly as Devan could manage in his human form. Nell knew that the last thing he wanted to do was draw attention from any prying eyes by shifting into a wolf.

Devan stopped abruptly.

"Can you smell it now?" he asked.

"Yes," Christopher and Nell both said in unison. Sanya's scent. The one they registered back at the hotel.

"We must be very close, if you guys can detect it," Devan said, possibly oblivious of the dig, but more than likely not, assumed Nell.

They came to a narrow ravine. Clear water flowed along its length. Just beyond it were the ruins of what looked like medieval huts. They were made of a bleached stone and once had steep roofs made of darker slabs. Devan came to a halt by the water, looking disturbed. Nell knew why. The smell was the strongest right in the very spot they were standing. When you moved away the scent began to weaken. It could only mean one thing.

"She must be buried here," Devan said, giving voice to what they were all no doubt thinking.

But that didn't make much sense. Zachariah wouldn't have given Sanya the dignity of a burial. He viewed her as a lesser species. Judging by the merciless way he snapped her neck in that awful video, he saw the spell-caster as less than nothing. To be abused then murdered.

The three of them remained silent and still, digesting the situation. The trees swayed in the wind. Water sloshed as it traveled along the ravine. Birds chirped on high branches. A musty, earthy smell emanated from the dense flora.

"We need to know for sure," said Devan, facing them. His face set.

Nell and Christopher nodded, grimly. It had to be done.

Devan threw off his backpack and unzipped it. He took out a retractable shovel and extended the shaft to its full length.

"Let me," said Christopher, reaching out a hand. "I can do it faster."

Devan handed him the shovel and Christopher began digging. The earth was moist and it came away easily. The scent grew stronger as Christopher dug further into the earth. After he had excavated a hole two feet deep and the scent became almost overwhelming, Christopher tossed the shovel aside.

"It's not right..." he began. "I mean...if we..." He didn't want to say it.

"I know what you're saying," said Nell, sparing him.

She sank to her knees and began scooping the earth out with her bare hands, gently, with care and respect. The other two knelt beside her and began doing the same. Soon Nell came to a solid surface. She took a long moment before softly, almost reverently, wiping away the dirt. She revealed a forehead, then eyes, nose and mouth. Sanya. The brave, warmhearted, masterly spell-caster who had come to their aid when all others had abandoned them.

They continued to carefully pull the mounds of dirt away from her. Then stopped suddenly, recoiling with horror at what they saw. Nell screamed. Devan gasped. Christopher had to cover his mouth. There was no more body underneath the neck. Sanya's decapitated head was all that was there. It was a sickening sight.

Nell looked up at the trees, trying to regain her composure. She couldn't look down. It was too painful. Too horrid.

"The bastards!" Devan grunted, balling a fist and slamming it into the ground.

Nell saw movement just ahead of her. Her sharp vision picked up the disturbance in the landscape.

"We need to leave," she said, quietly. "Now."

While they had been digging, a group of Crimson Claws had crept up on them. They emerged now from behind the trees. Four men and a woman, all dressed for the hiking trail in padded jackets and canvas pants. Yet their eyes gave them away. They had that blood-thirsty look, coupled with the maniacal grins. They moved in unison, one step at a time.

CHAPTER 25

Every move was mirrored exactly by each of them. The legs, arms, fingers, even mouths all moved in perfect synchronicity. It was darkly mesmerizing to witness.

"Too late," breathed Christopher.

"Then we fight," insisted Devan.

He quickly stood and shifted form. Limbs elongating, muscles growing, thick fur sprouting from his skin. He towered above the two vampires, a menacing growl emanating from deep in his chest.

The Crimsons paused as Devan changed before their eyes. But now they approached again, seemingly undeterred by the feral beast in their midst. They progressed slowly, mechanically, methodically.

Knowing what the Crimson Claws were capable of, Nell thought that their best chance was to make a run for it. There was no way they could take out five Crimson Claws. It would be a near impossible feat even if the numbers were evenly matched. She glanced at the hulking snarling werwulf between her and Christopher, and counted her blessings that Devan was with them. Surely he counted as two. But even so, the odds were still against them. She had to think on her feet.

She quickly stood up and squared her shoulders.

"We don't want to hurt you," she shouted, without a hint of irony. Her voice sounded brave, betraying her feelings. "Turn around and go back and you will not be harmed," she added. "This is your first and final warning."

The Crimson Claws stared at Nell in disbelief. Five identical expressions of shock. Eyebrows raised, mouths open, foreheads creased. Their shock quickly morphed into mocking smirks, then all five heads were thrown back and loud cackles echoed into the forest, scattering birds from high up in the trees.

On cue, Christopher and Devan pounced. Christopher flew through the air and landed behind the Crimson on the far right hand side. He wrapped his arms around the vampire's chest, locking his arms by his side. The vampire was too surprised to react in time. Devan closed the distance in a single bound and slashed savagely across the Crimson's neck. Christopher was still holding him as his head rolled off and landed with a crunch on the dry leaves that littered the ground. The mocking cackles came to an abrupt end as Christopher's shoes were showered in a pile of dark ash.

The odds were suddenly more manageable. Four Crimson Claws against two vampires and a werwulf. Not great, but certainly better.

The remaining four Crimsons' shock quickly turned to anger. Four twisted mouths and pairs of hard eyes were focused on Nell. Their fury and vengeance was directed squarely at her. The one who had tricked them so easily. In a blur of motion they simultaneously pounced towards her.

She had to think on her feet again. Her natural reaction would have been to back away. She made the split-second decision to leap towards them instead. She was hoping that her speed and their single-minded determination to attack her would mean they flew right past her.

Nell allowed herself only a millisecond of satisfaction as she realized her ploy had actually worked. She found herself standing alone while the Crimson Claws darted past her. They stumbled, losing their balance, as they snatched at thin air.

Christopher and Devan didn't miss a beat. While the vampires were momentarily flailing around, the duo once again pounced. They picked off the vampire closest to them.

CHAPTER 25

Christopher slammed into his back at full speed, sending him sprawling onto the dirt. Devan was on him in a flash. Snarling and tearing with razor-like claws and sharp teeth. In a matter of seconds he held aloft a severed head. Thick black blood dripped onto the forest floor from the torn neck. Nell looked on, almost mesmerized, as the flesh quickly dissolved into particles of dust before crumbling to the ground.

Three against three now. Nell suddenly had hope. But the Crimsons had been tricked twice. It was unlikely they would fall for another ruse.

As Nell was considering their options, the female Crimson Claw sprang at Christopher, knocking him to the ground. Before either she or Devan could react, the vampire sank her teeth into Christopher's neck and began to rip and tear with an animalistic frenzy. Dark blood spilled from the gaping wound and coated the attacker's mouth. She straddled Christopher's chest, pinning him to the ground.

The other two Crimson Claws advanced on Devan. Both in perfect step, every movement identical. The female vampire lifted her head and glared at them.

"We're not here for the dog," she spat. The other two Crimsons Claws said the exact same thing, at the exact same time — with the exact same voice.

Nell recognized the voice of the macabre chorus. From the video. From the moment she was captured by him and Klaus outside Vhik'h-Tal-Eskemon. Zachariah. He was speaking through his minions.

"The bitch," all three said together in his voice. "Get the bitch."

Devan placed himself between Nell and the Crimson Claws. He was crouched low, teeth bared, a guttural growl emanating from his chest. But he didn't attack. He knew Christopher's life was on the line.

Nell could see that Christopher didn't have long. His neck was badly damaged. Dark blood spilled out onto the leaves and twigs on the forest floor. A few more rips and his head would be detached from the body. He would turn to ash before her eyes.

Nell stepped forward, standing beside the werwulf.

"Let him go," she said. Her voice shook. Any hint of bravery had vanished. Seeing Christopher mortally wounded and hearing Zachariah's voice coming from the mouths of the Crimson Claws had left her reeling. She was scared and desperate.

"We can't do that," Zachariah's voice chorused from the vampires.

"THEN WHAT DO YOU WANT?" Nell screamed, sheer terror overcoming her. She was failing Christopher, when he had done so much to save her.

Devan reached out an arm and held her back with the soft pad of his paw.

"I'll come with you," Nell announced, pulling her arm free of Devan. "Just let him go and I'll come with you."

Christopher tried to lift his head. It was a suicidal move considering his current condition. But he wanted to warn her off.

"It's the only way," Nell said to him. "Don't try to move."

She was taking a gamble. Her human blood had been turned into a weapon. But there was no indication that her vampire blood held the same potency. There was nothing to say that Zachariah could use her in the same way again. But she couldn't be certain.

CHAPTER 25

The female Crimson Claw suddenly started screaming. A shrill, blood-curdling cry. She fell off Christopher's body and began writhing on the ground. She clutched frantically at her face as her body spasmed out of control. She looked like she was possessed.

The two other Crimson Claws looked on, wide-eyed. They both raised their left hand and clutched at their necks, guttural noises coming from their open mouths. Without warning, they turned and fled the scene, running in perfect step with one another. In a few moments they were gone, leaving Nell and Devan staring incredulously down at Christopher and the screaming vampire.

Nell rushed to Christopher, kneeling by his side.

"It hurts," he whispered, pain contorting his face. His voice sounded child-like, broken. He tentatively touched his own neck, hardly aware of the Crimson Claw rolling on the ground in agony next to him.

The sight of him broke Nell's heart, yet the fact that he could still speak was an encouraging sign. It meant his vocal cords were intact. He would heal.

"It's okay, Christopher," Nell soothed. "You'll be fine. Rest. Heal yourself."

The Crimson Claw stopped moving and her cries died down. She lay in a fetal position, silent and motionless.

Devan approached and rolled her onto her back. She had dark hair cut into a short bob and pale skin marked with freckles. She also wasn't dead. That much was clear. A soft moan escaped her lips and her chest rose and fell rapidly as she struggled for breath. For breath. That was the first clue that something very strange had happened. She slowly opened her eyes and Nell noticed that the menacing glint was absent from her gaze. She looked exhausted and bewildered. Her eyes slowly regained their focus and she took in Devan crouched above her.

She let out another blood-curdling scream then scrambled away. But could only manage a few feet before she collapsed back onto the ground. Her strength appeared to have failed her. She no longer looked powerful, poised and deadly. In fact, she looked quite the opposite.

"What the...what the actual fuck is that?" she stammered, looking at Devan. "Where am I?" She looked around frantically. She found Nell and stared at her like a petrified child.

Devan kept his distance.

"What's your name?" Nell asked, trying to sound gentle.

The woman looked down at her own hands, as if seeing them for the first time.

"I...I don't know," she said, tears streaming down her face.

"You don't know your own name?" Nell asked, not unkindly

The woman's face suddenly hardened.

"You...did you drug me?"

Her eyes were wild with confusion and terror.

"Nell, do you smell that?" Devan whispered. But in his werwulf form, his attempt at speaking softly sounded even more sinister than a full-on growl.

The woman's eyes widened and she scrambled back a few more feet.

"Smell what?" Nell answered, a little irritated that Devan had interrupted her attempt at questioning the Crimson Claw.

"Exactly," replied Devan.

Then it hit Nell. She leaned in and sampled the air around the Crimson Claw. She also searched her feelings. She was looking for that familiar sensation that indicated she was in

CHAPTER 25

the presence of the undead. The sixth sense.

Nothing.

"She's...she's human?" asked Nell, hardly believing the words that had just left her own mouth.

Devan backed away and retrieved his backpack. He shifted to human form and quickly extracted fresh clothes from the bag. Nell recalled her earlier vision of him. The different clothes. It made sense now.

"How could that possibly happen?" Devan said, as he approached Nell, now fully dressed. "Is she really human?"

The woman sat up now. It seemed the shock was starting to wear off and her senses were returning.

"Of course I'm a bloody human!" she said. "Unlike you freaks. What the Hell else would I be?"

Nell glanced at Christopher. He was healing quickly now. His vicious wound was sealing itself. The blood had stopped leaking out.

"You were a vampire. Now you're not," Nell said, matter-of-factly.

"You're insane," the woman said. "Let me go. I just want to go home."

Devan turned to her.

"Does the phrase 'Crimson Claw' mean anything to you?"

She thought for a moment, then recognition flooded her face. The tears started streaming again.

"Crimson Claw," she said, bitterly. "That was what he said just before he attacked...no bit...me. I don't remember anything after that."

She looked around at their faces.

"It wasn't any of you that hurt me," she stated. "It was somebody else. Are you with them? You won't hurt me?"

"No, of course not," Nell replied, actually offended. "We aren't with them and I give you my word that we will not hurt you."

The woman weighed Nell's words, eyeing her with suspicion.

"Do you recall your name now?" asked Devan.

"Yes," she said. "It's Bernadette...Bernadette Girard. I come from Ermont, near Paris. Where am I?"

Devan exchanged a glance with Nell.

"A long way from home," he said. "You're in Italy. Mount Vesuvius National Park, to be specific."

Bernadette looked completely bewildered.

Nell felt completely bewildered. Then a thought struck her.

Christopher. His blood. She and he were opposites. Yin and yang. Male and female. She descended from a murderous tyrant, he from his noble and humane brother. He had the gift of hindsight. She had the gift of foresight. Her blood created Crimson Claws. So his blood...

"In the name of the Omni-Father," she exclaimed, in true vampire style. "If my blood can make Crimson Claws, then Christopher's blood has the potential to unmake them...to *'revert to the origin'*." She was quoting a line from the prophecy.

She also recalled how the prophecy ended. *'Blood connects all. Blood is the liberator. Blood is the destroyer. Blood is the answer.'*

Devan looked thoroughly confused.

"At this point, I'm prepared to believe anything," he said, throwing his hands in the air. "I think we need to throw this over to Amara and Kavisha. This is way above my pay grade."

Nell's mind was racing. Even if Christopher's blood did have the power to change Crimson Claws back to humans, how would that work? It's not as if he could invite a million crazed vampires to take a nibble on him. Also Sanya was out of the equation. She would have had the skills to potentially create something that could be used as an antidote. What hope was there now? Like Devan, the wider implications were above her pay grade. Nell had more immediate concerns.

She glanced over at Christopher. The nasty gash had almost sealed completely. The flow of blood had stopped. He seemed more lucid. He slowly sat up, once more probing his neck with his fingers to survey the damage.

Devan reached out a hand to Bernadette, who still sat on the ground. She tentatively took it and was helped slowly to her feet.

"Let's get you home," said Devan.

Nell hadn't heard a better suggestion all day.

Chapter 26

The Sacra di San Michele was more magnificent than Haiden could have imagined. Even from a distance, its centuries-old structures dominated Mount Pirchiriano. The monastery's cluster of ornate stone buildings loomed majestically over the lush valleys below. These were not the circumstances in which the Hunter would have liked to visit the historic landmark. But that was out of his control now.

They were still a few hundred feet away, approaching slowly up the foothills beneath. Stealth and safety were foremost in their minds. This was a scouting mission. Nothing more. Their task was simple. Find out if this was where Zachariah and his Crimson Claws were hiding. That was all. No battles. No bravado. Besides, they would need a hell of a lot of back-up before even considering engaging the enemy.

Amara had contacted the world Councils days ago to let them know that soldiers may be needed at short notice. Vampires were flooding into Italy. Similarly, Haiden had put the call out to the Vampire Hunter network. Amara had asked the army to assemble in Florence, which was roughly halfway between Turin and Naples. When the call for action came, they would have to rush either north to Sacra di San Michele or south to Mount Vesuvius National Park at a moment's notice.

CHAPTER 26

A large contingent of wolves were already in the country, having been on tracking duties for some time. Devan had spread the word among the packs that they should head for the huge Vallombrosa Forest just outside of Florence to make camp and await further instructions.

There was an element of 'friendly' competition between Haiden and Devan about Zachariah's whereabouts. They had both refused to acknowledge they could be wrong. With the benefit of hindsight, Haiden realized it was all a little childish. Macho posturing, in fact. As long as one of them was right, and they managed to pin-point where Zachariah and his legion were hiding, it didn't matter who 'won'. The only victor that counted was the world.

Haiden's mission was running parallel with that of Devan, who had Nell and Christopher with him. The Hunter was uneasy at the thought of either group finding Zachariah without the other. But, like Amara had said, it was the least worst plan. Time was of the essence. They didn't have the luxury of good options.

Somewhere in the woodlands of Mount Vesuvius, Nell, Christopher and Devan were on the hunt, while Haiden and his team were traversing the lush greenery in the shadow of Sacra di San Michele.

Haiden turned around to face his companions. Like Haiden, Ezra was outfitted in all-black combat gear with a utility belt packed with weapons and tools. Behind the imposing Hunter was Klaus, dressed in green fatigues and wearing chunky hiking boots. His red hair made him stand out amongst the foliage, but Ezra's massive form ensured he was out of sight from the vantage of the monastery.

"Any word?" asked Haiden.

Klaus looked down at the screen of the cell-phone he was carrying.

"Nothing so far," he said. He looked concerned. "Also the signal is weakening the deeper we travel into the foothills. It seems we're approaching a deadzone for the phone networks."

"That figures," mused Ezra, scanning his surroundings. "There's nothing out here to communicate with."

"We have to assume Devan's team has nothing to report. So far," said Haiden. "So we keep going."

"Where do we scope out first," enquired Ezra, crouching slightly so his imposing frame was less conspicuous.

"We find the room where Sanya was executed," said Haiden, not mincing his words. "We know Zachariah was there recently. That will allow Klaus to track his scent or aura or…" He looked at Klaus. "…whatever voodoo you can perform. Just give us confirmation that he's here so we can beat a hasty retreat and call for back-up."

"I'll do what I can," replied Klaus.

"From the angle of the Tower of the Beautiful Alda in that video still, Amara worked out the most likely location of where Sanya was taken," explained Haiden. "It's some kind of anteroom attached to the Sacra di San Michele monastery itself. She thinks it was probably used for storing furniture or religious artifacts back in the day. That's our first stop."

Ezra and Klaus both nodded. Haiden led the way through the thick brush. They trekked quietly for twenty minutes before they emerged from a copse of cypress trees. About a hundred feet in front of them stood the Sacra di San Michele monastery. Just beyond that loomed the Tower of the Beautiful Alda. Haiden took a moment to take in the historic grandeur of the buildings from such a close vantage point.

CHAPTER 26

He was about to continue walking when an arm reached out and blocked his progress. He turned to see Klaus holding him back. He was staring intensely at Haiden.

"There's someone there," Klaus said, his voice low. "On the tower."

Haiden turned and looked up ahead. Atop the Tower of the Beautiful Alda was a shape. It was moving slowly. But that's all Haiden could discern from this distance. A shape. It was too far to make out anything substantive.

"It's him," said Klaus. "It's Zachariah."

Ezra came forward to the tree line. He crouched and stared out, squinting his eyes for sharper focus. Then he turned to Klaus.

"How can you possibly tell?" asked the Hunter. "It's too far out from here."

"I can tell," said Klaus. "It's him. It's Zachariah."

Haiden looked at Klaus for a long moment.

"If you're sure then that's good enough for me," he said.

But deep in his bones something felt off. It was too easy.

"If we go any further we risk revealing ourselves," said Klaus. He took out the cell-phone and cursed.

"Dead signal," he said. "We need to head back."

Ezra was scanning the stone structures.

"These buildings aren't big enough to hide an army of Crimson Claws," he said. "Either Zachariah's only got a small, core contingent with him, or the rest are hiding close to the grounds."

Haiden considered.

"The tower could house maybe twenty or so Crimson Claws," he said. "But we don't know how many could be stuffed into the Sacra di San Michele complex. But you're right, Ezra.

There's not enough space for a huge contingent. We could be in luck."

"Only if we hurry," said Klaus. "We have to inform Amara. We need those reinforcements."

Haiden led the way back into the thick of cypress trees. Then he broke out into a run. Time was of the essence. The odds might be in their favor. For once.

Chapter 27

Klaus didn't even attempt to sleep. He knew it would be no use. Instead, he paced the grounds of the cheap Turin guest house. He trudged across the small gravel expanse, passing the disused moss-covered fountain and sad-looking pot plants before turning around again.

He had called Amara as soon as his cell-phone registered a signal. She had put the call out right away. Vampires, Hunters and werwulfs were converging on Turin right now. Things were moving apace.

But in the still of this night Klaus's thoughts turned to Loris, as they did most nights. His heart still ached for the one he loved. The one who had died to save him. That act had changed Klaus in ways that even he couldn't fully fathom. He was human in terms of his need for sustenance and sleep. He would age. Yet his strength and senses were growing stronger and stronger. The change had left him both vulnerable and powerful. It had given and taken away in equal measure.

Klaus considered the prophecy, which appeared to be the source of his extraordinary fate. The words were ingrained on his brain, because they would always be tied to the loss of Loris:

Salvation lies in one soul. A death-walker turned young. One of tainted blood. He will endure a betrayal, a loss and an awakening. He will love, as no other of his kin has before. He will abandon those he serves. He will develop abilities unknown while reverting to the origin. These abilities can corrupt and besiege, for they stem from the transmutation of loss, the most powerful emotion. He must drain the one he loves, filling his essence and ending theirs. This act alone brings forth the genesis.

Klaus stopped pacing and looked up at the canopy of stars. If the prophecy was true, and so far it seemed to be, then he and he alone had to defeat Zachariah. *Salvation lies in one soul.* That phrase stood out to him. It quietly haunted both his sleeping and waking hours. *One soul.* It was Klaus against Zachariah. He was certain of it. Taking him out would make the Crimson Claws easier to defeat. But, with Zachariah, nothing was ever as simple as it appeared.

An idea began to build in his head, now that they were so close to what could be the end. What if the prophecy was an instruction rather than just a description. A call to action for one soul. What if he had to take this war into his own hands. Perhaps if he went into battle accompanied by others they would fail. *Salvation lies in one soul. One soul.*

He took a deep breath. He felt as if he was at a crossroads. Leave right now and go it alone, or stay and fight with his comrades. The news that Nell, Christopher and Devan were on their way, along with scores of vampires, Hunters and wolves, convinced Klaus that they could handle the Crimson Claws. But none of them would be able to touch Zachariah. That was a private battle. One that had been ordained centuries ago in an obscure book called the *Adumbrate Invictus*.

CHAPTER 27

If he made the wrong decision now it could end in disaster, not only for those he cared about, but for the world. He studied the heavens for any sign of an answer. The stars appeared silent on the subject. With divine guidance evading him as he peered up at the constellations, Klaus decided to practice his new-found talents. After all, the prophecy had been clear that they would come into play. He was changing for a reason.

He took another deep breath, centered himself and then cast his mind out to see what he could find. The thoughts of people in nearby rooms were mundane enough. He skipped over Haiden and Ezra out of courtesy. He pushed further. Through the trees and valleys, towards Sacra di San Michele. He heard nothing. Nothing at all. He had hoped to hear the thoughts of the Crimson Claws. Perhaps even Zachariah at a stretch. But he was disappointed. He pushed his mind further, past Sacra di San Michele, past the Tower of Beautiful Alda. Onward to the small town beyond.

His mind was suddenly filled with chatter. He took a moment to discern the jumble of thoughts. A group of English schoolgirls on a trip to Italy. He thought it best to withdraw his attention swiftly. Klaus pulled his focus back towards himself.

He again searched the Tower of Beautiful Alda, then Sacra di San Michele. Nothing. Silent. No thoughts. Not even a sense of presence. Yet it was clear that his ability was as sharp as ever. Was he being blocked somehow? Was there another explanation?

Klaus was suddenly worried. Had they been seen by Zachariah, or one of his minions, when he and the two Hunters were on their scouting mission? Had Zachariah fled as a result? Had their chance evaporated?

Cursing under his breath, Klaus tried to form a plan.

Assuming that Zachariah and the Crimson Claws had fled, then they were once more a step ahead. But Klaus had seen Zachariah in the flesh earlier in the day. So he couldn't be far. There was still a chance. The only choice to make now was whether to run blindly into the night or tell the others. The old Klaus would have disappeared with no regard for those around him. The new Klaus weighed up the pros and cons. He knew his friends would want to be involved. That they would be hurt if he just vanished. Klaus had to smirk at that. The fact that he was considering the feelings of humans and wolves. He really was changing.

"I thought I heard you," said a voice behind him.

Klaus turned sharply to see Haiden, fully dressed in his combat gear.

"I thought not even an earthquake could disturb your slumber," said Klaus.

"We have to look after a prize asset," said Haiden, eyeing Klaus. "Ezra's getting his head down now."

"Your concern is touching," said Klaus. "But I fear we have to wake your friend."

He went on to explain his reasoning.

"There were no minds in the tower, or the monastery?" asked Haiden.

"Not that I could discern," said Klaus.

"But that doesn't necessarily mean they're not there," said Haiden.

"Perhaps," admitted Klaus.

"We need to let Amara know," said Haiden.

"But wouldn't she..." began Klaus.

"No one is sleeping tonight," interjected Haiden. "Least of all Amara, if I know her at all. Come on, let's go." He turned

CHAPTER 27

back to Klaus before setting off. "Oh, and Klaus, thanks for not just taking off into the night. We need to do this together."

Klaus smiled back. But inside he was torn.

***

Haiden, Klaus and Ezra sat on the bed staring at the phone while Amara outlined her thoughts. Klaus felt the weight of the world on his shoulders. He wasn't sure if this was the right course of action. Was he placing his friends in unnecessary danger? Hunting for Zachariah without waiting for back-up could well be a suicide mission. But the choice had been taken out of his hands. The Hunters had been keeping a close eye on him. Fleeing into the night hadn't been an option.

"The rest of the reinforcements will be there in a matter of hours," said Amara. "They're making good progress."

"It might be too late," said Klaus. "Wolves and vampires are flooding into the region. That will not go unnoticed. Zachariah could flee into the shadows. We must act now. We have a small window of opportunity and it is closing further and further the longer we just sit here. There's no point assembling an army if it has nothing to fight."

"Haiden?" asked Amara. There was an edge to her voice.

"We're on board," said the Hunter as he glanced at Ezra, who nodded back resolutely. "Klaus is right. We can't leave it too late."

Amara let out a long breath. Klaus knew this was about much more than strategy to her. It was about Haiden.

"Okay, go," she said, reluctantly. "But be safe. Well as safe as you can be. If you see Zachariah then withdraw immediately and wait for help. Don't engage. Just track. Where are you headed first?"

"Back to the monastery, to start with," said Haiden. "It's the location of the last confirmed sighting."

"Okay, best of luck," said Amara, trying to sound stoic. "And Klaus," she added. "Thanks for deciding not to run off on your own."

Klaus was getting tired of hearing that praise. Especially as he had an uneasy feeling in the pit of his stomach that going it alone would have been the right move.

Chapter 28

They crouched low at the tree line. Sacra di San Michele was silhouetted in the darkness ahead of them. It was a still night. The moon was bright. Crickets chirped nearby. Wolves howled in the far distance. Klaus knew those howls would grow louder and more numerous as the minutes passed by.

Klaus reached out with his mind to sense if anybody was there. Nothing. He reverted to his human senses and breathed in deeply. Only the musty, earthy smell of the trees and soil around them. Haiden looked at him.

"Nothing," said Klaus.

"Then let's go," instructed Haiden, walking out into the open towards the monastery.

Ezra followed with Klaus trailing at the rear.

They reached the entrance of the monastery. A tall wooden door carved with images of shields, helmets and swords. At the top were two snakes wrapped around daggers. The door was housed within numerous arch patterns that were carved into the white stone of the building.

Klaus was marveling at the intricate carvings when a heavy object slammed into his back. He was thrown forward into the heavy door. He instinctively reached out a hand to cushion his impact, barely able to keep his balance. He looked down and saw a large rock by his feet. Klaus turned abruptly to find about a dozen robed figures standing in a semicircle twenty feet away. Haiden and Ezra immediately flanked him, so he was protected.

Klaus looked at the figures incredulously. It didn't make sense. He hadn't sensed anyone in the area. But now, in the cold light of the moon, they were surrounded. Was this how it ended, with the prophecy unfulfilled? Zachariah would go on to enslave the human race and subjugate other supernaturals?

"My brother, how I have missed you." The words came from each of the hooded figures, perfectly in unison and with one voice. Zachariah's.

Nell had described the phenomena when she debriefed Amara about the expedition to Mount Vesuvius. But hearing it in person was another level of creepy.

"I am glad that you have returned to me," continued Zachariah, through his vassals. "To your *true* Family."

The figures reached up and lowered their hoods in perfect union. Klaus's eyes widened and his pulse quickened. These were his former brothers and sisters. The original Red Claws he had lived with, fought with, fed with, spent a century in slumber alongside. He looked from figure to figure, putting names to faces. Joshua, Gabriel, Elspeth, Lenora, Horace, Darick, Nikolas, Velorina, Cassius, Briar, Drake, Ivy.

"Mind games," spat Haiden. "Don't listen to him." He placed a hand on Klaus's shoulder. "We're your family now."

Klaus should have been offended at the implication that he would simply switch sides, but he was oddly touched by Haiden's words.

"Too scared to do your own dirty work?" shouted Haiden into the night air. "Hiding behind your serfs, like a coward."

CHAPTER 28

"On the contrary," said Zachariah. This time it was a lone voice. It came from above.

Klaus, Ezra and Haiden moved a step away from the door and looked up. There, standing on a ledge above the entrance in front of a large arched window, was Zachariah. He was wearing the same full-length black robe as the others.

"I see that Klaus is the one who is afraid to do his own dirty work," sneered Zachariah. "Had to bring venal human scum to fight his battles. Hunters, no less. That is the true definition of a traitor."

That stung, Klaus had to admit.

"We are Family," chorused all of the Crimson Claws in unison. "We are one." The vampires began advancing on the three of them.

Ezra and Haiden pulled out menacing-looking scythes from their belts and adopted a fighting stance. They advanced a few paces so Klaus was once again protected.

The Crimsons moved forward as a single entity. Every step, every movement, every gesture and facial expression was mirrored by all twelve of them. It was hypnotic to witness.

Klaus registered a flash of movement before hearing a thudding sound. Zachariah had jumped down from the ledge and was now standing next to him. Klaus just had time to look into his dark menacing eyes before the world went black.

Chapter 29

Klaus awoke to find himself slumped in the corner of a room. He slowly moved his head to take in his surroundings. Hard gray floor, white stone walls, one small circular window placed high up. He was jolted upright as recognition flooded him. He'd seen this room before. In the gruesome video of Sanya's execution. That didn't bode well.

"Wakey wakey, dear brother."

Zachariah's voice on his neck sent a chill down his spine.

"I've missed you, Klaus. I've missed you more than you could know."

The words were not kind. They were spat from Zachariah's mouth like venom.

Klaus's body ached with stiffness. He had no recollection of being brought here to the anteroom inside the Sacra di San Michele monastery. He wondered about the fate of Haiden and Ezra. Judging from the final moments they were all together, it didn't seem like a happy one. He was accosted by a stab of guilt. They should never have been here with him. His initial hunch was correct. But he couldn't deal with that now. He had more immediate concerns.

"Alone at last," said Zachariah. "How I have *longed* for this moment," he added in a saccharine tone.

CHAPTER 29

He was mocking Klaus, making fun of the feelings the red-haired vampire once had for his master. Zachariah was well aware of the hold he previously enjoyed over Klaus.

Klaus felt nothing but disgust now. Loris had shown him that true love came with kindness and humility, not fear and control.

Klaus reached out with his mind to tap into Zachariah's thoughts. At such close quarters he was certain he could make a connection. He was disappointed. Nothing. Not even the undertone of another presence in the room. If Zachariah wasn't standing right before him, Klaus could almost have believed he wasn't there. He wanted desperately to know what Zachariah planned.

In the end, he didn't need special abilities. Zachariah willingly obliged.

"I have to say, Klaus, I'm very disappointed in you. On top of failing me miserably, you also have forsaken your Family," said Zachariah. "I always thought we had a special connection, *you and I.*" Once again the taunting.

Zachariah spread his arms wide then stared directly at Klaus.

"And now I have to kill you. Before you kill me." He raised his eyebrows. "Because that's what you're here for, isn't it? You're here to kill me. To destroy the one who created you. That is to be my thanks for giving you the gift."

"I'm here..." said Klaus, peeling himself off the floor, standing up and squaring his shoulders, "...to make you pay for what you've done. You're a monster, Zachariah. Make no mistake about that."

Zachariah looked amused.

"These people, these others you dismiss as worthless," continued Klaus. "They have qualities that you cannot fathom, such as honor, compassion and mercy. You are the plague on this Earth, not them."

Zachariah laughed. His cackles echoed off the stone walls.

"You think I'm the abomination?" replied Zachariah. "No Klaus. It is you. You are the one fighting against his very nature. Just look at you. Pathetic. You should be thankful I'm putting you out of your misery."

Zachariah shifted his body slightly to reveal something at the back of the room. Klaus registered it, then his eyes widened with horror. A black tripod with a phone attached on the mount. The camera lens was facing into the room. Recording. Zachariah was planning another show for the world. Another sick death video. This time Klaus was to be the 'star'.

Zachariah grinned when he saw the look of shock on Klaus's face.

"The world must come to understand that crossing me has consequences," he explained with unnerving calm. "My brethren must know the price of betrayal. You are to be that example, Klaus. Your death will have some purpose. For that, be grateful. Your end will be meaningful…but not quick or without the exquisite agonies reserved for traitors."

"You are truly sick, Zachariah," said Klaus, his voice low.

In a flash Zachariah reached into his pocket and pulled out a glass vial. Klaus didn't have to wrack his brain to figure out what it contained. The answer was depressingly familiar.

Zachariah pulled out the stopper and drank down the blood. As always, the transformation was near instantaneous. Zachariah seemed to grow by three inches. His posture became straight as a board. His face flushed and his eyes took on a crimson luminescence. His whole being seemed to hum and crackle with energy.

CHAPTER 29

Klaus knew what Zachariah had become in that instant. Yet Zachariah had no idea of what Klaus had become. He was oblivious to how his former devotee had changed since he had taken Loris's life essence. But right now Klaus couldn't even read Zachariah's thoughts. What use would any of his other enhanced abilities be?

Looking at Zachariah thrumming with vigor, a thought occurred to Klaus. It was a line from the prophecy, the very end part:

Blood connects all. Blood is the liberator. Blood is the destroyer. Blood is the answer.

Klaus had an idea. He just needed to remain alive long enough to put it into action.

Zachariah lunged forward at lightning speed. He threw a fist into Klaus's chest. Klaus went flying backwards into the wall. His back crunched against the stone and all the air was knocked from his lungs. He was winded and in agony. He fell to his knees and slowly looked up.

Zachariah didn't move to finish him off. He was true to his word. He was going to make this last. To put on a show for the camera. His hubris might present Klaus with an opportunity.

Klaus recovered quickly but remained kneeling on the ground, looking pained.

Zachariah approached and stood over him.

"Don't make this too easy, Klaus," he said, derisively. "We need to prolong the suffering to really get the point across to the audience. Now be a team player for once and..."

Before he could finish his sentence, Klaus launched himself from his crouching position and slammed into Zachariah. His shoulder made impact with Zachariah's midsection and the Crimson Claw leader went stumbling backwards. He was on the verge of losing his balance but managed to right himself at the very last second, taking a few more steps backwards before coming to a halt. A smile spread across his face.

"That's more like it," said Zachariah. "Make an effort, Klaus. Show them what a Red Claw is…."

He stopped speaking and his eyes went wide. He stared at Klaus, who held up the glass vial he had snatched from Zachariah's pocket when he had barreled into him.

Wasting no time, Klaus ripped open the stopper and drank down the blood. Nell's blood, from when she was human. The elixir that had proven so powerful and so destructive.

Suddenly, the floodgates opened in his mind. Zachariah's thoughts burnt white hot inside Klaus's head. Surprise mixed with fury alongside humiliation for being tricked. Now other voices came flooding in, from outside the building. The other Crimson Claws. Anger, fear, violence, triumph, alarm, disgust. He couldn't tell what was happening out there. He was only picking up on the volatile mix of emotions in the air. It was too much. A cacophony of thoughts and feelings coming at him at once.

Klaus placed his palms on his ears in an effort to block out the mental assault. But it did no good. He wasn't dealing with mere sound. Instead, he imagined a brick wall in front of his forehead. The imaginary wall allowed the thoughts to pass through, but they were less violent, less piercing. It worked. It wasn't perfect, but the psychic onslaught had diminished. After a few seconds he was able to at least think again.

Klaus felt other changes. All the pain had evaporated from his body. But it was more than just the absence of negative sensations. He felt charged with energy. Limitless. Whatever gifts he had been granted since Loris's passing had been

CHAPTER 29

amplified after drinking Nell's blood.

He got to his feet and faced Zachariah.

"You think we're evenly matched now?" asked his former master. "Far from it, Klaus. I was always superior to you. This changes nothing. It only makes your end more satisfying."

Zachariah charged at Klaus, who simply stood still.

Before Zachariah made contact with him, Klaus saw precisely what he intended to do. In his mind's eye he saw a flash of Zachariah lunging for his throat, his talon-like nails gliding through the air.

Klaus remained still as a statue and then, with milliseconds to spare, he ducked low in a lightning quick blur of motion. Zachariah had no time to react or respond. He went sailing over Klaus's head and crashed into the stone wall behind, landing in an unceremonious heap.

Zachariah roared with rage, spitting and gnashing his teeth, as he picked himself up.

Klaus turned and stood calmly facing him.

Zachariah went on the attack again, this time using the wall for traction. He propelled himself off the stone. Once again images flashed in Klaus's mind. He saw that Zachariah intended to take out his legs in an attempt to pin him down and make easy work of him.

Klaus, in response, lunged towards Zachariah, pressing a palm against his chest and slamming his body back against the cold, hard stone. The room actually shook with the force of the impact. Dust cascaded down on both of them, peppering their hair. Klaus could feel the shock and anger physically pulsing through Zachariah's body, so much so that the air around him was disturbed.

Zachariah hadn't expected Klaus to put up much of a fight.

He was seething, Klaus could sense, particularly as their encounter was being recorded. Zachariah reached down and pulled out another vial of Nell's blood from within his robe. Klaus could have easily swatted it away, but instead he decided to do nothing. He just held Zachariah in place as the Crimson Claw gulped the red liquid down greedily. Blood spilled down his lip and dripped off his chin onto the floor.

Klaus looked deep into Zachariah's eyes and saw the Crimson hue deepen. Red streaks began to criss-cross the whites of his eyes. He felt the electric charge cascading around Zachariah's body increase in intensity, yet Klaus still held him firmly in place, with one hand. Zachariah attempted to push himself off the wall, but he wasn't able to budge an inch. He looked at Klaus's hand in disbelief.

"You think we're evenly matched now?" said Klaus, echoing Zachariah's words. "Far from it, Zachariah."

Zachariah leaned forward and tried to push himself off again, but to no avail. His thoughts betrayed pure astonishment.

"You were right before," said Klaus, suddenly overcome with emotion as he stood eye to eye with the one who made him. The one he had adored. Loved. "You were my world, once," he continued. "There was nothing I wouldn't have done for you. Lie, steal, kill. But you abused that trust and threw me away. Threw away everything we were."

"We were *nothing*," Zachariah sneered, spittle lying from his mouth and flecking Klaus's face. "You were a barely competent lackey. I felt nothing for you, and I certainly didn't share in your...your...perversion."

That cut Klaus to the core. He swung his arm and threw the vampire across the room. Zachariah's feet didn't touch the floor before he was slammed into the opposite wall. He landed in another ungainly tangle.

Zachariah slowly got to his feet, his face bloody from the impact with the wall. He turned to face Klaus. His expression was twisted with rage and humiliation. Klaus didn't need to read his thoughts to know what he was feeling.

"Enough," Zachariah spat, glancing at the phone camera. "This ends now."

"So be it," replied Klaus.

For the third time Zachariah charged. Klaus saw a clear vision of Zachariah's teeth ripping into his neck. As Zachariah propelled himself forward, Klaus side-stepped at the very last moment, spinning on his heel and slashing across Zachariah's neck. He then grabbed Zachariah's head and twisted hard.

Zachariah crumpled to the floor in a heap. Klaus knelt down beside him and turned him onto his back. The vampire had a savage wound across his neck. His flesh and tendons were torn. He started coughing up blood.

Much to his own surprise, Klaus cradled Zachariah's head in his hands. He stared into the ravaged face of his creator. The one he had once idolized and cherished more than any other soul.

"I loved you, Zachariah," said Klaus, tears spilling down his cheeks. It was a deathbed confession, but not his death. "I loved you before I knew it was possible to love. But you broke me, just like you break and destroy everything around you. You are a curse made flesh, Zachariah. The seed of darkness. The obsidian."

Zachariah stared up at him, his mouth trembling. The vigor had dimmed from his eyes.

"I would have died for you," continued Klaus, shaking slightly due to the intensity of the emotions coursing through his body. "But you ruined it. Just like you ruin everything. Just like you ruined the world."

Klaus looked around the barren room, then closed his eyes and swallowed. He had to finish his thoughts. For his sake. For his own sanity. He looked down again at his former master.

"The funny thing is, if you hadn't pushed me away, I'd still be standing by your side like the faithful puppet I was," said Klaus. "I would have never realized how wrong I was. How much of a monster I was. Like you."

He studied the ruin of Zachariah's neck.

"You have finally reaped what you have sown, old friend," said Klaus, gently.

Zachariah coughed. More dark black blood spilled from his mouth. But he managed to speak. His words were raspy, barely a whisper. Klaus had to lean down.

"Do what you must, traitor," he said. "But know that I never loved you, Klaus. You were always worthless."

"That might be true," replied Klaus. "But I will die knowing that I *was* loved. Truly loved, and was able to love in return. You will die stewing in your hate."

Zachariah appeared to contemplate the words for a long moment.

"I'm glad you're the one to kill me, Klaus," he said, looking up. "Because it will haunt you for the rest of your life. I know you hate me, but you will never stop loving me."

Klaus had to look away, but Zachariah wasn't finished speaking.

"I gave you life, Klaus," he continued. "I gave you Family. You are like me in ways you will never truly understand. You are kin, Klaus…and she will find you."

The words disturbed Klaus. He studied Zachariah's dark

CHAPTER 29

eyes.

"Did you really think that I tortured you and left you for the dogs because you failed me?" said Zachariah. "I've been failed more times than I can count over the years and simply killed those who disappointed me. But your failure wounded me, Klaus. It hurt most of all. Do you know why? Because the blood that flows within you, flows within me. And it pains me to think of my kin as weak and impotent."

"More of your lies," said Klaus, dismissively. "It's a bit late for them now, don't you think? They will not save you."

"You think you know everything about me," said Zachariah. "But that is far from the truth. Before I was turned so long ago, I fathered a son. That son went on to father another son. I think even you can work out how this goes. And here you are, Klaus. A true Redclaw. At heart."

"I don't believe a word of it," said Klaus. "I'm tired of your games."

"Damien, my brother, was able to trace you," said Zachariah. "You were the one remaining branch until the family tree blinked out. How...circular...it is that now you kill the creator. Does it make you feel proud?"

Zachariah laughed. Speckles of thick, dark blood exploded from his mouth, flecking the ground.

"You're lying!" Klaus shouted. Rage enveloped him. Once more Zachariah was manipulating him. Even at this stage.

"Think about it, Klaus," continued Zachariah. "Why would I, the head of the most powerful vampire Family in existence, travel to some flea-infested backwater in Pennsylvania to bring a dull, feeble-minded red-haired loner into the fold? What did I have to gain from it?"

Klaus had no words in reply.

"Nothing!" spat Zachariah. "I owed it to the bloodline, that's all. I have regretted that sentimental decision ever since. You have been the ruin of my Family and a bane upon our noble line. You are the one who is a living curse."

Anger exploded within Klaus. Before he could process his thoughts, his hands reached and tore Zachariah's head clean away from his body. He held the decapitated head in his hands, staring into those dark, menacing eyes. Ones that would see no more of the world. The flesh began to disintegrate into ash, which cascaded through his fingers. It covered the robe that now lay flat to the ground, filled with more dark ash that was once a body.

Zachariah was no more.

Chapter 30

The troops aligned for battle.

Nell stood at the front flanked by Devan and Christopher.

Standing beside Devan, who towered over them in his feral form, were Haiden and Ezra. Weapons drawn. Eyes fixed on the enemy line.

Devan and his pack had raced into Sacra di San Michele as the robed figures were attacking the two Hunters, who were doing an admirable job of fending them off with their scythes. They cut and slashed with practiced skill. But it was just a matter of time before the outnumbered Hunters would have been overwhelmed by the vampires.

The wolves raced in among the melee and quickly shifted form. The vampires backed off at the sight of dozens of angry, ferocious werwulfs in their midst with sharp claws drawn. They scurried off towards the Tower of the Beautiful Alda.

Behind Nell and her friends were an army of vampires, Hunters and werwulfs. Together as one. Ready for battle. It was a sight to behold. The banding of three different legions, three different races. Vampires and black-clad hunters stood shoulder to shoulder while werwulfs, clustered in their respective packs, were spread across the field.

One notable absence was Klaus. Haiden had told Nell that

he had no idea where the former Red Claw had disappeared to. He and Ezra were too busy fending off the vampires to take notice of his movements. Nell had to trust that the former Red Claw knew what he was doing. She remembered the vision when she touched his hand on the plane to Italy. A small shiver ran down her spine.

A werwulf stalked up to the front and stood next to Devan. He was slightly thinner than the others and had mottled gray and white fur, indicating his advancing years. Nell recognized him. Lupertico. Lupita's father. He had lost his only son to the battle with the Crimson Claws. Yet here he was, putting his own life on the line once more for the cause.

"The scouts have returned," he said in a deep husky voice, looking from Devan to Nell. "The enemy is congregated just beyond the ruined tower."

Devan placed a hand on Lupertico's shoulder. Something unspoken was communicated between the two of them. The older werwulf dipped his head slightly.

"Thank you," said Nell, who only had her words.

She looked to Christopher and Devan, who both nodded, then at Haiden and Ezra, who grabbed their scythes from their belts and adopted a fighting stance. The sudden call to action seemed to radiate through the assembled army of its own accord. Growls and howls rang out. Hunters swiftly grabbed weapons from their belts. The vampires hissed from deep in their throats.

Devan led the way forward, followed by Nell, Christopher and the army. About thirty werwulfs broke away from the ranks and joined Devan at the front. Devan must have summoned his pack using their shared mind. The move made sense. They needed their strongest troops at the vanguard.

CHAPTER 30

Nell looked around at the towering, brutal werwulfs walking in step with her. She suddenly felt a lot more confident.

They walked past Sacra di San Michele and headed towards the Tower of the Beautiful Alda.

The werwulfs suddenly stopped in their tracks.

Standing in front of them at the base of the ruined sandstone tower were the Crimson Claws. The robed figures stood at the front while a sea of vampires stood behind them. Rows upon rows. There had to be hundreds of them. At least twice the number that Nell had behind her. She swallowed hard. A leftover human reflex. The odds were not in their favor, considering how vicious and strong the Crimson Claws were.

Nell scanned the assembled horde with her sharp vision. No sign of Zachariah. She thought about Klaus again, then the prophecy. Was he fulfilling his pre-ordained role? The vision of Klaus flashed into her mind again. She fought to cast it out of her head. No point dwelling on things she had absolutely no control over.

All the werwulfs moved to the front now, forming a mass of feral bodies. They crouched low, ready to attack. A deep growl emanated from every throat. Nell's heart was in her mouth as she waited for something to happen. Behind her, Hunters and vampires stood in formation. Poised.

Nell looked to Christopher, who stared back at her with a concerned look. She remembered that his blood was an antidote. But that fact was of little use now. It was a weapon that they could not use. She missed Sanya more than ever at that moment.

The only way out of this was to fight. Fleeing wasn't an option. She looked around her. No one seemed to be in the mood to back down, anyway. Faces were set, weapons were drawn. This was only going one way. She thought of Klaus again, then out of nowhere her thoughts landed on her Aunt Laura. A pang of sorrow convulsed her. But now wasn't the time to get emotional. Now was the time to fight for everything she believed in.

The robed figures in front of Crimson Claws suddenly moved off to the side and the crowd of vampires surged forward like a tidal wave. They were completely in step with each other, with identical expressions of wrath etched on their faces. The wave of vampires broke against the werwulfs, who were ready for the attack. They used their teeth, claws and powerful limbs to rip, slash, tear and bite. The Crimsons screamed in fury and anguish while the werwulfs growled and howled as they ripped heads from bodies, but also sustained injuries.

The werwulfs had formed a first wall of defense, but the Crimson Claws were starting to break through in places. Haiden and Ezra sprang into action, picking off the intruders. They were joined by the other Hunters. Scythes, axes and short-swords swung through the air. Heads were lopped cleanly off charging vampires. A cloud of dark ash hung in the air as flesh dissolved. Nell's side was doing most of the damage, but she knew it wouldn't last.

Her premonition came true only moments later when greater numbers began breaking through the ranks of the werwulfs. They charged at the Hunters, who began to fall, their weapons flailing in the air impotently. The Crimsons landed on their bodies, pinning them down, before leaning down and ripping at their necks. Screams, shouts and howls echoed into the air. Nell saw at least ten werwulfs lying unmoving on the ground in front of her. Two Hunters screamed in agony as

CHAPTER 30

Crimson Claws ripped and tore at their necks. Their screams eventually died, along with the Hunters.

Now the vampires joined the fray, charging at the Crimsons who had the Hunters pinned down. They threw themselves at the Crimsons, knocking them to the ground before raining down a barrage of blows. Two to three vampires targeted each of the Crimsons. They had been told to attack in groups, as they would be overpowered in one-on-one combat. So far it was working. The vampires had managed to save a number of Hunters, who had regained their feet and joined the melee once again, their weapons arcing through the air.

But quickly the battle descended into absolute chaos. The sheer number of Crimson Claws meant that the werwulfs and Hunters couldn't contain them. Amara's carefully formulated battle plan was rendered obsolete by the savage reality on the ground. It was now a free-for-all with werwulfs, Hunters and vampires spread haphazardly in the shadow of the Tower of the Beautiful Alda. All were fighting desperately to stay alive and hoping to inflict some damage on the enemy.

Nell had lost sight of Christopher and Devan, as well as Haiden and Ezra. In the midst of a battle raging as fiercely as this one, the only thing you could do was watch out for yourself. Things were happening too quickly to take account of others.

Crimson Claws threw themselves at Nell with no regard for their own preservation. She fought with all the strength and skill she had. Biting, ripping, tearing, punching, kicking, doing everything she possibly could to stave off the relentless attack. But for every Crimson Claw she was able to fend off, three more joined the fray.

Nell looked around her frantically. Once mighty werwulfs

lay bloodied and broken on the unforgiving earth. Hunters with their necks ripped, torn and bent at horrible angles were still and silent on the ground. Vampires were being picked off systematically. The group formations had fallen apart and now the vampires fought alone against a far stronger enemy. Clusters of thick dark ash cascaded through the air and littered the ground.

Everything became a blur. Nell redoubled her efforts. She ripped limbs from bodies, tore out insides with her bare hands and beheaded as many Crimson Claws as she could with the Hunter weapons that lay scattered on the ground. Their owners would never need them again.

And still the Crimsons came. Wave after wave after relentless wave.

This would be a fight to the death. Of that Nell was certain. Previously this realization would have broken her. But now, in the frantic rush of battle, she felt oddly serene. The way ahead had narrowed down to just one path. Take down as many Crimson Claws as possible before meeting her end. She owed that to the world for helping to unleash this dark plague. She owed her last nerve, sinew and all of her remaining strength to mankind. To her family. Images flashed in her mind of her mother, father, Aunt Laura, Christopher, Devan, Amara.

Three Crimsons Claws charged towards her. Nell crouched down ready to fight. If this was to be her last moment on Earth, she was going to make it count.

The vampires closed in on her in a flash. Nell threw a punch at the closest one. But before her fist made contact with the Crimson Claw, he staggered backwards as though he'd already been hit. Nell noticed the other two Crimsons stumbling back as well. It was as if they had come up against an invisible

CHAPTER 30

barrier just in front of her.

Nell quickly scanned the battlefield. Something wasn't right. The Crimsons Claws were silent. Silent and completely stationary, as if they had been frozen in place. The werwulfs, Hunters and vampires looked on incredulously. They didn't attack right away, in case this was some kind of ploy by the enemy. No one could make sense of what was happening.

Then the Crimson Claws spoke with one voice. An all too familiar one.

"Enough," they screamed with fury. "This ends now."

Moments later they collapsed onto the ground, clutching at their throats.

"Do what you must, traitor," they chorused, now with pained, raspy voices. "But know that I never loved you, Klaus. You were always worthless."

A Hunter seized his opportunity and swung his axe at the prone Crimson Claw in front of him. The head came off cleanly. The body began to disintegrate into ash.

Other Hunters moved forward, weapons raised.

"NOOO!" screamed Nell, at the top of her voice. "Stand your ground, but do not attack."

Hunters, vampires and werwulfs turned to look at her with utter bewilderment. This was their chance to vanquish their enemy. To end it. Yet Nell was telling them to hold back.

"Please trust me," shouted Nell, looking around beseechingly.

Nell cast her mind back to the encounter with the Crimson Claws at Mount Vesuvius. The female vampire, Bernadette, was able to be saved. Nell scanned her surroundings. She studied the Crimson Claws lying on the ground. These were all people once. Individuals with lives and families. It was so easy to view the Crimson Claws as a mass of evil. But they were innocents in reality. Changed, twisted and corrupted by the one who was speaking through them now.

"I'm glad you're the one to kill me, Klaus," they all chorused. "Because it will haunt you for the rest of your life. I know you hate me, but you will never stop loving me."

The assembled army looked on in astonishment as the words poured from the vampires. Nell was suddenly more certain she had made the right decision. Klaus was on the verge of ending Zachariah, it appeared. The prophecy was being fulfilled. Destiny was asserting itself.

"I gave you life, Klaus," the fallen Crimsons implored in unison. "I gave you Family. You are like me in ways you will never truly understand. You are kin, Klaus…and she will find you."

Zachariah, through his hundreds of minions, went on to explain how Klaus was his direct ancestor. The revelation stunned Nell. Yet the words spewed on, laced with hate, regret and venom. Fitting emotions for Zachariah, Nell thought.

"You have been the ruin of my Family and a bane upon our noble line," screamed the Crimsons. "You are the one who is a living curse."

Then nothing. Silence. Stillness. Were they dead? Was Zachariah dead? Klaus? Nell had no answers.

Nell took in the bizarre scene around her. In the far distance she spotted Christopher. Her heart suddenly lifted. She studied his face. It was bruised and bloody, but he was alive. He was alive! Christopher looked around, confusion etched on his face. Their eyes met. He looked overjoyed to see her, then they both shrugged, shaking their heads.

The Crimsons began moaning. Some cried out in pain from

their wounds. Others just cried. The connection to Zachariah seemed to have been broken. They were no longer one entity.

Nell spotted black robes dotted across the field. These were all that remained of Zachariah's former brethren. The original Red Claws. It seemed that their blood connection to Zachariah had reduced them to ash the moment his existence ended. At least that was what Nell surmised. She couldn't be completely sure of anything right now.

Some of the Crimsons sat up, dazed and disoriented. They looked around with bafflement. Many screamed on seeing the werwulfs standing over them. Others recoiled from the black-clad Hunters holding their deadly weapons aloft. The anger and rage had left them. They looked vulnerable, scared and all too human.

Nell felt a wave of relief wash over her. The Crimson Claws didn't need to be defeated, because there were no Crimson Claws any more.

Chapter 31

Klaus laid his head back against the white stone wall.

He surveyed the black robe on the ground, littered with ash that had once been the flesh of his former master.

Various emotions churned within him. Elation, sorrow, regret, horror, relief. Plus a host of more hard-to-define feelings. It was a heady mix that overwhelmed him.

He averted his eyes to the ceiling and took a series of deep breaths. He noticed that his breathing was becoming labored. Each inhalation rasped in his throat. He began to feel lightheaded. His body wasn't getting the oxygen it needed.

Klaus began clutching at his throat, trying desperately to get enough air. Panic overcame him. He was dying.

That was a bleak irony. By killing Zachariah, his creator, Klaus had signed his own death warrant. However much he tried to renounce his past, the fact remained that he had been a Red Claw, turned by Zachariah himself. His former master had used Nell's blood to link his family, old and new, to him. To speak with his voice. To see through their eyes. Zachariah's brother Damien must have had a hand in it, thought Klaus. He was a Magister with deep knowledge of the arcane.

Fate had been cruel to Klaus in so many ways. Yet he had played his part. Reluctantly. Begrudgingly. With an indignant

CHAPTER 31

scowl on his all-too-human face. The prophecy said that the Red Claws would be defeated. While Klaus had escaped from his past in so many ways, in other ways he was trapped in time. He would die alone in this bare room.

His breaths became excruciatingly difficult. He was sinking deeper into the void.

For the first time in his quickly diminishing life, Klaus prayed. He wasn't sure if there was a God out there, especially one who would listen to a tainted soul such as himself, but he had to try. There was nothing left to lose. He couldn't speak the words, so sent them out in thought:

Dear God, please let what I have done be enough. That this will be over. That my death will mean something. I pray that my Loris is safe in your care and that I may join him. Or, at the very least, let him know he was loved. I don't deserve your favor and don't expect it but, if it means anything, I truly repent for all the pain I have caused in this life...

Klaus toppled forward onto the robe that had belonged to the vampire he both loved and despised. He stretched out a hand with what remained of his strength.

A fingertip darkened, then tuned to ash. Followed by the whole finger. Then the entire hand. Soon nothing remained but ashes and dust.

Klaus was gone.

Chapter 32

"Klaus!" Nell yelled in a moment of clarity, peeling herself from Christopher. "We have to find him." The vision on the plane suddenly accosted her again.

She had been too preoccupied by grim and equally bizarre scenes on the field of battle. Werwulfs and Hunters lay dead and wounded while piles of ash were scattered across the hard earth. The dark material served as the only reminder of the vampires that once battled to help save humanity and those they fought. Then there were the humans who suddenly found themselves in a field in the shadow of an ancient tower. They had no idea how they got there and were fearful of the strange creatures that were trying to help them.

Christopher, Devan and Haiden had survived the battle, along with Lupertico. But all were bloodied and bruised. Haiden would have a fresh batch of scars to add to his already impressive collection. Devan was limping, while Christopher had deep lacerations criss-crossing his face. But in time they would disappear as his healing ability regenerated his flesh.

Ezra, the huge Hunter, wasn't so lucky. He hadn't made it after he was ambushed by a group of Crimson Claws. Nell made a point of not viewing the body. It would have been too painful. She left it to Haiden to show him the final respects he

CHAPTER 32

deserved.

Ezra was gone, but they still had a chance to help Klaus.

"The monastery," said Nell, urgently, nudging Christopher.

She sped off towards Sacra di San Michele, followed by Christopher. They forced open the imposing wooden doors and hurried inside.

"Klaus…Klaus," Nell shouted.

Her voice echoed around the cavernous interior.

No response.

Arches led off in various directions. Rows of pews were lined in the center of the floor. There was no sign of him.

Nell spotted a small set of concrete steps that led up to a simple wooden door. She raced up the stairs and flung the door open before charging into the room beyond. The walls were made of white stone and a small circular window was placed high up in the far wall. Her blood ran cold. She'd seen this place before, in Sanya's harrowing execution video.

She looked around frantically then spotted the heap of clothes on the floor. Green combat fatigues sitting atop a black robe. The garments were covered in thick, dark ash. She instinctively knew who both sets of clothes belonged to.

Christopher approached behind her and placed a hand on her shoulder. Nell went down on her knees. The strength seemed to have left her legs. She stared wide-eyed at the discarded heap of clothes.

Christopher knelt beside her, placing his hand on her shoulder again.

"He's gone," whispered Nell. "He's gone."

She thought about her Aunt Laura again. Was this the price Klaus had to pay for taking her away? Had the scales of justice rebalanced? No. Nell had already forgiven him. She knew he'd been brainwashed during his time with the Red Claws.

Nell's throat hitched and she stumbled backwards. Christopher caught her.

"On the plane, when I touched his hand," said Nell. "I saw him opening a glass vial and drinking blood. My blood. I was sure of it. Then a barrage of sounds and feelings assaulted my brain. I had to let go of his hand, break the connection, or I would have gone crazy. I had no idea what to make of it. It was just so weird, but it didn't seem to bode well."

"He did his part, however he did it," said Christopher. "We couldn't have asked any more from him."

Nell reached out and placed a hand on the pile of clothes.

"I'm so sorry, Klaus," she said. "It shouldn't have been this way, but we'll forever be in your debt. Forgive us."

"I don't think there was anything we could have done," said Christopher. "That prophecy had to play out the way it was intended. And as selfish as it sounds, I'm just glad it wasn't about us."

He paused for a long moment before continuing.

"But who would have thought that the chosen one was himself a Red Claw."

Chapter 33

The news reports kept flooding in.

Amara sat beside Haiden on the large ornate sofa. The once-rich ochre fabric had faded over time and was threadbare in patches. Sitting opposite them on an equally huge and time-worn sofa were Nell and Christopher. All eyes were glued to the flickering TV set, which was at least ten years out of date. But it did the job.

The videos from all over the world were as eerie as they were bizarre. They showed what looked like random people in the streets suddenly staggering backwards as if they'd bumped into a wall of glass. They looked shocked for a few moments before screaming something and collapsing to the ground, clutching at their necks.

The TV set was showing phone footage from a street in Girona in Spain. Four figures lay on the cobbled streets of the old town, surrounded by shocked tourists and the distinctive tall buildings made from rectangular stone blocks. They began screaming in a strange voice, as if possessed. Two of the fallen were women, yet they spoke with the same venomous male voice.

"Do what you must, traitor," they chorused, in raspy tones. "But know that I never loved you, Klaus. You were always worthless."

People on the street looked on in confusion as the prone figures continued to shout what sounded like utter nonsense.

With the final scream of "You are the one who is a living curse", the figures went silent and remained perfectly still. Seconds later they seemed to awake from a dream, looking around in confusion. They padded their own bodies before taking in their surroundings, seemingly for the first time.

This same scene was repeated all over the world, simultaneously. At first, the 'event' was blamed on a global psychosis or shared mental breakdown. Then rumors swirled of chemical warfare using neurotoxins. Other theories included hostile nano-tech that could seize control of the nervous system or electric pulse waves that could disrupt the neocortex.

It wasn't until Zulima Vargas from the United States vampire Council of Elders issued a video statement that the truth was revealed. The world learnt that the victims were in fact dormant Crimson Claws hiding in plain sight. The sudden episodes were brought on through a blood link with their leader. Zachariah had used the connection to control his minions but, in his heightened state with death imminent, it switched on of its own accord. As a result, millions of his slaves around the world simultaneously broadcast his final moments. To the public, the explanation was even more astounding than nano-tech or electric pulse waves.

Amara turned the sound down on the blocky remote control and turned to her friends.

"If only Klaus knew he had saved the world, I bet even he would crack a smile," she said.

Nell wasn't ready for humor. It was too soon.

"I wonder what he was feeling in those final moments," she

said, somberly. "He must have felt so alone."

Amara considered this, then let out a long breath.

"I think it played out the way it was meant to, Nell," she said. "The prophecy, at least from what I can gather, says that it would come down to a battle between light and dark, embodied by two vampires. Yes, the future of the world was at stake, and yet it was also a very personal fight. Between Klaus and Zachariah. But also within Klaus, I believe. He had to fight his past, his own nature, to become something new."

"Then make the ultimate sacrifice," added Haiden. "After all that."

Amara looked at him sharply.

The room remained silent. Amara pondered the prophecy, which she had dedicated to memory after spending so long studying it.

When the multitudes disperse across the hemispheres, the seeds of darkness will be relegated to the shadows. They will live by rules unwritten, designed only to keep them behind the veil. One brood will ascend into the new dawn. This Family is the obsidian, representing replete darkness. Its proliferation will herald the end of all things. For darkness must exist in shadow.

The obsidian faction will spread like a disease, growing vast enough to engulf all that is. The seeds of darkness will struggle but fail to tame the affliction. A war will rage and devastate the landscape. Creatures of the night will come together to fight as one. Unlikely allegiances will be forged. They will be tested. They will be sacrificed. They will be broken. Creation teeters on a perilous balance between light and dark.

Salvation lies in one soul. A death-walker turned young. One of tainted blood. He will endure a betrayal, a loss and an awakening.

He will love, as no other of his kin has before. He will abandon those he serves. He will develop abilities unknown while reverting to the origin. These abilities can corrupt and besiege, for they stem from the transmutation of loss, the most powerful emotion. He must drain the one he loves, filling his essence and ending theirs. This act alone brings forth the genesis.

Yet the Eminence of abominations will rise again. Out of light comes darkness, out of darkness comes light. Out of love comes hate. The blood of destruction. The blood of creation. A new Family is born. Tainted blood will clash in the final apocalypse.

Blood connects all. Blood is the liberator. Blood is the destroyer. Blood is the answer.

Certain phrases stood out in Amara's mind as she silently recited the words to herself. They seemed to tell the story of Klaus. Yet other parts left her with a lingering feeling of unease, particularly the ending. She had a feeling that nothing was simple and straightforward when it came to ancient vampiric prophecies.

The quiet contemplation of the room was interrupted when Christopher stood up.

"I think it's time," he said, looking around the room.

The three others nodded and also took to their feet. Nell made her way over to a dark mahogany side-table where a small gold urn was resting. She picked the container up delicately and cradled it like a new-born baby.

Amara watched her walk gingerly out of the room. The three of them followed in solemn silence. This had been Nell's idea. She wanted to give Klaus an honorable send off. It was the least he deserved, she felt. Klaus's ashes had been collected from atop his clothes at the monastery in Turin and brought

CHAPTER 33

here to the mansion on the outskirts of Angel Falls. The place Klaus had called home for a time.

Although she didn't draw attention to the fact, Amara knew that some of Zachariah's ashes had to be in the urn. Both vampires had died in the same spot. It would have been impossible to discern which ashes belonged to whom when they were collected. But it didn't really matter, she concluded. This was a symbolic gesture.

The four of them made their way out of the house, along the gravel path and through the imposing iron gates. They then followed the perimeter of the house until they were standing in the lush woods directly behind the property. Nell still led the way.

Amara took a good look at her friend, moving slowly and serenely through the brush and foliage into the trees beyond. Amara knew that Nell felt wracked by guilt. For Loris. For Sanya. For Ezra. For Klaus. For the thousands upon thousands of innocent human casualties who found themselves at the sharp end of Zachariah's maniacal plan. For everyone who had perished in the war. It was her blood that helped create the Crimson army. Her blood that Zachariah and his brother Damien discovered they could use to empower them. Her fateful decision to flee Vhik'h-Tal-Eskemon in the dead of night would haunt her for all eternity.

Amara wished that there was something she could do to stop Nell from carrying the weight of the world on her shoulders. But she knew that her words did little to soothe Nell's soul. Her wounds ran too deep. Amara had told Nell that the prophecy would likely have played out whether or not she had fled from the vampire headquarters. Amara was sure of it. She recalled the words of the Magister Jiangshina: *'These prophecies have an uncanny way of making their way into the world, despite any efforts to the contrary'.*

Now here they were at the end. But the final victory was bittersweet. It came at too high a price. How did you celebrate? How did you mark the end of violence when you had lost so much in the fight? Despite being a lifelong seeker of knowledge, Amara had no answers.

The four friends traversed the woodland for about twenty minutes until they came to a clearing. A narrow stream babbled with clear water and ran off into the distance. Surrounding it were a variety of yellow and purple wildflowers. The long branches of red maple trees formed a natural scarlet canopy overhead. Red leaves carpeted the ground around them.

"Here," said Nell, stopping. "This spot."

"Good choice," agreed Amara, taking in the natural beauty of the surroundings. "It's lovely."

"I'm sure Klaus would have been enchanted by it," said Haiden, with more than a hint of irony.

They decided to let the comment pass.

Nell knelt down and held the urn over the gentle running water. The other three joined her on the ground, forming a huddle. Nell gently unscrewed the lid of the urn. Her hands trembled slightly.

"Thank you, Klaus," she said, addressing the urn. "For all the sacrifices you had to make. For giving up the life you should have had. For turning our world away from darkness." Tears began to run down her face. "I forgive you. That's something I never had the chance to tell you in life." Amara knew she was thinking of her Aunt Laura. "There's no hatred left in my heart for you, Klaus," Nell continued. "You were a lost soul, but you finally found your true family in us."

Nell looked at her friends. Amara was the next to speak.

"Klaus was one of the bravest souls I know," said the librarian. "What we asked was too great, yet he did not hesitate when the time came. He met death as he met life. Unbowed. Unyielding." Her eyes were wet with emotion. "I hope Loris has found you, old friend, and you once again find the love and belonging that you so craved in life."

Amara glanced at Christopher, who looked a little surprised. He evidently wasn't expecting to take part in the eulogy.

"Farewell, Klaus," he said simply.

The others kept staring at him. He had to think on his feet.

"You taught me that nobody is beyond redemption," he added, after a long pause. "You taught me about forgiveness and what it means to fight every day to be better. For that I will always be grateful."

Christopher quickly looked at Haiden, hoping to pass the metaphorical microphone.

"Klaus, buddy," said Haiden. "You'd probably tell us to pull ourselves together and stop with the sentimental crap if you were here. So it's probably good that you're not."

Amara gave him a sharp look.

"Not that I'm glad you're dead," he quickly continued.

Now Nell gave him a piercing glance. There was a hint of a smirk on Christopher's face.

"What I mean to say," added the hunter. "Is that though you were stubborn, aloof and gruff in life…"

Amara raised her eyebrows.

"…underneath there beat a tender heart. You seemed to be out of step with the world. I hope you can find your footing in the afterlife…"

"That's, umm, lovely, Haiden," injected Amara, before he could place his foot any further down his own mouth. "Thank you."

Haiden got the message.

"Nell," said Amara, gently.

Nell nodded then slowly tipped the urn on its side. The ashes poured out. Most of it was carried away by the running water. The finer dust dissipated in the wind. Some of it landed on the earth around the stream.

Earth, wind and water, mused Amara. Essential elements of the planet. A planet which Klaus had saved.

Chapter 34

When Devan caught sight of Lupita his heart began racing. He quickened his pace, charging towards her on his powerful four legs. He closed the distance in no time and then shifted into his human form. He didn't care at all that he was stark naked. Among the wolf people, that sort of thing mattered little.

Lupita took him in with her large hazel eyes before opening her arms. Devan collapsed into her embrace, burying his face in her neck and inhaling her earthy, sweet scent.

"God, I missed you," he breathed, his arms slipping tightly around her upper body.

It took all his self-control not to break down in her arms. He had so longed for this moment. The thought of it had sustained him throughout the grueling mission in Italy. Devan suddenly noticed that her belly was flat as he pressed against her. Even he could work out what that meant. Devan pulled back, staring into Lupita's smiling face.

"Where is he?" he asked, urgently.

Lupita's eyes crinkled at the corners as she smiled. Devan noticed the faint bags under her eyes. Tell-tale signs that she was a new mother.

"She," Lupita said. "You have a baby girl."

At the words, Devan fell against Lupita, allowing himself to be enveloped in her arms once more. All the worries of the world fell away from him in that moment. It felt like shedding a heavy suit of armor.

"I have a baby girl," Devan said, more to himself. He felt tears spring to his eyes. "Did you name her?"

Lupita looked a little wary at the question. She hesitated slightly before answering.

"Well…of course, nothing is official yet," she began. "I didn't want to set anything in stone without your input. But, well, we've been calling her…Leona."

Devan felt his knees go weak. His heart skipped a beat and he forgot to breathe. Leona. His mother's name. Lupita had named the baby after his mother. A wave of love flooded through him for all three ladies. One of them being a very little lady.

Lupita appeared worried by Devan's reaction. The fact that he hadn't taken a breath didn't help.

"Of course…" she began, "…it was just an idea…we can always…"

"It's perfect," said Devan. "It's absolutely perfect. You couldn't have chosen a better name. Thank you."

Lupita beamed before taking Devan's hand and leading him through the trees. She took him to a large clearing where a sizable log cabin stood. It was rudimentary but sturdy, with a pitched roof and stairs leading up to the entrance.

For the first time, Devan noticed other people. They watched him warily. A man in plain overalls was collecting branches to the side of the building while a woman wearing a simple cloth tunic carried a large jug of water up the stairs. Devan suddenly felt self-conscious in his nakedness.

Three small children burst out of the hut and raced down

the stairs. The woman was almost knocked over. She cursed as some of the water sloshed to the ground. The kids, two girls and a boy who looked to be between three and five, chased each other around the perimeter of the cabin, laughing and screaming. They were completely naked and barefoot. Devan could hear more than one baby crying from inside the cabin. He remembered that children were reared collectively in a pack. It was a community effort to nurture young ones until they were ready for the change.

Lupita led the way up the rickety stairs and pushed the door open. The interior was basic, to say the least. A large dining table sat in the center of the space surrounded by unmatching chairs honed from wild trees. Rudimentary cots and small beds lined one wall, while shelves containing pans and an array of utensils adorned another. The woman with the jug was emptying the water into a large pot that sat atop a primus stove. Steam rose from the pot as she poured in the water.

Lupita grabbed some clothes from a pile on a shelf and handed them to Devan. He quickly dressed in a rough cloth shirt and worn denim pants.

Devan's eyes were drawn to one of the cots. Standing beside it was an old man with a stooped posture. He bent down and picked up a baby from the cot and slowly approached Devan and Lupita. The man had thick white eyebrows that grew wild, dark skin like worn leather and strands of white hair sprouting in various directions on his mostly bald head. He shuffled across the uneven floor slowly and carefully. Both because he was carrying a baby and on account of his advancing years.

As he approached, Devan sensed who he was. This was the first time Devan had seen him in human form.

"Lupertico!" said Devan, his eyes wide as he took in both

man and baby.

"Hello, son," said Lupertico, looking slightly abashed. "I think I shape up better as a wolf than a human," he added, noticing Devan's lingering gaze.

Devan was too polite to share his opinion.

"I have something for you," said Lupertico, handing the bundle to Devan.

Devan stood there frozen, not daring to move. Not even daring to breathe. He simply stared down at the little life in his arms. His body felt hot and cold at the same time. He was both elated and scared rigid. He took in his daughter's soft skin, wisps of brown hair, closed eyelids, button nose, full lips, chubby cheeks, angled chin. He drank her in, transfixed by every part of her as his eyes glided over her tiny form.

He reached out a hand and stroked her cheek with his finger, so lightly he could barely feel her skin against his own. He was scared he might break her. Leona's eyelids suddenly fluttered open to reveal deep brown eyes, flecked with gold. Exactly like the lady she was named after. Devan was in love instantly.

"Hey," Devan whispered to her gently. "I'm your daddy."

Leona's eyes widened as she studied the new face peering down at her. She didn't appear upset at the sight of the stranger.

"Sorry I wasn't there when you arrived," soothed Devan. "But I'm never going to leave you."

Devan gently rocked his daughter back and forth. He felt like his heart might explode. He never knew that such a pure love existed.

"Don't make promises you can't keep," said Lupertico, jovially. "The world might need saving again."

Devan noticed Lupita stiffening. Her smile faded a little.

CHAPTER 34

"The world will have to cope without me," he said.

He spent the next few hours refusing to put his daughter down, much to Lupita's alternating exasperation and delight. Devan finally gave in when it was time for her nap. Lupita showed him how to swaddle Leona in a tight package so that she felt safe as she slept. It took a few attempts but Devan finally managed it and, reluctantly, placed his baby in the crib. Even then he studied her as she slept, hypnotized by the rhythm of her breaths and the rise and fall of her little chest.

"Let's go and sit outside so we don't disturb her," Lupita said, quietly.

It was hard for Devan to leave his daughter's side. He felt a magnetic pull towards her. In the end Lupita had to grab his hand and drag him away. A few moments later they were sitting on the wobbly steps outside the cabin. The sun had sunk low in the sky. It occasionally pierced through the gaps in the trees, forcing them both to shield their eyes.

Devan nudged up close to Lupita, so their shoulders were touching. Then he took her hands in his.

"We have things to talk about, Devan," Lupita said, looking at him.

The bottom suddenly fell out of his world. His stomach lurched. He dreaded what might be coming next after the bliss of meeting his daughter. He hated the thought that this all could be snatched away from him. The way that his mother was snatched away from him. He wanted so much to give this new life his best shot. For Leona to grow up with two parents who adored her, and loved each other...or so he hoped.

"We can't just pretend that nothing happened," Lupita continued, somberly.

She squeezed his hand. But Devan couldn't look at her. Tears stung his eyes. He felt like his entire life was hanging in the balance. Lupita reached up and gently placed her hand on his chin before slowly turning his head to face her. She studied his pained expression and seemed to come to a decision.

"I don't blame you anymore," Lupita breathed, piercing him with her clear hazel eyes.

The tears ran down Devan's cheek. There was no holding back now.

"I don't blame you," she repeated. "For Lupo. You did the best you could. We all did. I was wrong to blame you for what happened to my brother." Lupita choked as she said 'brother'.

Devan squeezed her hands.

"I'm sorry for everything, Lupita," he said. "I truly am. More than you could ever know. You and Leona mean absolutely everything to me, so much so that it hurts." The words came flooding out of him. "I will do everything I can, every single day for the rest of my life, to show you both that you mean the world to me. You are the bravest, kindest and most beautiful soul I know, Lupita. I don't want to live without you, or my baby."

She leaned over and gently kissed him on the lips. It was the best answer he could have hoped for. Words be damned.

"We can do this, can't we?" Lupita said, turning to stare at the fading sun.

"Do what?" Devan asked, wrapping an arm around her shoulder.

"Be normal parents, without any of that other crazy stuff," Lupita replied. She suddenly turned to face him. Concern was etched on her face. "But what if we don't know how to be normal together? We've only ever been joined in war, Devan.

CHAPTER 34

What if you find you don't like a boring, mundane life? What if you want to go back to hunting…to fighting?" Lupita's voice shook.

Devan could tell she was expressing her deepest fear.

"I will *never* leave you," he said. "You and our baby are my life now, and I can't tell you how good boring sounds right about now."

Lupita smiled. This time Devan leaned in and kissed her. Deeply. Passionately. She responded in kind.

"I love you," he said, coming up for air momentarily.

She wrapped her hands around his face.

"I love you, too, dufus," she said. "Let's do this."

Chapter 35

Kavisha felt like she was banging her head against a brick wall.

She looked around at the somber faces assembled around the table.

Dragos Vacarescu, Speaker of the Council of Elders, was addressing the room. Kavisha studied the countless scars that criss-crossed his ancient face. His withered left arm hung impotently at his side.

The other three Council members looked on with rapt attention. Loshua Dascălu, Zulima Vargas and Shing-Lei Zan. Loris Valkari had sadly permanently vacated his seat while Gustav Nielsen was apparently taking care of a matter of the utmost urgency.

"She served her purpose in extenuating circumstances," explained Dragos, pointing with his one good hand at the High Chancellor. "But now she has to be removed. Immediately. Her continued presence on our highest body is an affront to our kind. Immortals will tolerate bowing down to a mortal no longer."

"When were you ever asked to bow down to her?" Kavisha snapped back. She couldn't contain her anger. "Without Amara, would we be back sitting here in Vhik'h-Tal-Eskemon with the Crimson Claw threat behind us?" She looked around at the assembled faces. "It was Amara that helped forge the aliases that proved so vital, she who formulated the attack strategy, she who served as a bridge with the humans."

"She is not of our blood," protested the Speaker. "This is not our way."

Kavisha banged a fist on the table.

"And where did the old ways get us, Dragos?" she demanded. "It was only recently that you yourself warned that we faced being eradicated by the *nocturnae hostium*. But an understanding has been reached with the Hunters, as with the humans, thanks to the 'mortal'."

"And what kind of perverse understanding is this?" argued Dragos. "The librarian went behind our backs to sell us out to the humans. We are now to become their pets?"

Kavisha exhaled sharply.

"Amara did no such thing," she said, trying to maintain some degree of composure. "She only engaged with the humans to explore a way for us to co-exist without the need for killing. The humans have far superior scientific capabilities than us. They are able to synthesize blood plasma. From what Amara has told me, it has all the requisite ingredients needed to sustain us. Proteins, sugars, albumin, enzymes. It means we don't have to take lives indiscriminately."

"So we must live like slaves now, feeding on their unholy mush like farm animals!" Dragos was almost screaming. "We have become the cattle, now? Once-proud immortals are to become subdued livestock while the humans have the whip hand?"

"That is not the intent," replied Kavisha, feeling exasperated. "And nothing has been agreed upon."

"This is not our way, High Chancellor," said Zulima Vargas,

in a far more measured tone than Dragos, yet bitterness still infused her words. She was a strikingly tall woman, even sitting down, with sleek long black hair that cascaded down her back. "We are predators, we are hunters, we are the shadows in the night," she continued. "We do not beg. We do not accept charity. Especially from mortals."

Loshua Dascălu and Shing-Lei Zan both nodded in agreement. Dragos, the oldest of the vampires who existed in a time when the undead had free reign over life and death, still looked like he was ready to explode.

Kavisha felt hopeless. The Council was sounding like the Crimson Claws. She had held out a small flicker of hope that things would change once the war was over. That a new dawn would emerge and the alliances forged under such turbulent conditions might endure. But it wasn't to be. Nothing seemed to have changed. The old ways of operating and thinking were firmly entrenched.

She wished Amara were by her side now. She could use the librarian's wise counsel. But in reality her presence here would only further antagonize the Council members. Kavisha felt trapped. She felt impotent. She felt threatened.

She looked around her. The faces remained angry and sullen. Yet anger also blossomed within Kavisha. Those gathered around this table had not participated in the war. They had not put their lives on the line. They had remained safely ensconced within this gothic fortress protected by its ancient talismans. They had claimed that they were taking care of administrative matters critical to the war effort. But Kavisha knew the truth. She knew they were hiding, ready to crawl out once the coast was clear to dictate how vampires must exist in the future. A future they risked nothing for.

CHAPTER 35

Amara, the mortal woman who they so scorned, berated and belittled, had spent her every waking moment fighting on their behalf. She had lost sleep, peace of mind and her life as she knew it. Kavisha knew that Amara would have gladly taken up arms if she was asked to. Yet here were these gutless immortals speaking about her as if she was worthless, lesser than them. It made her blood boil.

Kavisha felt like everything was spiraling out of her control. She recalled the premonition she had in Italy about her own mortality. At the time she had assumed that her demise would come at the hands of the Crimson Claws. Zachariah himself, most likely.

Her mind flashed back to their deal struck close to a century and a half ago. It was made in Caledonia, part of the Northeast Kingdom of Vermont. Wooden shanty houses lined the dirt tracks. The Red Claws had lain waste to the local populace. Kavisha and members of the Council had witnessed the carnage firsthand on the ground. Whole families slaughtered in their sparse homes. The Red Claws' rampage across the country appeared unstoppable.

Kavisha managed to send word to Zachariah. A meeting was held out in the open, underneath a waning crescent moon. Zachariah was arrogant and bloodthirsty, but he wasn't without a finely-honed instinct for self-preservation. He was looking for insurance. If there ever came a time when the ruling vampires he so disdained turned on the Red Claws, he wanted an assurance. That he and his Family would not be marked for death. The sanction imposed had to stop short of annihilation. In return, Kavisha also wanted a guarantee, sealed by a blood oath, that she and the Council would be spared from their killing spree. The terms were agreed and the accord was sealed.

Decades later when the Red Claws needed to be dealt with for the greater good, Kavisha had ordered they be placed in a forced sleep state for a century. Other councils had remonstrated with her to enforce a final solution. To eliminate the plague that was exposing their ilk to death by the Hunters. But Kavisha's hands were tied. An oath was an oath. It was a decision she had come to bitterly regret over the past year as she once again witnessed the carnage unleashed by Zachariah.

In Italy, Amara was sure that Zachariah would find a way to finish her. That she would be part of the toll he was exacting on the world. Now, looking around the table at the contemptuous faces of her so-called 'brethren', she had a feeling that the hand of fate would be dealt from much closer to home.

Chapter 36

The letter landed on Amara's doorstep about a week after she'd returned home to Angel Falls.

Her tiny one-bedroom apartment was a world away from the grandeur of Vhik'h-Tal-Eskemon. But home was where the books were, as far as Amara was concerned, and her flat was crammed with piles of paperbacks that she had loved and stacks more that she hadn't had the chance to read yet. That was one reason to envy immortality, she reflected. You had all the time in the world to catch-up on your reading list.

Amara sat on the plastic chair at the compact kitchen table, holding the sheet of paper. The letter was penned in a beautiful flowing script that was the polar opposite of Amara's uneven scrawl. She'd read the words over and over again, hearing the voice behind the writing.

My dear Amara,

I'm sorry that you've received this letter rather than hearing from me in person. I know I'm being a total coward, but I'm not ready to talk just yet.

First of all, don't worry. Christopher and I are safe. After what happened this past year, we decided to get away for a while. Actually, scrub the 'we', it was all my idea. I just couldn't face coming back and having to deal with the aftermath. I'm sorry for leaving it all to you and the others. Told you I was a total coward.

If truth be told, I'm not doing too well. I don't want to worry you, but I also don't want to lie to you. You deserve better. You've always deserved better from me.

Now that the immediate danger is over, my mind is constantly racing. I'm having to face up to everything that happened to me. Memories are coming back from my time with the Red Claws and, well, it hurts, Amara. It hurts deeply.

Christopher is trying his best to help me move on, but it's slow progress. I don't want you to see me like this or to become a burden to you. I know how you have a soft spot for lost causes, but I have already asked too much of you. We all have.

I won't hide forever. But for now, I need to stay away. I really hope you can understand. I will come back to you one day. Once I've defeated my demons, or at least found a way to keep them at bay. Until then I'll try to take each day as it comes.

I hope you and Haiden can do that, too. Just be you, two people in love, without the weight of the world on your shoulders. You deserve every good thing, Amara. I hope you are truly happy.

Please don't try to find me. I know you can be quite the detective when you put your mind to it. We'll be back when we're ready.

I love you and I'm sorry for dragging you into this. From that first moment in Angel Falls when you helped me start my car in the dead of night, you have been my personal angel, Amara.

I wish I was more like you. You are the smartest, strongest person I know.

See you soon(ish),
Nell (and Christopher) xxx

CHAPTER 36

Tears crept down Amara's face as she studied the letter. She cried for her friend, for the pain she was enduring. She cried for Ezra, Sanya, Loris, the young wolves, Aunt Laura. She cried for the senseless loss of life endured by the entire world.

She was torn from her sorrow by a knock at the front door. She quickly wiped her tears with the sleeve of her baggy pullover and took a few heaving breaths to compose herself before going to see who it was.

She opened the door to see a delivery driver, with his cap pulled low over his face. He was looking down at a clipboard.

"Amara Dalmar?" he asked, without looking up.

"Yes, that's me," she replied.

"Good," he snapped back, before throwing a palm into her chest.

Amara stumbled backwards along the passageway. The man quickly entered the apartment and shut the door behind him.

"Wh…What do you want," stuttered Amara.

The man took off his hat and glared at her. His skin was deathly pale. Sharp teeth protruded at the sides of his mouth. Amara had seen him before. She searched her memory for his name.

"Nielsen," she said, at last. "Gustav Nielsen. You're on the Council of Elders."

"Well, it appears to be true," he replied, regarding her imperiously. "Nothing gets past you, librarian." His sharp tone made the statement sound like an insult rather than a complement.

"You didn't answer my question," said Amara, keeping her distance.

"Your response to me is the answer to the question," he replied.

"You're not making any sense," said Amara.

"You think you can make demands of me?" spat Nielsen, angrily. "You think that we answer to you? A mortal. You have no authority to dictate rules that govern how we, your superiors, conduct our lives." He took a step forward, pointing a slender finger at her. "You think you can feed us ungodly false blood, poison us with your sacrilege…blasphemy…your desecration." Spittle flew from his mouth.

"But Kavisha…" began Amara.

"The High Chancellor is a fool," snapped Nielsen. "We kept quiet while the war was waged and, perhaps, you were of some little use in that endeavor."

Amara felt the heat of anger rising in her chest, but she kept her emotions in check.

"Who is this 'we' you talk about?" she asked. "How many others feel this way?"

"Do you not listen, mortal?" he admonished. "You are not in a position to ask anything of me. I do not serve you. Your impudence is galling."

"Then what do you want?" Amara replied, realizing too late that she just asked another question.

"Let me show you," the vampire replied before extracting a silver dagger from a pocket and moving towards her down the narrow hallway.

Amara turned and rushed into her living room. It was such a small space that she reached the far wall in only a few steps. Her back was pressed against wooden shelves containing rows of her precious books.

Nielsen crossed the threshold and took a step into the room, his dagger raised. A sneer was plastered on his face.

"Give my regards to that other interloper Klaus when…" he

CHAPTER 36

began.

Amara heard a whooshing sound as the scythe sliced through the air. Moments later Nielsen's head came rolling towards her. She kicked it away in disgust with the tip of a foot. The headless body crumpled to the floor as Haiden went over to Amara and embraced her. She buried her head in his chest.

"Well, that's one time I'm not annoyed my nap was interrupted," he said, rubbing her back.

They both turned to survey the room. A small pile of ash now lay where the head had come to a stop. The delivery uniform was covered in more of the dark material.

"He said 'we,'" informed Amara. "He's not the only one who wants me out of the picture."

"Makes sense," replied Haiden. "In a sick, twisted way, of course. No good deed ever went unpunished. Now that you served your purpose they want to go back to the old order, without the likes of us polluting their ranks."

"But that's ridiculous," said Amara. "The world has changed, irrevocably. Their secret is out. I thought that things would be better. That we'd all do better."

"It was a slim hope at best," mused Haiden. "They've had centuries upon centuries of being top dogs, at least in their own minds. That mentality can't be undone in an instant. Add in lashings of hubris, pride and a colossal superiority complex, and you get blood-suckers who don't want to play ball. Some things don't change, Amara. They just don't."

She looked up at him, not knowing what to say, but feeling her heart sink. She knew what was coming next.

"Just the essentials," he said, as if reading her mind. "We need to move light."

She nodded, reluctantly, taking a last look around her little home. She took in her books, pot plants and various knick-knacks. She thought about her life in Angel Falls. Stamping books for senior citizens and curating the volumes of titles in Henry Freeman Memorial. Then she recalled the exhilaration and iron-clad sense of purpose she felt while engaged in a battle against an undead army. Yes, it was dangerous. Yes, it was crazy. But she had never felt so alive.

Haiden cupped his hands around her face.

"I'll keep you safe," he said. "I promise. I won't let anyone hurt you."

Amara looked deep into his eyes. She might be losing her home and most of her worldly possessions, but she had Haiden and she had an open road ahead of her. That was a deal she would make every time.

Chapter 37

The streets of Paris were filled with a surprising number of undead.

Nell found herself checking for Crimson Claws in the faces of each one they passed. The usual etiquette when encountering another vampire was a quick knowing look or the subtlest of nods. Nell's lingering stares were putting the other vampires on edge. They looked spooked, as if their cover might be blown.

She knew it was a bad habit, but it was beyond her control. The part of her brain in charge of self-preservation was constantly scanning faces for that maniacal glazed look that indicated the vampires were in thrall of a hive mind. She knew it was ridiculous. Zachariah was dead. The Crimson Claws had been released from his blood Magick. They were human once more.

Nell had expected to feel light and free once she and Christopher were unburdened from the shackles of war. But nothing could be further from the truth. Instead, she felt like she was balancing on a tightrope, struggling not to fall off into a dark abyss.

Writing the letter to Amara had been tough. She had wanted to phone, but couldn't find the courage to talk to her friend. Amara's natural concern and sympathy would have felt overbearing. So, a letter with no return address was Nell's solution. At least the librarian would appreciate the written word, she reasoned. It was the weakest of justifications, but all she had.

It was tough enough to be open with Christopher about how she was feeling. The cloud of sadness, the shadow of physical pain, the nerves constantly on edge. They were all a reminder of what had happened. Now that the danger had passed, her subconscious was serving up more and more glimpses of her time in captivity. The torture. The humiliation. The blood-letting. The mockery. *Here, deal with it,* her brain seemed to be saying. *You can't keep it hidden in the dark recesses for eternity.*

Christopher never left her side. She knew he was scared that she would do something stupid. Something final. But she wouldn't. She could never do that to him. His love was keeping her going, helping her to face each new dawn.

They sat on a bench looking out across the River Seine. The water lapped gently against the banks. Christopher had taken her to galleries, museums and various historic sites across Paris. All the things she loved to do as a mortal. It was his attempt to distract her from her own mind. It worked to an extent, but she still found herself dwelling on her traumas.

"Hey, look over there," said Christopher, pointing to the Cathedral of Notre-Dame.

Nell glanced at the medieval facade of the historic building, but her focus quickly shifted to the deck of a barge sailing across the calm river. She noticed a young couple embracing by the railings. They looked so carefree and in love that it made Nell's heart ache. She reached out and grabbed Christopher's hand.

CHAPTER 37

"I'm sorry," she said, studying his face. "For being like this."

Christopher looked at her, gathering his thoughts.

"You've been through a lot, Nell," he said, squeezing her hand. "More than most go through in a lifetime. You have nothing to be sorry for."

He leaned over and pressed his lips against her forehead. Whenever he touched her, she felt a ripple of relief. His contact made her feel safe and supported. His body reminded her on a visceral, physical level that she had someone on her side. She had craved his affection more and more recently, as she sought respite from her spiraling thoughts. When Christopher's hands were on her, it was the only time that she felt truly at peace and in the moment.

"Let's go," Nell said, standing up abruptly and pulling on his hand.

Christopher arched his eyebrows and smiled. He knew where this was going, and he seemed more than happy to oblige.

Back at the hotel room, Nell shed her clothes the second the door closed behind her. Christopher sat on the edge of the king-size bed. He wrapped his arms around her waist as she approached him. He began peppering her stomach with light kisses. Then suddenly stopped. He just sat there staring at her. He then gently reached up and grabbed hold of her hips before slowly swiveling her around, so she stood sideways on. Again, he just stared at her. Silent.

Nell was just about to say something when he spoke.

"Ummm, Nell," he began.

"Yes," she said, annoyed by this point at his odd behavior, which was taking her out of the moment.

"Your stomach," he replied. Christopher's eyes flicked

upwards to meet her own. "It's…different."

Vampire bodies remained the same after they were turned. They were frozen in time. If they were damaged or injured, they would heal. Always reverting to the exact same state.

Nell peered down at her stomach. It protruded slightly. That was something new, she had to admit. It had always been perfectly flat, even as a human. More to do with her genes than diet and lifestyle.

She hurried to the full-length mirror fixed on a wardrobe, turning to her side to take a closer look at her figure. She ran a palm down from her chest over her stomach, then stepped closer to the mirror.

A current of shock ran down her spine all the way to the soles of her feet. She looked as if…as if she was… No, that wasn't impossible. Vampires couldn't bear children. The undead were turned, not born. She shifted her angle. Then once more. But there was no escaping the fact that her stomach was gently curving out.

She turned to Christopher. He stared at her wide eyed. Transfixed. She could tell that he was thinking the exact same thing as she was.

"I…can't be…can I?" Nell's voice shook as she turned back to the mirror.

"I don't…I mean I can't… No." Christopher said, finally coming to his senses. "No. It's not possible. We're technically dead. We can't create life. Especially in *that* way."

"But we're not exactly like the others," Nell said, tentatively. "Those things we can do…what if…"

"Come here," Christopher interjected. He held out his hands. Nell slowly walked towards him. He wrapped his arms around her once again and then placed an ear to her midsection.

CHAPTER 37

Nell remained perfectly still, just watching for his reaction. She knew his hearing was extra-sensitive. After a few moments he drew his head back and stared up at her open-mouthed. He seemed to have aged ten years in an instant, even though he would never grow older.

"I can hear it," he said, in barely a whisper.

"Hear what?" asked Nell, though a part of her knew the answer before Christopher spoke.

"A heartbeat."

Nell's mouth dropped open. Then the bottom fell out of her world. The room began to spin. Christopher had to catch her in his arms and place her on the bed.

After what seemed like an eternity, she finally regained the ability to speak.

"What the hell do we do?" she asked.

Christopher turned to look at her. He appeared dumbfounded.

"I don't have the first clue," he admitted.

Chapter 38

The primary maternal instinct kicked in. Protection. Nell felt the overwhelming need to safeguard this baby at all costs. They had to get away. Nell's brain, body and very soul was instructing her to flee to safety. To evade prying eyes, particularly those of the other vampires. Their situation was unique in the vampire world. To Nell, that meant unwanted attention, and unwanted attention meant danger.

After arguing for weeks about where to relocate, Nell and Christopher finally agreed on the northern tip of Scotland. After researching the area, they narrowed it down to the settlement of Scarfskerry on the north-east coast. The location was isolated, yet not too far from the major town of Thurso. The local population spoke English and were used to occasional tourists visiting to take in the natural beauty of the area. Nell and Christopher could pass for a couple of rich Yanks who wanted to take an extended sabbatical out in the unspoilt wilderness. Funds from the Vampire Council's unlimited reserves allowed them to travel quickly and relatively privately.

***

CHAPTER 38

The house stood alone on a large field of swaying wild grass. It was made of old stone and wood and looked like it had taken a battering from the elements over the years. Roof tiles were missing, the timbers were cracked in places and chunks of stone had fallen away from the square blocks flanking the dark wooden door. But the property had lasted this long, so it wasn't going anywhere. Plus, Nell and Christopher were on the outskirts of civilization. It didn't leave them with a wide range of options. This wasn't London or New York, where they could have chosen from thousands of rental homes simply by scrolling a phone app.

After making a few basic repairs, including patching up the roof, the place began to feel like a home. There was a lot more to be done, but they had plenty of time on their hands to fix it up. Perhaps an eternity. It was their own little hideaway from the rest of the world.

The two of them would take long walks along the windswept pebble beach, exploring the rocky coves and wild fauna that lined the coast. They could look out at the tiny island of Stroma and beyond it to the much larger Shetland Islands. They would occasionally wave at the boats carrying supplies to and from the islands.

For sustenance they had to rely on what nature could offer them. There was no way they could take human lives in an area so remote and unpopulated without it going noticed. Plus, Nell was repulsed at the thought of killing people, especially after the Crimson massacres and with a new life growing inside her body.

The blood from stray sheep was their staple. Locals stumbling across the carcasses would assume the sheep had been picked off by Scottish wildcats, which were a long-standing menace to the area's livestock. Most vampires would no doubt be repulsed at the thought of surviving off the blood of animals, but Nell couldn't care less. It was a price worth paying for the safety and isolation they enjoyed in Scarfskerry. Christopher didn't complain, but Nell had a suspicion that he was far less enamored with having to live off animal blood.

Yet in other ways, Christopher had taken to this austere, remote life with relative ease. It appeared he was in the grip of the nesting instinct as much as Nell. The pregnancy had brought out a new array of emotions in both of them. The sight of Nell's growing belly was a source of joy and fascination for Christopher. He would spend hours with his hand on her stomach, his eyes lighting up when he felt movement under the skin. She would beam back at him, placing her hand over his.

Most evenings were spent reading by the light of a log burning stove. They didn't need the stove to keep warm. Cold weather did not trouble the undead, but the glow of the dancing flames served to make the house warm in the sentimental sense. Christopher would make a weekly trip into Thurso to expand their growing library of books. Nell requested literature classics and supernatural thrillers, while he opted for graphic novels and music books. He even bought an old guitar from a charity shop and began playing again. Nell would sit mesmerized as his fingers flew across the strings, picking out intricate melodies. The stone walls of their small home made the music sound even more ethereal. Christopher still had that magic touch when it came to playing the guitar. He began writing nursery rhymes and lullabies for the baby, much to Nell's delight as he performed his new creations.

One evening Nell was sat by the fire as usual, spellbound

CHAPTER 38

by Christopher's playing, when there was a knock at the door. Christopher's fingers abruptly stopped strumming the strings. He looked at her. She stared back at him. They had never had a visitor before. The owner of the house lived in Germany and all communication took place via email.

No one from their old life knew they were here. Nell was more intrigued than worried about who it could be. She suddenly thought of the dead sheep. Perhaps it was a local farmer inquiring about their livestock. That seemed the most likely explanation. But there was only one way to know for sure. She gave a small nod to Christopher.

He carefully placed the guitar down before standing up and walking to the front door. Nell followed a step behind him. Security wasn't a primary concern in these parts. Christopher retracted the bolt from the latch then twisted the rusty round handle beneath it. The mechanism complained with a screech before the door opened.

Standing beyond the threshold was a figure in a long black robe. Their head was covered by the robe's hood. They were silhouetted by the orange glow of the setting sun behind them.

Nell jumped back and gasped. She remembered Zachariah's Family at the monastery in Turin. They were dressed in the same way. This was a Crimson Claw. Her heart leapt in her chest. They had come for her and Christopher...and the baby. The war wasn't over. More blood would be spilled. Starting with theirs.

Christopher blocked the door with his body and made a hissing sound from deep in his throat. An instinctive vampire warning cry. He crouched low, ready to spring. Nell could see the Crimson Claw in the space above his head. The robed figure suddenly reached up and swept the hood back, revealing their face.

Female. Oriental features. Flawless alabaster pale skin. Sleek jet-black hair pulled back. Recognition hit Nell.

"Angajamentul de neintervenție," said the visitor in a soft sing-song voice. She had just recited the Magister pledge of neutrality.

Jiangshina, Nell recalled. That was her name.

Christopher stood up straight again then turned back to look at Nell. She raised her eyebrows and opened her mouth, but didn't say anything.

"Angajamentul de neintervenție," repeated Christopher, turning back to the Magister. "How did you find us?" he asked, in a far more abrupt tone.

Nell's heart was hammering. She wanted the same information. Also to know what the Magister wanted. Nell's mind raced ahead of her. Was the war still raging? Did Zachariah somehow survive? Was the threat to humanity still alive? Was it about one of the others? Devan? Amara? Haiden? Kavisha?

"I cannot come in unless invited," said Jiangshina, softly.

"I know," replied Christopher, his tone anything but soft. His body still blocked the door.

Nell moved closer to him. She felt safer in the knowledge that the Magister could not enter the house unless expressly invited. She also didn't make any attempt to hide her bump. She had a strong feeling that her present condition was the reason why their peaceful evening had been interrupted.

"We are the watchers," said the lone Magister. "We are named such that we are the keepers of lore and heritage, we are among the…"

"Spare me the PR crap," interjected Christopher. "Just answer the damn question."

CHAPTER 38

A small sigh escaped Jiangshina's narrow lips.

"It is our duty to know, young Christopher," she said. A slight emphasis on the 'young'. "We watch. We chronicle. We monitor all..." She glanced at Nell's swollen stomach. "...anomalies."

"Then what do you want?" demanded Christopher, getting straight to the point

"I mean you no harm," said the Magister, calmly.

"That didn't answer the question," replied Christopher.

"Simply to impart some advice," said Jiangshina, her tone still amiable. "And to give you a choice."

Nell had a bad feeling about the final part of that statement. She moved closer to Christopher. He placed a protective arm around her.

"Be quick," said Christopher. "Then leave us."

"I would like to remind you of the final part of the prophecy contained in the *Adumbrate Invictus*," said Jiangshina.

That damned prophecy again, thought Nell. Would it haunt their lives forever?

"I don't see what that's got to do with us now," said Nell, finding her voice. "The war. It's over."

"If only it were that simple, child," said Jiangshina, again with a slight emphasis on 'child'. "If you recall, the concluding part of the prophecy states:

The Eminence of abominations will rise again. Out of light comes darkness, out of darkness comes light. Out of love comes hate. The blood of destruction. The blood of creation. A new Family is born. Tainted blood will clash in the final apocalypse.

"Blood connects all. Blood is the liberator. Blood is the destroyer. Blood is the answer."

The Magister stared at both of them. Christopher was silent. Nell mulled the words carefully, repeating them in her head, trying to find anything that could relate to them. She wasn't prepared to be lectured on what it meant by the Magister. She had sacrificed control of her life too many times. She wanted to think for herself. Act for herself.

'The blood of destruction'. That could refer to Nell's ancestry. She was descended from the bloodthirsty medieval ruler Vlad Tepes. *'The blood of creation'* could refer to Christopher. He was distantly related to Vlad's noble brother Radu. There was more. *'Out of light comes darkness...Out of love comes hate..."*

She suddenly looked down at her bump and placed both hands over it protectively. Then she glared up at the Magister, her face a mask of anger.

"Are you saying that our child will be this *Eminence of abominations?*" She couldn't keep the rage from her voice.

The Magister was quiet for a long moment.

"*A new Family is born,*" Jiangshina said, finally, quoting from the prophecy and once again staring at Nell's bump.

Nell's mouth fell open. A rush of cold fear surged through her body, turning her veins to ice and her heart to rock. Christopher turned to her.

"What's she saying?" he asked, not quite following the logic.

"She's saying that you and I are the light and the dark," explained Nell. "That our child will be of tainted blood and will bring about the final apocalypse," she added. "That the baby...our baby...is an...abomination."

Nell turned back to Jiangshina.

"That *is* what you're saying, right, Magister?" she asked, coldly.

"*I* am saying nothing," Jiangshina said, almost kindly. "These are not my words, child. I am merely the messenger. Yet the prophecy has so far proven to be accurate."

"Bullshit," said Christopher, incensed. "The prophecy might be accurate, but *you* haven't been right about anything." He jabbed a finger at the Magister. "Let's not forget that it was you high-and-mighty Magisters that proclaimed the prophecy was about me and Nell, when it turned out to be about Loris and Klaus. Major fail there."

There was a ripple on the surface of Jiangshina's calm veneer.

"And now here you are here again," continued Christopher, raising his voice. "Laying the fate of the world at our doorstep once more. Well, you were wrong the first time and you are wrong this time, too."

"Fabian Bamford..." began Jiangshina.

"Zachariah Redclaw's brother, you mean," shouted Christopher. "The one who was leading your merry band for decades without any one of you realizing who he really was."

"Yes," breathed the Magister, conceding the point. "Bamford, he misled us all. He deliberately misinterpreted the prophecy to protect his brother. But this time..."

"This time nothing," said Christopher. "It's another steaming pile of horse..."

Nell interrupted, hoping to calm the situation.

"You said before that there was a choice to make," said Nell. "What did you mean by that?"

Jiangshina crossed her arms. She looked visibly uncomfortable now.

"This is not something that you will want to hear," she began, "but it is my duty to put it forward."

"We're all ears," said Christopher, cynically.

"It is my firm belief, and that of my fellow Magisters, that the child Nell is carrying will become the…eminen…one…mentioned in the prophecy. Her entry into the mortal realm risks 'apocalypse'. That was the specific term used in the prophecy. But there is a way to ensure that that risk is never taken…if you act now."

Nell listened to the words and processed their meaning. Then exploded.

"How dare you even suggest it?" she spat. "Who do you think you are? To end my child's life because of your 'interpretation' of an old piece of text."

"That old piece of text has proven…" began the Magister.

Christopher crouched low and began hissing again. He was done with words.

"GET OUT OF HERE," screamed Nell, placing a hand on Christopher's shoulder. "Or we won't be held responsible for what happens to you. Any rules of hospitality are over at this point, as far as we're concerned. Screw your pledge of neutrality. You have overstepped the mark."

Jiangshina looked genuinely scared as she stared into Christopher's eyes. She took a step back.

"So be it," she huffed, her placid exterior now in tatters. "We are Magisters. We chronicle. We advise. We watch…and we *will* be watching."

"Well, watch this," said Nell, before slamming the door in her face.

Epilogue

The memories of a difficult birth were washed away as Nell gazed lovingly at her new baby. Faith, they'd decided to call her. Given everything they'd been though, it seemed to fit perfectly. Faith Laura Deverell was her full name.

Holding tiny Faith to his chest, Christopher gently rocked her back and forth. He kissed her on the top of her head before laying her down in the cot for her afternoon nap.

Nell stood over the small bed, looking down at the little bundle with her chubby cheeks, snub nose, blue eyes and wisps of light hair. Various emotions flooded through her. Love, apprehension, joy, insecurity, pride, wonder. But most of all love.

Nell knew that she should leave Faith be, so she could settle into sleep, but she just couldn't resist. She reached down and stroked her hand. Faith's fingers instinctively curled around her own.

Then it happened. That familiar sensation gripped her. Nell felt unbalanced for a moment and then she was thrust into the future. Sounds and images came flooding towards her.

***

Searing heat. Towering flames. The world was burning around her. Buildings were reduced to rubble. Screams rang out from all directions.

In the middle of the chaos stood a woman. Faith. She looked so much like Nell, but with Christopher's sharp blue eyes and strong chin. Her clothes were torn and burnt. She looked exhausted.

A shadow leapt towards her. Nell strained to see. A wolf. Large with dark russet fur. Nell thought she recognized her. Lupita. No, not her. But like her. Nell couldn't tell if the wolf meant to hurt or help Faith.

Nothing was clear.

Nell could hear a woman laughing above the various screams. It made no sense.

The heat was suddenly too much. The flames were rising. Nell had to let go.

***

She was thrust back into the sparse bedroom in Scarfskerry. She gripped the edge of the cot to steady herself. She was gasping, as if the flames still surrounded her.

Christopher rushed over and took her in his arms. She collapsed into him. The ominous vision was still fresh in her mind.

Nell looked down at her baby as Christopher held her close. Faith was asleep now. A look of peace and serenity on her face. Nell wanted that peace to last for eternity. But she feared that wouldn't be the case.

So she made a vow. To be there for her daughter for all time. The future was uncertain, but her love for her little girl was not. The same held true for Christopher. Nell had to trust in that love to save her daughter when the time came. Faith was made of their blood…and blood connects all.

Blood is the liberator. Blood is the destroyer. Blood is the answer.

***

Dear Reader,

Thank you for reading my book series. For the final time, I'd like to make a humble plea.

As a part-time indie writer with a full-time job, I would be truly grateful if you could leave me a review on Amazon, as I have no other way of raising awareness. Even just one simple sentence would be perfect. Thank you so much in advance.

If you would like to contact me for any reason (such as to point out a mistake!) or simply to say hi, that would be great. My email address is:

anyakelner@gmail.com

Printed in Great Britain
by Amazon